sinning *like* hell

USA Today Bestselling Author

TRILINA PUCCI

sinning like hell

Cover Design: Ashes and Vellichor

Formatting: LJDesigns

Editing/Proofing: One Love Editing, Erica Edits, My Brother's Editor, All Encompassing, Rumi Khan

Printed in the United States of America IBSN: 978-0-578-32022-9

Prologue

I slide my hand through the long strand of beads forming a curtain, lined neatly in a row as I pass through the doorway, hearing only the sound of them rattling around my face.

Each year is the same. I come to this dark room, thick with the smell of incense in the back room of a Queens candle shop, to meet with familiar dark brown eyes that see all.

"I was expecting you," she says with a rasp that comes from too many cigarettes and a decaying body.

I don't answer, just smirk as the old woman takes a deep breath, sweeping her long gray hair over her shoulder. She brushes her hands over the colorful scarves draped over her small wooden table, whispering to herself. Maybe praying before she reaches for the deck of tarot cards next to her.

My fingers curl around the top of the old wooden chair, dragging its heels over the floor before I sit.

"I'm here. Like you expected. So tell me the future, old woman."

Her perfectly arched brow raises as she flips over the top card. One I've come to understand represents the past.

"Five of cups…" Her eyes lift to mine. "Grief over what is lost."

I lean back into the chair, legs spread, hands joined in my lap. "You say that every year."

She shakes her head gently. "That's because the past never changes."

I stare across at her, waiting for the next card. She turns over two nude people with the label *The Lovers* underneath.

"Looks like the present doesn't change either," she says under her breath.

It's always the same. The Romani woman tells me they still grieve the past, that their fate is intertwined, but in the end, the future is always just out of reach. Unseeable. Like it's being guarded—kept secret by the devil himself.

As the third card flips, the one that represents the future, her eyes narrow, and I tilt my head to the ceiling, waiting for what's a foregone conclusion.

Fuck. I don't know why I come, and yet I still do, every damn year. Bullshit—I'm struggling to hold on to that lie because the reason's etched onto my bones.

That night, the night when she called Calder by his name at the carnival. A part of me wondered if the witch cursed him to his death with all those things she'd said. And in case she really is that powerful, the other part of me hopes that somehow their story, Calder's and Sutton's, can be resurrected. And that all the wrongs that happened can be made right.

I vowed to him that if I protect him—I protect her. And I won't break a promise to my brother.

So here I sit, hoping this witch can tell me what's coming.

Hold up. Why hasn't she said anything?

My head drops to hers, but what I see has me sitting up straighter. Magda's frozen, staring down, her lips moving ever so slightly as if she's speaking. But no sound's coming out. What the fuck?

"Magda?"

She says nothing, fixed to the card, lips moving faster. So I snap my fingers toward her face.

"Hey. Witch. What the fuck do you see right now?"

My eyes dart to the card before looking back at her. It looks like a tower on fire as people fall from it. That's never what she pulls.

"Hey. What does that card mean?"

Silence.

I reach across the table, grabbing her arm as a whoosh of breath leaves her, eyes fluttering back. She falls back against her seat, pulling from my hold, eyes locked to mine.

All I see is fear. It's so potent that I can almost smell it.

Her sun-soaked leather skin is pale, and her breath comes out in ragged draws as she makes the sign of the cross.

"So much death. So much destruction…" She trails off, shivering, reaching for a wrap that's slung over the back of her chair.

"Death always waits for men like us," I level calmly as I sit forward, chasing the fear on her face, "as does hell, Magda. What have you seen?"

Her head shakes, eyes avoiding mine as she pulls her wrap tight. The sound of her chair scraping the ground pierces the silence with the quickness of her standing up.

"Take your money and go."

My brows furrow as I slowly stand.

"You will tell me what you saw first. Because I ain't leaving until you do."

Her eyes grow cold as we stare at each other. "*O maćho o baro xàla e tikinen.*"

My hand slaps down on the table, making her shoulders jump as my voice bellows, "In English."

The old woman takes a step around the table, moving like the slither of a snake.

“I said, ‘Men are like fish,’ Roman Wolfe. ‘The great ones devour the small.’”

She stops in front of me as my chin drops so that I can see her.

“And which are we?”

“You are the madness he creates. You are the great fish. But Calder”—she shivers—“he’s the ocean, and he’ll swallow everyone whole. This is the last time I will speak his name. Because to say it calls to evil. But you are wrong. Death isn’t waiting for Calder. It’s listening for his instruction.”

Chapter One

Sutton
Present

My body feels like it's floating, but my eyes are so heavy that it feels impossible to open them. Am I dreaming? Or have I died? I always thought death would be peaceful, but all I feel is fear. It's coursing through me, holding me by my throat, and all I can think is to call out his name.

Calder.

Cold rushes into my body, and I feel my eyelids begin to flutter. Oh God, I can feel my heart beating and my lungs burning. I don't think I'm dead, but then why am I so scared? It's as if my mind knows something irrevocable has happened—something worse than death.

Because I'm afraid to open my eyes. Fearful of what will be in front of them.

Calder.

Muted voices fill my ears, but I can't quite make sense of what's happening around me. They get louder and louder until it feels like they're yelling at me, making me wince and try to lift my arms to my ears.

Pins and needles shoot through my arms, making me gasp, and this time I feel my lips mouth his name.

Calder.

"Can you open your eyes for me? Hey. Come on…what's her name?"

From behind me, someone says, "Her name's Sutton."

The next voice is closer, as if it's hovering above me.

"Sutton. Can you open your eyes?"

I blink them open, eyes unfocused, lips trying to move, but still no sound comes out of my mouth. My tongue feels like it's coated in chalk as I try to swallow.

Memories flick through my mind, causing my pulse to quicken—Hunter making unimaginable threats to Calder. Me swallowing pills. Then everything's gone.

"No, no. Stay with me, Sutton."

I feel my arms rubbed vigorously. So I drop my face toward the feeling, only to realize my eyes have closed again before I reopen them as wide as possible, letting my head fall to the side.

My entire world slowly and painfully comes into focus, making my body shudder with fear. I want to scream, but I'm held hostage by the scene in front of me as stuttered breaths draw from my lungs.

Calder's tan skin is gray, hair slicked across his forehead, his eyes closed before they're forced open by the men working on him as they shine a light on them. They're jerking him around like a rag doll, tearing his blood-spattered shirt open. The paramedics press something to his chest, scrambling to stop the blood from leaking out as they shout directions over him.

Oh God. No.

Blood seeps closer to me from Calder's lifeless body as I stare, unable to see anything but him.

"Calder," I whisper, slurred and too quiet.

"He's bleeding out," I hear yelled out, but unsure from whom.

My mind feels detached, unable to make my body listen because I need to get closer to him. I have to. He can't leave me.

"No," I drag out, feeling like my stomach might turn over.

Every bit of the panic I felt swallowing those pills descends upon me in full force, electrifying my nerves and jump-starting my heart.

"Calder," I say a bit louder, but I'm drowned out by louder voices around me.

"Let's get her on the stretcher. Narcan's working. Vitals are stable."

The sound of fingers snapping in my face makes me blink rapidly.

Calder. The gauze on his chest is soaked with his blood. *Oh God. Please no.*

"Sutton. Focus on me. Can you tell me what you took?"

My head turns toward the men kneeling over me, my garbled words rushing out. "Why is he bleeding? Why is Calder hurt? Make it stop."

"Tell us what you took."

"Make it stop," I all but scream.

I reach for Calder, ignoring the question as I'm slid onto a stretcher. But my movements are slow, making my hand land in thick, wet crimson pooled around him instead of his arm.

My wrist is yanked away and tucked in next to me as the rip of Velcro cuts through the air.

"No," I breathe harshly, trying to reach for him again, but I'm strapped in, unable to move.

They're taking me away. *No.* Adrenaline pumps through my body as I grind my teeth together before gritting out, "Stop."

My head swings uncoordinatedly back and forth as I try to shake it.

"I can't go. I need to stay with him."

Voices bellow from the side, calling my attention.

"I don't have a pulse. Paddles."

Oh my God. No. Calder. Tears cascade down my face as I try to struggle against the hold of the straps, but I'm so weak.

A voice at my feet says, "Try to relax, Sutton," but I ignore it, wiggling, hoping it will force them to leave me where I am.

But I'm just too weak.

A pulsing sound echoes around the room, sending the fear of God through me as I clench my fists tight, begging, protesting as the legs of the wheeled gurney click into place.

"Leave me here. Please. Leave me with him. He can't die alone. Please, God. Anyone. Please."

The paddles in the EMT's hands are pressed to Calder's chest, sending the voltage straight to his heart. I stare as his back arches off the ground and then relaxes, feeling as if I'm fracturing into pieces.

He's dying. This isn't real. This can't be happening. No. I won't believe it. This is a nightmare. It has to be.

A voice carries. "Nothing. Again."

I strain to see him, but he's disappearing as they roll me away.

"No," I say through my teeth, voice cracking as I begin to sob, looking between the men on either side of me now. "Help him. Leave me and help him. Please."

He can't die in this room without me.

Another click of the paddles, and then the sound of his body falling back against the floor pulls a gut-wrenching sob from my chest.

"Calder. Stay with me. Please. I love you."

My vision blurs from the tears pouring down, soaking my cheeks, as I stare at the ceiling. Panic infused with fear wracks my body as my head shifts, looking between the walls of the hallway.

I have to go back.

I did all this to save him. I tried to save him. Please, God. Please don't take him from me. Not like this. Not with me still alive.

"Her pulse is through the roof. Sutton. Look at me, take a deep breath. We need you to calm down."

"No. Take me back to him," I growl, trying to stay awake, feeling like I'm going to be sick.

But they just keep carrying me down the hall. Farther away from him. Until I can't even hear what's happening, and all I'm left with is the unthinkable.

I can't do this. I'm not strong enough. I need you...please, Calder. I love you.

"If you're taking him, let me go too," I whisper through my tears. "Please, please, please. You can't be this cruel. I've listened and prayed. I do what I'm asked, what I'm told. You can't punish me like this. I'm begging you. I can't *live* without him."

"Calm down. They're doing all they can. Focus on breathing. You're going to be okay."

It doesn't matter what anyone says. My words are for God. They're a prayer because nothing will ever be okay again.

My eyes close, wishing for the darkness I felt before to come again and take me away. My lips part, whispering the words I know he'll never hear.

"It was all worth it. You are mine, and I am yours."

The lights above my head pass in a flash as I drift in and out of consciousness. I'm rushed down the hospital corridor as people speak above me, talking about an overdose and spouting medical terms that I don't understand.

"I couldn't let him be hurt," I slur, but nobody's listening.

My eyes land on a man in a white coat. He's looking at the EMTs as he places a hand on the metal rail of the gurney.

"Mrs. Prescott."

I blink, trying to focus. Wait. He's not looking at me. *He said Mrs.* My head turns to the side to see my mother standing beside me.

"Sutton will be escorted to our psychiatric ward. We'll assess her and keep you informed. I've spoken with the Senator. Rest assured, we'll keep this matter private."

I shake my head, wanting to speak, to scream at her. To tell her I hate her, but none of my words come out fast enough.

The movement of the bed rolling jostles my body, pulling my attention back to the doctor. "Wait. How long are you keeping me here? What about Calder?"

The doctor looks down at me. His cheeks wear a warmth that his eyes lack.

"You're lucky to be alive, Miss Prescott. But you'll need to speak to someone because not everyone had the same fortune as you."

My entire chest feels like it's cracked wide open as I try to refuse what he's saying.

"No. No. They were helping him. He's not dead."

The doctor ignores me, nodding to the orderly. "Let the staff know we're holding her until further notice."

"Listen to me. He's. Not. Dead."

But nobody hears me. I'm shaking, tears falling into the corners of my mouth, leaving the taste of salt on my tongue as I shift my head from side to side.

The doctor speaks over me. "Call psych and tell them we need a consult. And that it's hush-hush."

"No. I'm not crazy. You can't keep me here."

Both men flick their gaze to my panicked face before looking away, continuing with their instructions. Oh my God. My breath turns into short huffs as I begin to break into a full-fledged panic attack because I'm alone. Terrifyingly alone. They're locking me up and throwing away the key just to keep us apart.

"Calder," I rush out as loud as I can before taking a deep breath and calling for him again.

"Miss Prescott, take a deep breath."

There's no more time for that. They forced me from the room, away from his side. But I won't let them steal him from me now. I'll never let them do that.

"He's not dead…I prayed. I asked God. He can't be dead. I won't believe it. It's not true."

Both men stare down at me, saying nothing. My chest rises and falls faster and faster until this time, his name leaves my lips as a scream.

There is no me without him. No world I'd be forced to exist in without him in it. The thought is unbearable. Physically fucking unbearable.

I keep screaming because it's a herald's cry. I hope the heavens fall to earth and the devil rises to imprison it here.

Because there are no stars and no purpose.

Without Calder, nothing exists.

Chapter Two

Sutton

"No," I scream, kicking my feet as I buck off the bed. "Get off me."

"Hold her. Tighter," the nurse directs with a needle in hand.

Male orderlies grip my arms and legs. One on each side of me, struggling to hold me down because I'm a maniac—screaming through ground teeth, spit flying from my mouth as I flail all over the rigid strip of a hospital bed, tears streaming down my face.

"Let me go."

My head thrashes from side to side as I groan, straining all my muscles, trying to break free. Because I don't need another fucking dose of that shit that turns me into a zombie. I want to get to him, even if I have to tear through everyone here.

Calder's not dead. Fuck their lies.

"Screw you. Your lies won't keep us apart," I growl. "Why are you doing this?"

I scream again, deep and guttural, trying to pull my arms free. My scalp stings as my hair's caught under the hand of one of the orderlies holding me down. But it's nothing in comparison to the pain inside of me.

He's not dead. I won't believe it. I'll never believe it.

"You're sick, sweetie. Still affected by the drugs you took," the nurse lies because I've been here for days, and those drugs are well out of my system.

But this is what happens every time I refuse to cooperate. Apparently, being locked up and isolated isn't enough. They have to dope me up to keep me quiet.

I buck again, fighting as before while she snaps at the men, "Hold her still. She's tiny."

"No. I want Calder," I scream, knowing he won't hear me but needing to say his name.

"Stop fighting, Miss Prescott. Just give in and rest."

"Calder," I yell again, feeling a prick on my hip, making my sob draw out along with my protest. "No."

Tears rush down my face as I stare up at the white, ugly dropped ceiling tiles, familiar with the next sensation—the warmth that will wrap my body in its vise grip, making me mute.

But only on the outside. Inside, I'm still screaming his name. Over and over.

The drugs work swiftly, coursing through my blood, pulling me deeper into the mattress, making it impossible to move or fight.

"I want Calder," I whisper.

The last of his name bleeds out, almost slurring as my eyes blink away the wetness left over on my lashes.

"He's dead, Sutton," the nurse says under her breath, wiping my eyes as she stares down at me with sympathy etched on her face. "You can let her go, gentlemen. She's not any trouble for us, now."

If they do release me, I can't tell because my legs feel like lead. My head falls to the side, feeling as if it's sinking into oblivion.

"Close your eyes now," the nurse instructs. "That's it, sleep away this nightmare."

I do as she says only because I know it's his face I'll see and his warmth I'll feel because Calder's with me in my dreams. And my nightmares. He's always with me, protecting me, loving me. Until I open my eyes again.

"Better," I whisper as my dreamworld begins blending with my reality, and everything fades into darkness.

Chapter Three

Sutton

I can hear them speaking—the doctor and my parents—but I don't roll over from where I'm lying. Instead, I'm motionless, staring at the sweat beading over the cheap mauve plastic hospital cup that's next to my bed.

It's been ten days since my psych ward incarceration, isolated from everyone I know. This is the first time either of my parents has come to check on me.

Not that I expected them any earlier.

But it's weird to think that I ever believed either of them truly loved me. I knew there was a line to toe and that I wasn't their top priority, but I never realized that I wasn't one at all.

They really don't love me.

My mind drifts back to the day everything happened, to my mother's words and the cruelty that played out in her eyes as she said them.

My head shoots sideways as my hand covers my cheek. Tears well in my eyes as the sting smarts my skin.

"I should've had an abortion."

I blink, the memory fading but the pain lingering. The way she looked as if she was relieved to finally tell me the truth, and the sneer of her lip as her eyes dismissed me. I'll never forget that. Jesus, I'm not sure anyone can ever prepare for knowing that you've always been alone. Unwanted. That the joke's been on you your whole life.

My hands curl up under my chin as I try to reason with the despair I feel. I won't let them beat me. I won't. My chin trembles, but I squeeze my eyes shut, giving a small shake of my head.

No. Calder will come. Just hold on.

He has to because he's the only person that fills all those cracks and crevices inflicted on my heart.

God, I don't know if I'm strong enough to endure this…this reality without him.

More hushed talking ensues behind me, and I keep ignoring it. Because I don't care.

Nothing I have to say matters anyway. That's the lesson I've learned.

I'll stay locked in this fucking room until I stop fighting for him.

They're trying to beat him out of me. But I'll never pretend he's dead.

He's not. He's just not.

Cold spreads over my body as I squeeze my eyes closed harder, refusing any thoughts born from *their* deceit to stay inside my head.

The taste of bile taints my mouth, my stomach sick with panic, as I begin telling myself the same story I've held firm to since the moment I was committed to this hellhole. It's a mantra of hope.

Calder will come for me.

"He will," I say under my breath.

And he'll make them pay for what they've done to us.

Then he'll take me away from this nightmare, just like we planned.

My shoulders begin to tremble, fingers curling around the blanket as I pull it closer to my face.

I just want to tuck myself away and disappear so they can't see me anymore because I want to be left alone. Left to fade away, into my memories, locked inside my own mind until he frees me.

Go back, Sutton. Go back to the day you first met.

My eyes close as I try to remember how blue the sky looked when he graced our off-limits basketball court. I take a deep breath in, wishing I could smell the ocean or the faint scent of cigarettes that always lingers on his neck.

We were perfect. All the beauty of beginnings and him—the possibility of love.

The doctor starts to speak louder, but I keep my eyes closed, concentrating on Calder's beautiful face.

"She's clinically depressed. And it's getting worse. She's not eating. She's combative with the staff, refusing to speak. The hospital has been very accommodating, Senator Prescott. Inventive even, considering we didn't have cause to hold her this long. Now we need to talk about real solutions. Because your daughter—"

My father's gruff voice commands the room, interrupting the doctor, barging too loudly into my mind, tearing down the walls I built.

"Thank you for your input, Doctor. But we *have* a real solution. Sutton will be fine once she gets to Madison Prep. They're aware of the situation."

"Good luck getting her there without putting a feeding tube in her. A prep school isn't exactly a hospital, Senator. I don't think you understand the gravity of the situation."

I squeeze my eyes tighter, trying to feel the breeze or hear the sounds of birds chirping from that day. My head shakes, anger building because I'm trying like hell to imagine the thunder of his basketball hitting the ground, but I can't. It's slipping away.

Goddammit. I can't hold on to him.

Another image flashes in my mind.

It's him behind the confessional screen. *Yes, come back to me.* Even in the dark, his eyes are so blue. His lips tug into a smirk at the same time mine do. As if he's feeling the same emotions I am. He is, and we do.

Can you feel me now, Calder? Because I love you. And I need you. I'm trying to be strong, but I don't know how long I can live this hell before I break. I'm so tired. Please come. Please.

My mother's voice comes from behind me, yanking me from my thoughts, throwing me to my knees in the present.

"Sutton. Roll over and look at me when I'm speaking to you. You need to let this go. Calder Wolfe is dead. And you need to move on for all our sakes."

My fingertips wipe the tops of my cheeks, smearing the constantly flowing tears over my dry skin as I bury my heart down deep.

I just wanted to hold on to him for a moment longer, but I need to not feel so that I can be as cruel as she deserves. Because I hate her, and I wish I could strangle every last lie from her throat until she chokes on her fucking entitlement.

For all our sakes? As if she has a place here.

"Save the faux tough love speech," I breathe out. "He's not dead. We both know that. So I won't go along with this bullshit. Fuck *your sake*…I only care about him."

"How dare you speak to me that way," she hisses.

My lip lifts into a sneer, hating the show she's putting on as if she's a good mother deserving of my respect.

I twist, shifting around quickly so that I'm facing her, locking eyes before she draws back.

Her brows draw together, disgust staining her features.

"That's right. Take a good look, Elizabeth. This is your handiwork."

At least she has the moral compass to pale. She's seeing what I do every single day in the tiny, smudged plastic mirror they give me. *Can't have me slitting my wrists with glass, after all.*

I search her face as her gaze drifts over the dark circles under my eyes.

"The dark circles are from the nightmares. They have a way of keeping you awake. But I bet you can't relate. You probably sleep like a baby since you *are* the nightmare."

She swallows, jaw set in anger, but her eyes drop to my cheekbones which are too pronounced because I'm gaunt.

"It's hard to eat when people are always sticking you with needles to shut you the fuck up. Then again, lying bastards never want to hear the truth. Do they, Senator?"

My father clears his throat, looking away like the coward he is. But she doesn't. No, my mother is never one to cower from confrontation.

I push myself up to sit, lifting my chin to give her a better look at the scratch marks clawed over what used to be smooth and unmarred skin.

"This is really the best part. See, sometimes, I want to crawl out of my skin. That's how unbearable life feels without him." My voices cracks as it begins to tremble. "And no matter how strong I try to be, sorrow is fucking drowning me. It won't let me breathe, so I dig my nails into my neck and try to tear myself apart."

Her lips part as if she's going to say something, but I throw back the covers, hanging my legs over the side of the bed, punctuating my words.

"I *bleed* for him. Calder isn't something I move on from, you callous whore. This is what misery looks like. But then, what do you care, right? You wish I were dead. Remember?"

This time she looks away, crossing her arms, staring at my father. Silence suffocates the space as everyone looks anywhere but at me. I guess the outcome of their evil is hard to witness.

Good. I hope it fucking haunts them.

I laugh, but it's tinged with rage. "If you're not letting me out, then go. Just. Fucking. Leave."

The doctor clears his throat, closing the distance between us, worry on his brow.

"Sutton. Grief takes many forms. Your parents care deeply about you—"

My head shoots to his, feeling myself snap.

"Fuck grief. That's not what I feel." My fingers claw at my chest as I spit my words, screaming them at his face. "The absence of him makes death favorable when I'm fucking weak."

My fists ball in front of me, lifting to my head before pounding down to the mattress. "I love him. Don't you understand that? I love Calder."

I place my bare feet on the cold speckled tiles, hurling my words, crying them out of my body.

"He's not dead. He's not fucking dead. You just accepted the lie they told. You're a fucking puppet."

My father turns toward me with anger behind his eyes. In the past, it would've terrified me, but this time I smile back, full of animosity and spite.

Because there's nothing more they can do to me that would be worse than how I feel right now.

He hurls his words at me with vicious intent.

"How could you do this to our family? Look at where we are, Sutton. In a goddamn psych ward because you tried to kill yourself over a drug dealer. You're acting like a selfish child. And now you look like this…like some kind of… Jesus, what will the press say—"

His voice trails off as he turns away. But I huff a laugh, tucking my hair behind my ears, feeling unhinged, unpredictable.

"What do I look like, Senator? Like a girl who's lost everything? And don't kid yourself—my childhood died the minute you locked me in here."

My hospital gown brushes my calf as I step forward, wanting to hurt him. To say everything I've kept quiet, locked inside of myself because I loved my parents.

But I've been surrounded by monsters, and now I see them for who they really are.

My finger stabs into the air, shifting between them.

"I'm in this place because of *you*. I look like this because of *you*. Blame yourselves," I spit, face distorted, neck burning red from my anger. "Then you should figure out how to repent. Because when Calder comes—"

My mother steps in front of my father, swiping her hand in the air harshly.

"That's enough. Stop this," she snaps, but I don't, shouting over her as I shake my head.

"No. I won't. When Calder comes for me—"

"He's never coming," she hurls.

"Yes, he is," I scream back.

Her teeth grind as her hand darts out, gripping my chin roughly between her fingers. Our eyes are locked as she speaks her words with quiet, sinister violence.

"Don't you dare speak that filth's name ever again. He. Is. Dead. And may he burn in hell."

I lunge, screaming, hearing her shriek as I reach for her neck to choke the life from her. The doctor throws himself between us, thrusting me backward.

"I'll kill you," I howl as I'm pinned by his body against the bed, still trying to reach for her.

Orderlies rush the room as my mother breathes, "Jesus Christ. She's crazy. You're not my daughter."

"Oh yes, I am, you bitch. I'm just the daughter you deserve."

My chest is heaving as my wrists are restrained, but my eyes stay locked to hers. I'm wild, filled with hatred.

"One day, everything you've built will burn to the fucking ground. And I'll be there to strike the match."

My father wraps an arm around her waist, pulling her backward out of the hospital room door, but our eyes stay locked on each other the whole way out.

It's not until the door closes and they disappear that I fall to my knees, arms held above my head by the men surrounding me. Sobs thunder out from my opened mouth as I dangle, unable to escape my emotions.

"It's okay. Let her go," the doctor says quietly as I cry.

My arms fall to my sides, palms smacking the ground, making them sting as I hang my head, barely holding myself up. Water pours from my eyes, spilling over my cheeks onto the floor, blurring my vision. But it doesn't matter because I can't see past this feeling.

This fucking sadness.

"I hate them. I hate all of you," I scream.

My fingers curl into the ground before I slap it.

"Where are you? Goddammit. I need you. You're not dead."

I hit the tile again.

"You're not."

And again.

My hands hit the floor faster and faster as I repeat, *You're not dead*, until my arms give out, and I slide down to my belly, feeling the chill on my skin. My head lies to the side, staring at the empty floor next to me, remembering everything about him.

A part of me is scared that the longer I'm here, the harder it will get to find him when I close my eyes. But at this moment, he's staring back at me, eyes the color of the ocean, lips the same blush of my cheeks.

He's here with me.

"I love you, baby," he whispers before disappearing piece by piece into the night sky like the stems of a dandelion blown away to make a wish.

I reach into the space, feeling nothing but emptiness, closing my eyes because I'm alone again.

"Hold on for a little longer," I mumble to myself, feeling the needle pushing into my hip again.

Chapter Four

Sutton

"Calder," I rush out, sitting up quickly from the stiff hospital bed as I wake from my dream.

I wish it *were* only a dream and not a memory because the pain that sears straight through my heart kills me every time I wake up.

It's too visceral to remember the way he looked on the floor of my bedroom—the emptiness in his eyes, the way he was so still even as they tore his shirt, scrambling to stop the bleeding… There was so much blood.

My hand comes to my forehead, feeling the dampness beaded over my brow before I lower it, noticing my tremble.

Jesus, my hands are shaking.

I lift my eyes to the darkness of my room, save the light filtering through a small rectangular window in the door from the hallway. It must be late because it's quiet.

God, how long was I asleep this time?

Looks like they doped me up nice and good after my parents left this morning.

My feet kick out from under the blanket, trying to rid myself of it, but I'm still slow from whatever they sedated me with. *I hate this feeling.*

Twisting toward the table next to my bed, I reach for the cup filled with water. But as I do, I'm suddenly halted, body frozen in place.

There's a man next to my bed.

He's in a black suit, jacket open, sitting in the corner of my room with one leg casually crossed over the other, hands folded on his thigh, staring back at me.

"Who the hell are you?"

He takes a deep breath but offers nothing.

The light from the door cuts across half his face, spotlighting it just enough to see him. But he tilts his head, bringing his eyes into view, making me frown.

There's something that feels familiar about him, but I know we've never met. Or maybe we have. I can't count the number of doctors and shrinks that have been through my room. All with the same bullshit questions.

His eyes search over my face as I grab my cup, gulping down the coolness. The way he's looking at me is like he's hoping to discover an answer to a question he hasn't asked yet.

My eyes roll as the thwack of the cup back to the table accents my words.

"You must be the new shrink? I'm surprised you guys even pretend to evaluate me, considering you're going to say whatever my parents want you to. But like I told the other guy, I'm not unstable. My parents are just assholes."

He shakes his head, and for whatever reason, goose bumps spread over my neck.

What the hell is going on? Why the mystery?

Butterflies flicker in my stomach, but I'm not nervous. Maybe they're trying to run away. I narrow my eyes, wondering if I should too.

My voice is cautious, laced with my unease, uncomfortable with our sudden game.

"Okay then, did my parents send you?"

He grins, and it pisses me off. *Oh, fuck them.* I should've known.

"I know Calder's not dead. So you can save your breath and leave."

He licks his lips, seemingly deep in thought. So I spit my words at him, feeling all the familiar anger from earlier soaking them.

"I said, get the fuck out."

"Ha." He chuckles. "You're a firecracker. I would've never believed it from the way you were described. What a nice surprise."

"Life's full of those," I huff.

I scoot back up against the wall, pulling the blanket back over my lap dismissively before I scowl, adding, "So, how about you try to surprise me now and listen? Get out of my room."

He hums a laugh.

"I suppose life is full of those, but it's not often I feel that way. And in answer to your question—no, Sutton, I don't work for your parents. In fact, it's quite the opposite. And I'm not a shrink either. Care to take another guess?"

My shoulders tense as all the tiny hairs on the back of my neck rise up like hackles. The longer I look into his eyes, the more violence I feel behind them, and I'm scared.

Because it's as if he's patiently waiting to be unmasked.

Suddenly, everything Calder said about his father begins to flood my mind. What if Tyler sent this man…here…to hurt me? It's what he promised would happen.

I exhale, teeth finding a raised piece of skin on my dry lips as I inconspicuously begin to slide my hand over the bed for the button to call the nurse. But he smiles, eyes flicking to my hand as I do.

"Go ahead, call for help." He's completely unbothered. Almost amused. "It won't change my presence. People tend to give deference to a man like me." His eyes lift as he leans forward, his entire face coming into view.

Oh my God. How could I have missed it?

It's in the eyes—they look like Calder's. Not in form or color. It's the lack of fear behind them they share. Ordinary people don't have that trait. I saw it once before in Tyler's eyes when he argued with my father on the steps of the church.

It's something I've come to envy.

"You're Connor O'Bannion."

He grins. "And she's smart. No wonder my nephew likes you so much."

"Loves…" I correct boldly.

If Connor's here, then he knows everything. And no matter how scary that is, love is what we feel. And not even *he* gets to say otherwise.

"Oof. Fearless too, I see. My God. You are something," he offers, staring in predatory awe.

I wish that were true, that I was fearless. Because my heart is beating out of my damn chest, and I feel like I'm going to throw up. The only thing keeping me from screaming for help is that I'm desperate to know where Calder is, and I bet Connor knows.

"Where is he? And don't tell me he's dead. I'm tired of the lies."

He takes a deep breath like he's choosing his words carefully.

"You're so sure he's alive."

He's not asking a question. He's stating a fact as if it's remarkable.

My chin lifts as chills cover my body because I won't back

down. I want to know where Calder is. I want to hear Connor make liars out of everyone.

I need to hear that my life isn't fucking over—that the man I love is alive.

Connor smirks, his hands clasping together.

"You remind me of my sister, Lena, Calder's mother. I can see why he's so taken by you, Sutton. She was strong-willed, committed to her faith. And stubborn. Oh, the arguments we'd have. I miss her every day. So for that, I'll give you something you want."

He cocks his head as he straightens the cuff of his shirt, adding, "A gift…before I take everything away."

Oh my God. I blink, heart thudding to a stop, because absolute fear snakes around the organ, holding it in a vise grip.

My gut was right. Connor's here to hurt me.

Calder. His name rings out in my mind, calling to him like a lifeline.

Connor bites his bottom lip, eyes narrowed, as my voice comes out barely above a whisper.

"Are you going to kill me?"

The answer that takes seconds feels like an eternity because life is cruel. I know that now. My lips part, wanting to beg, *I can't be taken. We've fought so hard.* But I don't. Calder would be strong. He'd never let anyone see his fear. So I'll do the same.

Connor shakes his head in answer, never breaking eye contact, but I don't feel relief.

My mind is screaming at me. No part of me believes Connor isn't here to hurt me. So, if I'm not dying today, then he's going to make me wish I were.

"Let's get to the gift…you're right, Sutton. He's alive."

My chest caves the moment he says it, a whoosh of air emptying my lungs. My entire body begins shaking as I stare down at the blanket over my lap, clenching it, trying not to let the tears fall that are pooling in my eyes.

I want to scream, to weep, to fucking explode because he's alive. He's alive.

All the fractured pieces of my mind fall back into place because I'm not crazy. They're liars.

I take a deep breath, steadying my breathing as Connor continues.

"He took a clean hit right through the chest but hasn't woken up yet. The bullet barely missed his heart. I guess the saints were lookin' down on him that day. I had him quietly airlifted into the city and out of this..." He motions around the room with a look of disdain, not offering any more before he continues. "It's as if he was never here. Calder doesn't exist in St. Simeon anymore. He's a ghost."

I search his eyes, my brows furrowing, wanting more information like why he was shot, who shot him, and what the fuck happened that day?

But he offers nothing else, and I won't ask because survival keeps my mouth shut. If he wanted me to know more, he'd tell me.

Silence fills the room as I nervously rub the stiff white sheet between my fingers, focused on the only thought owning my body—Calder's alive.

My eyes close, filled with tears that want to fall, but this time it's not because I'm drenched in sorrow. It's because I know he really will come for me. I feel it in my bones.

If death couldn't hold him, nobody can keep him from me.

The side of Connor's mouth tugs into a grin as I reopen my eyes. He wags a finger at me before standing, drawing my eyes up. He's tall like Calder, just not as broad.

I watch him as he walks to the foot of my hospital bed.

"She was wrong about you, you know. One look and I can see that you'd never roll over. There's a fire burning behind those pretty green eyes. It's a shame he can't keep you. Because you, girl, might be the most dangerous fucking creature I've met."

What the fuck?

"She, who?"

His vile grin turns into a smile as his fingers curl around the smooth edge of the footboard as our eyes stay locked.

"Sometimes enemies are forced to work together for a common goal. Your mother was so sure you'd be easily manipulated into believing Calder died. Seems she was wrong. I think the only real pussy in your family is your father."

They're working together? Oh my God. I'm struck silent, lost to the million thoughts flying through my head as heat creeps up my neck, spurred by the anger I feel. My head drops, staring at my lap.

All this time, she was plotting. It's not like I didn't know, but… no… I *didn't* really know.

I couldn't say those words—that he was dead. That it was true. My body rejected it, and I clung to that, telling myself it was a gut feeling. Promising my heart that he would come.

But I didn't *really* know. Because lunacy was preferable to reality. And all this time, I suffered while she was plotting, sticking the knife in deeper, hoping I'd die.

Because that's what I was doing…dying without him.

My head lifts, eyes locked to Connor's.

"The day Calder comes will be everyone's reckoning. And I won't even pray for your souls."

Connor's jaw strains, muscles rippling as he looks into my eyes. His whisper is sinister as he leans in.

"There it is…that fire. The anger. But I still can't tell if you're a scared little animal backed into a corner? Or a wolf ready to eat?"

Connor grips the footboard with one hand, reaching inside his jacket with the other, by his ribs, and pulls out a gun.

My eyes drop to the piece, blinking too rapidly as my mind begins racing, my heart pounding in my chest. *He said he wasn't going to kill me. Did he lie or change his mind?*

Even in his large hand, the black metal looks heavy, but he holds it like he's familiar. I'm staring at it, nerves feeling like I've been hit with an electric jolt as adrenaline courses through me.

Connor slowly taps the gun barrel against the footboard, making a tapping sound as he speaks.

"You wanna know what he said as he lay dying on that stretcher?" I swallow, lifting my eyes to his face. "It was your name, Sutton. He said it over and over. He begged for you."

"He loves me," I whisper, breath hitching. "And I love him."

I do love him so much that even now, here, faced with a gun, I can't lie. I will never stop loving him. It's impossible, like it's woven into my DNA.

"See, that's the problem," Connor grits out. "Love isn't for men like us. We're too selfish."

"He's not like you," I cut, anger still brimming.

The tapping stops, and Connor tilts his head. "But are you?"

My chest rises and falls quickly. My soul is engulfed and darkened by my rage. This is why Connor is here. It's not to take my life—he's taking Calder.

Connor places the gun at my feet, laying it down gently, smoothing a hand over the top. There's a challenge on his face as he takes a step backward, lifting his hands in the air.

"Let's see what you're made of. What are you willing to do to keep him?"

I don't hesitate, scrambling forward over my knees to grab the gun, jerking the heavy metal up toward his face, finger on the trigger. My hand shakes uncontrollably as tears fall from my eyes.

"Tell me where he is."

Connor smirks. "It's one thing to sacrifice yourself. Quite another to have someone else's blood staining your hands."

"Tell me," I snarl, spit flying from my mouth. "Tell me, or I'll shoot."

Connor's eyes grow wide like he's feeding off my anger.

"Will you? Because you look more like that scared little animal."

He takes a step toward me, so I stab the gun in the air.

"Tell me where Calder is."

The silence stretches out as we stand off, rooted in our places.

But then he lunges.

My shoulders jump, tensing, prepared for the bang as I press the trigger, but all I hear is an empty click. Connor laughs, grabbing the barrel of the gun, pressing it to his forehead as I shake, eyes wide with panic, clicking it over and over again.

No, no, no, no, no.

Our eyes meet, and before I can say anything, the gun's ripped from my hand. I open my mouth to scream, but barely a sound comes out as I scramble backward because Connor's already around the side of my bed, his hand clenching my throat as he hauls me further back, throwing me into the headboard.

"So brave," he growls, "and foolish."

I can't scream or cry because he's choking me. All my breath is trapped inside my body, burning inside my lungs, clawing to escape.

"Did you think I'd really give you a loaded weapon? Even weak bitches bite."

The mask he wears is replaced by sadistic amusement as he watches me flail and kick my legs. My hands circle around his wrist before slapping at him to let go, but he gives my neck a jerk, smashing the back of my head against the wall, making my eyes roll back as he tightens his grip even more.

I'm dazed, head wrung, as my mouth falls open, feeling myself begin to fade. My hands slap against his wrist slower and slower until I can't lift them anymore.

"This is what it looks like to be a wolf, little girl. This is Calder's birthright. I am who he'll become. And you don't fucking change that."

He squeezes tighter, making my eyes sting from the pressure before they begin to flutter closed, lungs burning. I'm losing consciousness.

Calder.

Warm breath tickles my face before Connor suddenly lets me go, whispering, "Not yet."

I release a breath in a whoosh, sucking in another just as quickly, feeling the color drain from my cheeks. My head hangs forward, eyes watering, staring down at the sheet-thin blanket as I press my palms into the bed, trying to hold myself up.

The heavy scent of cigars makes me want to gag as Connor sits next to me, pressing a finger to my forehead and lifting my head before wiping my hair from my face.

"You can't have him. Don't you understand? His allegiance is owed to this family, not you. And yet…"

Connor searches my face, maybe because he sees I know the rest.

When push came to shove, Calder left everyone to die, for me. He never thought about his brothers or himself. Only me. I am where his loyalty lies. Not to his name or the family.

I swallow, wincing past the pain as Connor continues.

"He risked this family for some little whore he's known for ten seconds. If I didn't love my sister so much, I would've killed him for his betrayal."

My shoulders shake, staring back at him. I close my eyes, wishing that this was a nightmare.

"No, don't do that. You're braver than that. Look at me, Sutton."

My chin trembles as I reopen my eyes to his cold face. Connor reaches up, taking a strand of my hair between his fingers and lifting it to his face, and inhales.

"Tell me that you understand that you have to let him go."

I nod, exhaling ragged breaths, saying whatever he wants me to as I stare past him at the wall.

He pulls away, looking up from my hair and tsking.

"I don't believe you. Let me explain what will happen if you don't obey me."

My hair falls back against my shoulder as my eyes meet his again.

"I will gut your whole useless, shitty family and those innocent little bitch friends of yours. Do you understand? They'll die, sweetheart, one by fucking one until you submit. It would be a shame to condemn that pretty little pixie of a blonde named Piper to a life of being passed around, fucked, and used up until we stick a needle in her arm and toss her body in the trash."

A sob tries to escape my lips, but I slap my hand over my mouth.

"Calder will find you, I'm sure of that, but what I also know is that you're the only one who can end this."

My hand drops from my face.

"How am I supposed to make him believe I don't love him?"

There's no version of us where Calder could ever believe that. Connor has to know that.

"You don't have to make him believe a lie. He just needs to see that love isn't enough to make the nightmares go away."

He is enough. He's all I need. Connor knows that too. Which drives fear straight to my heart.

"What nightmares?" I say on unsteady breaths, feeling led to ask the question.

Because I feel it coming—the destruction, the desecration of our love. All the evils of the world conspiring to ruin us.

Connor smiles before it turns into a frown. He reaches into his pocket, saying, "Shh," before caging me in as I dig my heels into the mattress, trying to scoot away.

His cell phone fills his palm as he brings it from his pocket. Our eyes meet again as his other hand slaps against my forehead, holding me in place.

"Stop. What are you doing?" I shriek, but his finger pulls at the skin around my eyes to keep them open as he holds the phone in front of my face.

"Providing the nightmare. Be a good girl and watch."

I flick my eyes to the screen just as laughter sounds from the video. Two men fill the screen, one older and the other… *Oh no. Please, God. Don't let this happen.*

My head tries to tug sideways, but Connor's fingers dig into my skin, keeping me facing forward.

"I don't want to see this, please," I cry, but it falls on deaf ears.

I try to close my eyes but only manage to half blink as they begin to burn. The guys on the video are walking down into a basement.

"It's right around that corner," one of them says.

"Where?"

My body goes numb. I stop tensing and fighting because I know what's going to happen. I see what Connor's showing me. And the pain, the unimaginable pain that's welling inside, makes my stomach turn, bile rising in my throat.

"He'll hate you for this," I whisper, tears pouring down my face.

My vision's blurred, eyes unable to blink, but Connor still forces them open.

"Sweetheart, this wasn't me. This is your fault. This will break him because how many people have to die for your love?"

My entire body shakes as I chant, *I'm sorry*, in my mind, over and over, wishing for this to all stop. Hoping and praying that what I know is coming won't.

Calder will carry this for the rest of his life. Connor's right—all I have to do is let him see me. Because I'm not sure love *will* be enough. Not for the horror burning into my memory.

The camera pans to the right as West comes into frame, fear on his face.

He's my age. He's too young.

Please, no. No, no, no.

"You had a job to do. Tyler told you to watch your brother and get him away from that fucking little bitch. He warned you what would happen if you didn't listen."

West shakes his head, hands reaching out in front of him as he backs up, pleading,

"I didn't know he was still talking to her. I didn't know. You have to believe me. I don't want to die." His head swings to the right. *"Please... Pops, don't let him kill me."*

My mouth falls open, sobbing, saying West's name through heavy tears, feeling his fear. Knowing he was alone with nobody to protect him.

Because of me.

I begin to whisper a Hail Mary because I'm hoping beyond hope that this is all a warning and not a consequence.

Until the bang.

West's body falls to the ground, a single hole burned into his forehead. I gasp, then again, catapulted into shock, hyperventilating as Connor lets me go.

My eyes squeeze shut, arms covering my head, trying to erase what I just saw. But I can't. All I see is his face when I close them.

I see West's sweet face, the floppy golden curls, and that smirk he wore like he knew a secret nobody else knew. And the way he looked at Calder like he was a god, always staring up because he wasn't quite as tall—like the little brother that tries on his big brother's clothes to pretend what it's like to be cool. He loved him so much. I saw it that day at the carnival because no matter the risk, he never stopped smiling at me as if he was happy I loved Calder.

Connor stands, silent, tapping a finger to the same place the bullet killed West.

"His brother's death is on your hands. Is that enough of a reason now?"

A hate-filled scream rips through my throat as I tilt my head back to the ceiling. Connor buttons his jacket and walks straight past all the people dressed in white, filling my room.

My mind isn't my own anymore.

People grab at my wrists, yelling, trying to calm me. But I don't care because I'm already dead.

A part of me died right there on that floor with Calder.

And the other died today.

We'll never run away. There won't be stars or blue skies filled with heavens staring down on us. All we have is death and destruction.

A life sentence, forced to survive within the absence of our love.

Chapter Five

Calder

The sound of beeping feels like stabbing on the inside of my fucking ears. Like nails being hammered inside my eardrums. I'm struggling to open my eyes, blinded by the light as my tongue darts out over my dry lips.

"Sut—" I'm trying to say her name, but only half comes out because the word scratches my throat.

"Oh shit. C—"

Footsteps gather closer to me as I blink my eyes open, everything fuzzy before slowly coming into focus.

"Nurse," I hear someone yell from my side as I shake my head, eyes closing again.

The lights are too bright. Fuck. *Where am I? What the fuck happened?*

"Sutton," I breathe out, deep and raspy.

A warm hand touches my shoulder, but I'm slow to react, lagging before turning my head to Roman's face.

Fuck, everything hurts—breathing, blinking, my whole goddamn body. What the fuck happened to me?

Roman's leaning in, staring at me.

"C, can you hear me? Can you see my face?"

I nod, feeling confused and out of focus, until a sharp pain shoots through me, making me groan as the beeping in the background grows faster.

"Fuck." I grunt, trying to reach for my chest, unable to because I'm caught around a mass of wires and tubes. "Romes… What is all this shit? Where's West? Tell him I need—"

My face falls heavily to my arm, seeing a needle piercing my skin along with a black band wrapped around my bicep. My eyes lift to where they're all connected, piped into machines next to my bed.

I'm in the hospital. What the fuck? The last thing I remember is Sutton. Where is Sutton?

"Get this shit off me."

Hot breath leaves my body as my mouth hangs open while I clumsily struggle to rip the tape on my arm.

"No. Dude. Don't touch. Calder. Stop."

Blood beads on my skin as the needle tugs from my veins, hitting the floor. Roman holds his hands out in front of him before running one through his hair, turning in a circle to look back at the door.

"Where the fuck is she, Roman?"

I rip the Velcro band off, and alarms begin to blare, making me wince and Roman panic.

"Brother. Come on. You gotta relax."

I blink, trying to get my bearings, feeling hazy and weak. But I don't give a fuck. If I have to crawl to her, I will.

"Sutton. I want her," I try to push myself upright, only to fall back down. "Fuck."

"Okay. Okay. But you got shot, C. Please chill. You ain't no good to anybody dead."

I got shot. Fuck. Do I remember that?

A flash of images imprisons my mind as I shake my head. They're coming on so fast it feels like the breath is knocked out of my lungs. I heave in short gasps of air as the memories descend.

Her beautiful face is so pale. All her wild hair spread out where she lay dead…pills scattered around her.

"*No*," I rush out, loud, vibrating my rib cage as I push myself to sit, immediately feeling the pain rock my chest again.

"Goddammit," I grind out, unstopping. "Where is she?"

Roman stares back at me, and for the first time in our lives, all I see is fear on his face. Straight up fucking fear.

"Roman," I bellow, "don't you tell me she's dead. If you say that, I'll kill you."

I hold up a hand to say something else, but I have to stop moving to catch my breath. People begin quickly filing into my room, all speaking at the same time. But my mind is only on one fucking thing. Sutton.

My head flops down as I drop an unsteady leg over the side of the bed, blood dripping down my veiny forearm.

"I have to get to her."

Someone touches my arm, but I jerk away, almost falling over.

"Where the fuck is she?" I yell through slurred words.

I blink, trying to get rid of the white dots in my vision. But they're multiplying.

Baby, I'm coming. I love you.

"Calm down, Calder" and "You need to lie down" are hurled at me. But my entire body is fueled with the rage I feel.

She almost died. All those pills…my precious fucking girl.

And it's all because of that little motherfucker Hunter, and my pops, and her fucking parents.

I already killed one of them. The rest better run.

Some asshole grabs my wrist.

"Settle down, Mr. Wolfe. You're still fresh from surgery."

I swing, hitting only air, feeling hot pokers branding me from the inside out.

My hand wraps around the hospital bed rail, holding me steady as I groan out a breath before putting my other foot on the ground. Fuck, it's so hard to breathe.

"Where's Sutton?"

The room is packed full of people, all with worried eyes fixed to me, but they don't fucking know what I'll do to every goddamn person here if I'm ignored.

"I heard her whisper my name. I know she's not dead. I've been chasing her voice back here from hell. Because no-fucking-body keeps *me* from *her*."

My hand curls into the sheet as I try to push to standing, bellowing my words.

"Bring me my fucking girl."

Another unbearable pain sears me, buckling my knees. Everyone lunges toward me, but it's Roman who catches me, arms wrapped around me, holding me as we sink to the ground, dragging the sheet off the bed.

"She's alive, C. She's okay, brother. I got her. Rest. You'll need your strength. Because everything after this will be a fight."

My breathing slows as he nods, repeating the last part over and over until my eyes close and all the sound fades into nothingness until I'm back, trapped inside my mind.

Swirls of black fog curl over and into itself, almost as if it's crawling toward me. It pools at my feet as I stare down into the vacant nothingness.

Where am I? What is this?

Sutton.

My head shifts around the empty void, stepping backward, but no matter which way I turn, it's all the same—endless black space vibrating with rage and hate.

This is hell.

Baby.

Frost chills my feet, rooting me in place as the dense black mist begins winding up my legs, creeping over itself to my arms, cold and blistering hot simultaneously.

It slithers and glides over my flesh, searing me as it does, scorching my skin.

I jerk my arms, but it has a hold on me, almost as if it's born from me, back to claim its space.

It wraps tightly around my neck, engulfing my face until plunging inside my mouth. My lungs feel like they're filled with tar, robbing me of any breath, drowning me in scorching liquid.

I'm devoured from the inside out by the profane feeling of desecration and violence.

But my only thought is Sutton.

I need to get to her.

I want to yell. My fists tighten as pain wracks my body, making my skin crawl and my stomach sick. Because I feel like I'm being burned alive and squeezed to death at the same time.

But I don't stop fighting, trying to reject my fate.

I hear my own words gritted between my teeth.

"She's my fate, you motherfucker, not this place."

If this is hell, the devil should worry because I won't be fucking kept from her. It's not my time to go, not when she's alive.

"I won't go."

I tense my shoulders, grinding my teeth. Devil, you can't take me from her. *My eyes close, seeing her face, hearing my name whispered from her lips.*

Her sweet voice fills my ears, "I love you," quelling the

scorching fire inside of me as I focus on it, holding it tight inside of me like my lifeline.

All I see is her. All I want is her.

My chest begins vibrating with a rumble as I stretch my arms wide and cry, "Sutton."

Her name draws out until there's no more breath left to say it, and I fall to my knees.

The thick cloud of soot inside expels from my mouth with wicked retreat, arching my back until I fall forward onto the palms of my hands.

My head lifts as I stare into the void, kneeling before standing.

"Sutton," I breathe out again as a voice from behind whispers in my ear.

"She doesn't belong here, Devil. If you claim her, she'll be damned."

I suck in a quick breath, overcome by the pure goodness at my back. It feels like her, like love and devotion. Goodness and life.

My thoughts sound too loud, hissing in my head.

Heaven or hell. Heaven or hell. Heaven or hell.

I have to choose. My eyes close, knowing there never was a choice for us. The only place Sutton belongs is with me.

"Then let her be damned, God, because I told you. Not even you can have her."

Chapter Six

Sutton

It's been two full weeks since Calder was shot. Four days since I was visited by Connor. And zero hours that I've felt whole.

But how could I feel whole? Nothing will ever be the same again.

I was a dreamy girl, staring at the moon. A good girl caught halfway between childish dreams and a shiny future. Always seeing my world through rose-colored glasses.

But it was all a lie.

Everything I thought about who I was is inextricably false.

Because that's not who I really am.

I'm selfish.

Connor was right. I'm willing to do anything to keep Calder—including loving him when it means ruin.

I'm the evil.

When I close my eyes, all I see is West, with fear marking his face.

I hear the way he pleaded with his own father. Scared for his life.

But something happened to me when Connor walked away, leaving me screaming for West's life on that hospital bed.

I shattered. Crawled into a corner of myself, too scared to come out.

My eyes half blink as I stare down at my lap, almost paralyzed by my numbness. He's dead. West is dead. And all I want is Calder. I'm so scared that if I let myself really feel this…this guilt, and heartbreak—all the fucking devastation of what we've caused—I'll shatter into too many pieces that can't be put back together.

And I hate myself because I've seen that we're unholy, condemned to our family names. Destined to destroy everyone around us because our love only begets hate.

And still, I love him.

The feel of beads fills my upturned palm as I lift my eyes from the back seat of the black SUV. This morning, I was released to my parents, quietly escorted to their car, where a bag was already packed waiting inside for me.

The single bag I'm allowed to take to my new home—Madison Prep, all-girls academy.

"Why are you giving me this?" I whisper, looking up at my father's face, closing my fingers around the rosary.

"You're going to need it in a moment."

His eyes don't meet mine as he speaks. Not that I expect them to. Neither of my parents have uttered more than two words to me since I saw them this morning. But what's there to say?

They've won. I'm doing as I was told.

My brows furrow, head shifting to look out of the tinted window. I always forget how tall the buildings are and how wide the streets are in New York. It's a place you could get lost in.

I turn my head to look out of the window past my mother, suddenly feeling uneasy.

"Shouldn't we be crossing the George Washington Bridge? I thought we were flying out of Teterboro?"

My mother's profile turns to mine, eyes locked.

"We're making a stop before you fly to Madison."

My father clears his throat as I look down at my hand. My heart begins to beat faster as my eyes search my lap. *Why did he give me these?*

"Where are we going?" I say quietly but with purpose as goose bumps spread over my arms.

My mother's voice is level, calm, and filled with her distaste for me.

"To see your boyfriend."

"Room 304," my father directs.

I nod, remembering that's what the nurse said at the station when we arrived, but I'm surprised I even heard her because it's almost as if there's nothing but buzzing in my ears.

Mount Sinai is a foreboding building with cold hallways and doctors in crisp jackets. It's a place where people escape death's grip, but I feel my heartbeat slowing with each step I take down the long corridor.

I feel like I've woken up inside one of my nightmares, and I can't escape.

"To see your boyfriend," my mother said casually, like it's just another day.

Not the day they're going to force me to look at the man I love and say unspeakable things. To tell him I killed his brother. That our love is a curse. That we can never see each other again.

This moment will leave an indelible mark. One branded on our hearts, turning the memories of our first kiss into ash and our touches into regret. Because today is when I condemn us to hell.

How can I do this?

The familiar panic that's permanently settled inside of me wells. I wrap my arms around myself as I walk, trying to stave it away, digging my nails into my sides, hoping the pain will win.

I can't do this. Oh God. I can't.

My eyes blink faster. I feel light-headed.

I give my head a slight shake, taking a deep breath because I have to do this. There's no other choice. We're not strong enough to beat them, not when they'll take someone like West.

My head bows, feeling my chest shake.

This has to be goodbye.

I glance over my shoulder at my parents following behind me, eyes dropping to where my father's arm is gently tucked behind my mother's back, guiding her.

We look like a family united to anyone watching, but all I feel is hatred and sadness. For myself, for them, for everyone. But I need to hold on to the hate. I need to dig my nails in, wrapping my arms around tightly, refusing to let go.

Or this might kill me.

My head swings back, eyes ticking to the gold plaques affixed to the sides of the doors. I count them quietly to myself as I walk past. Like a countdown to a bomb exploding, the steady ticks a person would hear before they know everything they've ever known and loved is about to eviscerate.

298, 300, 302…

My chest jerks as a singular thunderous sob attempts to crack me open. My hand darts over my mouth before I look around to make sure nobody is looking as I try to slow my breathing.

You're okay. You're okay.

But I'm not.

How can I destroy him when he never did the same to me?

My eyes flick to a nurse across from me, who smiles kindly as I drag the back of my hand over my lips before smoothing my hair. Her eyes dart away as she busies herself with some folders, giving me my dignity.

I suppose I look like every other person she usually sees. But losing Calder feels bigger than death.

"Keep a hold of yourself," my mother whispers from behind as I half blink, swallowing my self-pity.

That's what it is—selfish pity for a love I can't have.

West is dead. So it's fitting our love should die too.

I swallow, closing my eyes as I push the taste of bile back down my throat, along with the sadness.

"This is it: 304," my father offers, reaching past me for the door handle, forcing me to the side.

"I hate you for this," I whisper, turning my face to my mother, feeling nothing.

Hold on to the hate, Sutton.

My mother huffs a contemptuous laugh.

"One day, you'll thank us, Sutton."

My head shakes as I answer with nothing but honesty.

"The only thing I'll ever thank you for is dying."

The heavy hospital door sweeps open, but I stand there still, too much of a coward to lift my head.

This is it. Our end.

The last line in the book that will linger, leaving its mark on my heart forever.

"Come, Sutton," my father commands like I'm a dog as he walks inside.

My eyes lift, locking with the face staring back at me from the hospital bed.

Oh my God.

My head darts back over my shoulder to the smile on my mother's face.

"What have you done?"

She walks past me into the room, whispering, "What I had to do to please Connor. Just like you will."

The walls around me feel like they're caving in as my breath shortens dangerously close to a panic attack. I search the room, eyes darting from face to face, before landing on a man with a pad of paper and pen in hand.

A reporter? *Why is there a reporter here?*

I blink as a flash from a camera catches me off guard, making me drop my eyes and tuck my chin to my chest. My mind races, trying to put the pieces together as someone speaks.

"You must be so relieved, Miss Prescott, to know that your boyfriend will make a full recovery. I bet he's your hero."

My boyfriend? Full recovery? This isn't happening.

I dig my nails into my palms, needing to feel something visceral to pull myself back into reality as I blink down at the floor.

My feet are moving. I've entered the room.

Jesus, my body's on autopilot.

"It's not every day I get to report a happy ending to such a horrific beginning."

What the fuck?

My eyes dart to the unassuming man who's speaking, eyes narrowed, brows drawn together as I search his face. If he only knew what he was saying…the kind of disgusting fallacies he is spreading.

I want to scream at him, but my mouth won't move. I'm in shock because I know what's happening. I just can't fucking believe it.

"She's still in shock since the robbery, and with—" my father offers, not elaborating at the end.

A robbery?

Oh my God. That's their story. The one I'm expected to bear, like a goddamn cross. Everyone gets what they want. Connor, my parents. Tied up all nice and neat with a little bow, and I can't do anything but smile as they dredge me up to hang on that fucking piece of wood, nails in my hands, bleeding out.

I turn my head back to the hospital bed, walking closer, feeling my rage build.

"Of course, of course," the reporter responds. "I'm sure it was traumatizing seeing your boyfriend taken away by the ambulance. What was your frame of mind during that time?"

He's waiting for a response, but all I can manage is to stare forward as all the memories come crashing back to me.

Motherfucker.

Hunter's face looks almost unrecognizable, mouth swollen, cut open, and stitched back together. He's battered and bruised in deep shades of black and blue everywhere I can see. Purple and yellow peek out from bandages on his forehead, stained from the inside out with blood. And his arm is in a cast, held up by a contraption, making it impossible for him to move from the position he's in.

Calder broke him into pieces. This is why Connor wiped him off the map.

But I have no doubt that Calder did it for me. To protect me.

My heart almost leaps out of my fucking chest as I stare into Hunter's eyes, wishing like hell that Calder had broken his neck.

Everything Hunter said that day plays like a damn record in my head. All the vile and disgusting things he threatened, pushing me further into despair.

"We'd love a photo for the piece. It's scheduled to run on the front page…we're leading with the unfortunate sailing death of Mr. Kelly and tying in how these two brave kids have leaned on each other through tragedy. It's a real Romeo and Juliet story."

I don't turn to look at the reporter as he speaks, for fear they'll see the look on my face—morbid satisfaction.

I hope the whole Kelly family goes up in flames.

Marianne Kelly's voice fills the room, lifting my gaze. I didn't even notice her when I walked in. She's staring at me with the same hate I'm looking at her with.

"Take a photo of just their hands…joined. Hunter's been through enough. Memorializing his wounds doesn't suit the narrative," she directs, narrowing her eyes on me.

I look over my shoulder, seeing the reporter nodding vigorously before jerking his head toward Hunter and me for the photographer to get to work.

"Miss—" That's all the prompt I hear as I pick up Hunter's hand, staring into his eyes as the cameras click behind me.

Hunter's eyes search mine, but he doesn't speak. They're filled with disdain, not that anyone would notice past the blemished skin and bruises, but I see it.

I remember who you are, Hunter Kelly. And I won't forget.

My father clears his throat. "Sutton, you wanted to say a prayer for Hunter, remember?"

The side of my lip tugs into a grin.

Such a masterful manipulation they've conspired. The world will see me on my knees, at Hunter's bedside, praying for a love that doesn't exist.

Our families linked forever. And Calder, a ghost.

I reach into the pocket of my pants, pulling out my rosary, letting my thumb skim over the beads before staring into Hunter's eyes.

I don't have to look behind me to see the smug mask of victory my parents are wearing. Because it's in front of me, on Marianne Kelly's face.

No one's asking the right questions or second-guessing the story because they've handed the world precisely what it devours. A fairy tale.

Except everyone here is a fucking villain backed by the devil himself.

My hand rests against the mattress as I lower myself slowly to kneel at the side of Hunter's bed, bringing the rosary to my lips as I close my eyes.

Clicks of the camera go off in a flurry as I silently say the last prayer to God I will ever make.

Our Father who art in heaven. You abandoned me. Left me to this cruelty. You've taken the only man I love from me and allowed innocent people to be punished in the name of their hate. So this is the last time I'll pray to your name. If you're real, if you ever loved me, then commit Hunter to hell. And let them burn with him.

My eyes open, palms pressing to the bed as I stand, retaking Hunter's hand and wrapping my rosary around it. I lean down to his ear, whispering so that only he can hear.

"I wish he'd killed you. And one day, Hunter—he will. *That* was my prayer to God. For you to burn in hell."

The hate in his eyes follows me as I pull away. But I smile, lifting his battered hand to my lips, pressing a kiss to the top before saying,

"Amen."

Chapter Seven

Calder

My body's sore as I blink, bringing my hand to my chest. I don't know how long I've been asleep since the last time I woke up ready to brawl, but the hot pokers inside of me aren't there anymore.

"Nice to have you back, brother."

My head swings to where Roman's watching me from a brown leather chair in the corner of the room. The last time I saw his face, I was falling to the goddamn floor while he warned me about what was coming.

"How long have I been…" I trail off, looking around, realizing I don't know where the fuck I am, as he finishes my thought.

"New York-Presbyterian."

My eyes lock to his again as he says, "It's been three weeks, five days, and a couple of hours."

Three fucking weeks?

I run my hands through my hair, taking a deep breath.

"What do you remember?"

"Everything," I level, throwing back the blanket. "How come I'm not in cuffs?"

I push into a sitting position and swing my legs over the side of the bed. But Roman stands, patting the air with his hand.

"Whoa. C, you need to take it easy."

Fuck taking it easy. I'm going to get my girl.

My head shakes as I rip off a black band that's Velcroed around my arm.

"You need to get me some clothes." My hand drops to the hospital gown I'm in. "This shit ain't gonna fly when I walk outta here."

Roman closes the distance between us, and my head draws back.

He looks like he hasn't slept in weeks; his clothes are rumpled and disheveled. But that's not what's hitting me hard in the gut.

Roman's staring at the ground as if he can't look at me—shoulders turned in, hands shoved into his pockets.

My brother looks fucking defeated. And that's not something he's ever carried.

"What the fuck is going on, Roman? Tell me she's okay. Because I swear to fucking God—"

An unfamiliar feeling courses through me as I take a step forward. It's fear.

I'm scared to death something's happened to her. And it fucking shreds me. I'll never fucking forgive myself if... No. Fuck no, I can't think about it, or I'll lose my mind.

Roman nods. "She's alive. They've got her upstate at some fucking prep school called Madison. And you ain't in cuffs because of Connor."

I nod, fully understanding Connor pulled major strings to keep my ass out of jail. Strings that will come with shit attached. But right now, I don't care about that. I just need to get to her.

"C, a lot of shit went down that day. You need to chill because what I gotta say—"

He exhales harshly, not finishing his thought, as I take another step, pulled backward by the needle stuck in my vein. I grab the line, yanking it from my arm before tossing the whole thing on the bed.

"You can fill me in while we drive."

"Stand fucking still, Calder," he barks, drawing my eyes. "I gotta say this…fuck, how do I say this…"

Roman runs his hand over his head, shaking it before he drops his eyes, mouth opened.

"What the fuck is going on, Roman? Spit it out."

He can't even look at me. His hand grips the back of his neck as he speaks.

"It's my fault. I shouldn't have left him alone."

Oh, Roman. Don't say that. Oh fuck.

Rage courses through me. My mind pleads with itself. Begging for what I'm thinking not to be true. But as Roman looks up, the fucking devastation on his face fills every fucking pore of my body as my teeth grind.

My fingers curl over the side rail on my bed, squeezing so hard that pain shoots up my forearm. I raise the bed, letting it drop with a bang.

"*Who*? Who did you leave alone?"

Roman doesn't answer as he lets out a heavy breath. That look, it takes me back to when we were children.

To when we were twelve, and he'd found out his father died. It didn't matter that the dude was a deadbeat who'd abandoned him. Roman felt responsible. Like he could've somehow saved him if he was just better. He's worn that shame for the rest of his life.

And that's the look he has on his face right now. Like he

should've been better.

"West was found—"

I take a step backward, colliding into the machines behind me, hit in the chest like that fucking bullet with his words. Shit falls, crashing to the ground around me as I try to steady my feet before pushing off something hard next to me. The heavy equipment careens to the floor with a thunderous bang.

"No." My head shakes as I stab a finger at him. "You shut the fuck up. No."

He doesn't stop though, pulling his hands from his pockets, wiping them down his face as he steps toward me.

"His body was dumped by the side of Highway 27."

"Goddamn you," I grind out, feeling like I'm out of breath as I bring a fist to my forehead. "He was fine, Roman. He was going to be fine."

Roman's shoulders shake as he blows out an unsteady breath, eyes locked to mine.

"We take care of him, Romes," I growl, turning toward the heavy metal at my back.

I'm wild, murderous, destroying anything I can get my hands on.

A crash echoes through the room as I hurl machine after machine to the floor before pitching a metal rod holding an empty bag of fluid across the room, bellowing, "No."

The hospital door flies open, but Roman pulls his gun.

"Get the fuck out. He does what he needs to do."

My fists hurl against the wall, denting the drywall as I grunt and growl. I want to hit something until it's destroyed. Because that's what I am. Fucking destroyed.

My brother is dead. He's fucking dead.

And it's my fault.

"I did this. I fucking did this," I shout, feeling the wall give under my fist. "It wasn't supposed to be him. Not because of me."

Roman catches my arm as I connect a fist to the wall again, jerking me toward him.

I shove him away, but he fights to pull me back, gripping the back of my neck. We're eye to eye, pain to pain as he presses his forehead to mine.

"You gotta let it hurt, C. I got you. I got you. You can let it hurt."

My arms raise at my sides as my mouth opens, growling the pain of this loss, wishing I could make it all right. Knowing I fucking can't.

"Fucckkk," I grind out, body shaking. "It wasn't supposed to be him, Romes. Not him. I was supposed to protect—"

My body shudders as wetness coats my face, the rest of my words turning into sobs. Men don't cry. That's what everyone always says, but I'm not crying. I'm weeping. Hoping that if I suffer enough, he won't ever have to.

If I couldn't protect him in this life, then I'll give a pound of flesh to protect his soul.

Roman holds me as I grieve. He doesn't move as I begin to shout again, throwing my fists against him, cursing God and myself until my arms can't move anymore.

We stay there, locked together, because we're all we have.

My head falls against his shoulder, muscles weak. He wraps his arms around me tighter.

"Pops put a bullet in his head because West protected you. But his death isn't your fault, C. You can't carry that. This life ate him up, but seeing you and her together—that was what he talked about all the time when you weren't around. It's like he never knew people like us could be loved like that. He saw the change in you. We both did. That is what you gave him, not death. So don't you fucking dare turn your back on him now. He wanted you to live, C. You gotta do that for him. Swear to me, Calder. I fucking mean it. You don't let his death be in vain."

I pull away, staring at Roman, holding back the overwhelming agony I feel, burying it deep inside of me so it can fuel the anger I'll need.

"I'll make every single one of them pay, Roman. They'll suffer for what they've done to West and to us. I swear that to you."

He nods, stepping back away from me. Both of us take deep breaths, owning the men we are and what we have to be, before he says, "Let's get you to your girl. Because everything after this is gonna be a fight."

Those words echoed from before fill me with purpose. I know exactly what I need to do because nobody will ever take another person I love again. If death and destruction are my destiny, then I'm ready.

"First we see Sutton, and then we find Pops."

All it is, is dark outside. No lights, just sky. I don't think there are even stars out as we drive down the highway, windows down to try to mask the sound of my ragged breaths.

He's dead.

My brother is dead.

Roman was right. This life eats us up. But I should've saved him. I should've done what I needed to do, claimed my birthright, been the man I was born to be. Because then none of this shit would've happened.

I roll my window up as Roman glances over.

"You good?"

"Tell me everything I don't know."

His hands grip the steering wheel harder.

"C—"

He only gets my name out before I repeat myself.

"Tell me everything I don't fucking know."

The car slows, pulling to a stop as he shifts to look at me.

"All right, but you gotta stay chill."

I know he means because of my stiches and shit, so I nod.

"Fuck." He breathes, rubbing his shaved head before he lays it out. "Connor's working with her parents. He owns the fucking Senator now, and Kelly's wife was happy to step into place. And… Hunter's alive."

"The fuck he is. I beat that little bitch to death."

"No, you didn't. He made it. Barely. But he did. And *he's* their story—they made her pray at his bedside. Put that shit in the papers, called them a Romeo and Juliet story because he saved her from some bullshit break-in. That's the take, man. They're linked."

My vision blurs, black spots appearing in front of me before my fists hurl into the dash over and over as I growl.

"Fuck."

Roman lets me explode, staying quiet as I heave breaths staring into the darkness behind the windshield.

"What else?" I grind out.

Roman hesitates then locks eyes with mine. "Connor showed her West. He has a video that Pops shot of…" His face drops, and I squeeze my fists so hard pain shoots up my forearms before he takes a breath and finishes.

"He showed her. Threatened her friends, her life, yours. He told her she had to walk away. And he ain't playing."

"And he told you everything to make sure I got the message."

Roman nods.

My hands wipe down my face as my body stills. Because I know what I have to do. And so will she. I can't just kill all of them, because Connor's made it clear that I can't run from my birthright. They'll always be a bounty on my head. We'd never know freedom.

"I'm gonna end this, Roman. For all of us. But I'm gonna kill them all for her."

Chapter Eight

Calder

My head hangs, feeling the weight of my love crushing me as I stand in Sutton's moonlit dorm room, staring down at her sleeping body.

She's thinner, shadows under her eyes, hands tucked under her chin like she's haunted even in her sleep.

I did this to her.

Fuck. The shit she's endured, all the fucking pain she's gone through over the last few weeks. And I couldn't save her…or West.

I lift my head to the ceiling, still feeling raw over my brother as I grind my teeth together.

If I ever deserved any goodness, God...give it all to her.

I blow out a breath and open my eyes, looking around the room. The thought of her stuck in this fucking place with no pictures of her friends on the walls and only an empty twin bed across from her makes me want to burn it down and steal her away.

She shouldn't be here. *Goddammit.* She should be staring at the stars, red hair blowing in the wind with that fucking gleam in her eye that's a little bit trouble and a little bit heaven.

My hand wipes over my mouth, thumb carrying away a stray drop of grief falling down my cheek.

"I'm so fucking sorry I failed you. But I'll never do it again."

I think back to everything Roman told me as we drove here. The fucking details were like a knife to the heart.

He was right to do it. To be straight, no watering shit down. Because my brother knows I'll need that hate to have what I want. But every hour felt like torture because I gathered more and more rage, knowing I'd have to let it eat its way through me, patiently waiting until I could make them all pay.

Pay for every goddamn indiscretion and sin against her—from the psych ward to her parents working with Connor.

I'll make them eat their fucking tongues for the lies they told her, and destroy their goddamn names. Until they're splashed all over the front pages like that bullshit story about Hunter saving her.

And the next time I see him, I'll put a gun in Hunter Kelly's fucking mouth and make sure I do the job right.

Sutton rustles, sighing in her sleep. She rolls onto her side, gorgeous red hair spilling over her pillow, making her look like a fucking angel. Because that's what she is.

My angel.

Fuck me. I want to scoop her up in my arms and kiss every fucking place she hurts until all that's left is the wet imprint of my mouth on her flesh. I lean down, drawn into her as my eyes drift over her neck.

"Baby," I whisper.

My knees feel weak, palms coming to the mattress as I drop down to them, staring at faded scratches on her neck, darkened by faint bruises. My fingertips hover, scared to touch her because she might hurt, before they curl into fists, lowering down to the bed.

Anger boils inside my veins because I know this is Connor. He marked her, put the bruises here for me, as a reminder of my place.

He'll hurt the worst.

He threatened to take everything from her, but by the time he notices that I've done the same to him, it'll be too late.

Fuck. I can barely breathe. I'm gonna gut him from dick to throat for touching my precious girl.

"Baby." My voice breaks as I lean in, pressing a kiss to her lips. Anger and love are at war within me. "He'll find no peace in this life or after. I promise you that."

My head bows, eyes closing as I stay knelt in front of her, rocked by the fucking war inside of me. By all the goddamn love I feel for this girl.

How do I leave her alone?

I lift my head, ready to kiss her again but not ready to say goodbye as shiny emerald jewels framed by thick black lashes stare back at me.

All the air inside my body is robbed from me.

She blinks, unbelieving, like she can't trust her own eyes. Slowly, almost too cautiously, her hand comes to my beard. It's as if she's afraid I'll disappear, a shaky breath leaving her gorgeous lips.

"You're here."

Aw, fuck. That voice. It guts me, cracks me right the fuck open. My eyes close as my lips part, feeling like I just took my first real breath as she says, "I'm not dreaming?"

"No, baby," I whisper, bringing my eyes back to her. "I'm here."

We stare at each other, the world drifting away, not saying a fucking word. Hands brush over cheeks and palms press to faces, needing to feel the warmth on our skin to prove we're not in another fucking dream. One that'll become a nightmare the minute we wake up.

A tear from her eye pools against my hand before flowing over my skin as her shoulders shake. Her eyes drop, as if she suddenly feels the weight of the world on her shoulders.

Because she does. I see it in her eyes—the fucking agony and torment she's wearing over West.

"Calder…" Her voice is so shaky she can barely get her words out. "West—oh God…"

Her face draws in, devastated as I gather her hands between mine, pressing kisses to her palms.

"No," I growl. "That shit isn't your fault. Don't you fucking do that."

My face raises to hers, my hands cradling her face.

"Look at me. I know what Connor did. What you saw. I'm gonna make him pay for it. But baby, *they* took West. Not you. Not us. You understand me?"

Her voice is so quiet, so fucking delicate and raw that it cuts me open.

"I'm sorry. I'm just so sorry. I'm a curse."

I wipe my thumbs over her reddened face, bringing my lips close to hers, brushing over them with mine as I speak, the taste of salt lingering between them.

"I love you, Sutton. *You're* my magic. My forever, baby. Don't take that away from me."

She lets out a breath, fingers crawling along my jaw, pulling me closer.

"I love you too. So fucking much."

My mouth seals over hers, holding still, only for a moment, letting the divinity of her taste fill my body like my communion as her tongue dips inside my mouth.

I tilt my head, drawing her bottom lip between mine, letting it drag out. I'm high on her after one hit. We kiss like we're starved for each other, needing another taste, just to satisfy the hunger.

This is heaven. And she's the only version I'll ever want.

She blinks up, breathless, as I pull back, her words rushing out.

"I thought I'd lost you, Calder. I was so scared."

I grip the nape of her neck, pulling her forehead to mine, hating how strong she had to be as I grit my words out.

"Not even death, baby. Not even then."

She pushes her mouth back to mine, tongues dancing, craving more, as I grip her hair, wanting to devour her. To kiss her senseless. I love this girl so fucking much that nothing else matters—not her family or her friends.

I'd let them all die tomorrow to keep her.

A quiet moan pulls from her throat as her tongue licks over mine, her back arching toward me. The kiss grows faster, our heads tilting, lips crushing against each other.

I kiss her like it's the first time, rough, soaked in need.

Because I want it to last. Forever. *Fuck.* I feel rooted in place, knelt by the side of her bed, hands in her hair, pulling her closer. And floating all at the same time.

The taste of salt coats my lips, seeping into our mouths. She's crying.

I start to pull away, but she grabs the sides of my face, keeping me in place, breathing ragged breaths against my lips.

"What's going to happen to us?" she whispers.

I'll never lie to her. But I wish I could.

I press my lips to hers one more time, closing my eyes as I answer.

"You're always mine, baby. Even in goodbye."

Her breath hitches as her hands shake. *Fuck.*

"You're my home, Sutton," I whisper, slowly pulling back. I put my hands over hers and look into her eyes. "And I'll always come back. But we can't have magic and forever until *I* make the rules. Until *I'm* king."

A sob shudders through her chest before she shakes her head, growling no. My heart is physically fucking breaking, but she knows this is the only way. This is how I protect her and give her what she wants—our future.

She takes a deep breath, dragging her hands away from under mine before wiping them over her wet cheeks. Our eyes stay locked as I watch the girl I love trying to become the woman she'll need to be.

"Sutton," I whisper, wanting to tell her everything will be okay, but she shakes her head, bringing a finger to my lips.

"I would wade through hell to be with you, Calder. No matter how long it takes."

This beautiful fucking girl is stronger than she'll ever know. Everything I do for the rest of my fucking life will always be for her.

"And if we only had tonight—" she breathes.

I push her hand out of the way, grabbing her lip, and tug her mouth to mine, kissing the fuck out of her.

"Then it would be worth it."

Chapter Nine

Sutton

Calder's palms press into the bed, pushing him back to standing as he stares down at me. My bottom lip folds between my teeth, then drags out slowly, and my chest rises and falls quickly as I sit up.

This is our goodbye.

I reach for him, grabbing his belt with my hands as I tuck my knees underneath me so that I'm kneeling on the bed.

"Don't go. Please. Don't leave me yet."

He lets out a heavy breath, dropping his eyes to the floor for the longest second before meeting mine again.

"Baby, I'm not anywhere near brave enough to walk out that fucking door with you watching me."

The way he says it like he can barely get the words out past his emotions almost makes me break. Calder reaches behind him, dragging his shirt over his head.

God, he looks so strong, untouched by death, but I remember how close he came.

I lift my hand to the bandage covering the right side of his chest before leaning in to press a kiss to it.

"I'm okay," he offers, voice low and gravelly. He runs his hand down the side of my head, tucking my hair behind my ear.

But I'm still staring at the white square piece of gauze taped neatly over his pec, suddenly remembering every detail of that day. My lips part, needing air, feeling the familiar panic buzzing over me as I whisper to myself, "How am I going to exist without you?"

Calder gently grips my jaw, bringing my face to his, our eyes locked.

"You don't. There is no fucking difference between where I begin and you end. Not now, not ever. So we'll do what we have to so that we survive until we're together again."

He leans in, brushing his lips to mine so gently it makes my soul cry. My hands run up his chest, resting on the sides of his neck as he speaks against my jaw between dragging long kisses over my skin.

"It doesn't fucking matter what happens in the in-between, Sutton. Because I've seen the world without you, baby." His eyes meet mine. "And on my fucking life, we won't die before I know it with you again."

I suck in a breath, holding back more tears that are begging to fall.

"Promise on us," I whisper.

He's staring down at me with those blue eyes, piercing and haunted, not answering, making my chin quiver. A deep v cuts his brows as I shake my head.

My lips part, but before I can speak, he growls, grabbing my hand before forcing me to stand quickly.

"C'mere."

Calder steps backward, eyes on mine as I follow, our arms

outstretched.

He stops in front of the bay window on the far side of my room. I blink up as Calder draws back the heavy polyester navy curtains, letting in all the moonlight.

My eyes glisten as I stare out at the night sky. The moon is full and bright, tucked high in the sky, shining down on our faces and bathing us in cool light.

"You want me to promise? I'll do you one better, baby."

My face turns back to his as he takes my other hand. We stand facing each other, fingers interlaced, silent as the world cracks and breaks away around us, leaving only the stars and that moon.

His voice is quiet and deep, filled with the reverence of his love as he stares down at me.

"You told me once that this moon was a curse. You remember that?"

I smile weakly, biting my bottom lip, and I glance over as he continues.

"But I don't think it is. I think its magic is only for us. It was waiting for us to find each other. That's why it felt unlucky before."

His face is so earnest as he says it that I'm stripped of all my fears of the future. None of them matter because he is love, and he is mine.

A tear escapes, running down my face as I look into his eyes.

Calder blows out a shaky breath, eyes dropping to the floor, squeezing my hands tighter. His ocean-colored eyes, banked in the moonlight, lift to mine again as he speaks.

"I vow to always love you above all others. No matter what."

I blink as my heart races, realizing what he's doing. I'm almost unable to speak because his love is so big, so all-consuming that I drown in it.

My lips part, but only a shaky breath comes before he smiles down at me. Before he says anything else, I repeat his vow back to him as my own.

"I vow to always love *you* above all others. No matter what."

He brings my hands to his lips, kissing one, then the other before pressing them against his cheek.

"I will always protect you, even with my life."

My shoulders shake because I know he will. Always. He drops my hands back down, still holding them.

"And I will always protect you, even against yourself."

I lick my lips, tasting the saltiness left behind from my tears.

He lifts his hands to my face, cradling my cheeks. "I promise to die by your side when we're wrinkly and fucking gray. So that we'll never be apart again."

My hands grip his forearms to give me the strength not to fall to my knees as I stare up into his eyes.

"And I promise to love you even after death."

His lips come to mine, breathing his words against them, leaving them to burn into my heart.

"I'm yours. And you are mine. Not even death does us part."

"Forever," I whisper back, leaning into his kiss.

But this isn't just a kiss. It's the consecration of our love—our vows.

A declaration to the universe that we're fated and nothing can keep us apart. Our mouths meet again, reverently, lip over lip, as we fall into each other deeper. Existing only for one another.

No end, no beginning.

I don't know how much time will pass before I see him again, but I know deep down in my soul that I will.

And that's all I need.

Chapter Ten

Calder

I'm struck silent, too filled with emotion to open my fucking mouth. Because I love her down to the depths of my soul.

So fucking much that it makes me dangerous.

One day I'm gonna say these vows to her in front of a goddamn priest. But if I open my mouth right now and try to say that, I'll just take everything back that I shouldn't.

I'll tell her that we're running away and leaving the animals to fight it out alone.

That's how fucking wicked this girl holds my heart.

I already lost one brother, and I'm mired in fucking guilt and still only a breath away from risking another.

Those eyes stare up at me, begging for things she shouldn't, saying it all with a bat of her lashes as she licks her lips.

"Tell me what you want, baby. Because tonight I'll give you

everything."

Sutton reaches down between us, fingers coming to my belt, making the metal clank as she pulls the leather from the clasp. It falls open as we stay locked on each other, feeling the crackle of energy that passes between us.

Fuck. The connection I have with her is palpable, as if it vibrates off us.

Soul mate would be the easy word, but what I feel is deeper. I recognize *my* soul in *her*. Like it's split between us, and we're only whole when we're together.

My hips jerk as she pulls at the top button of my pants, unfastening my Dickies, saying nothing and everything all at once.

Her hands still as she blinks up at me.

"I want *us*, Calder. It felt like there was nothing between us when we did this before. We didn't have to be strong or brave. We were just raw, stripped-down, and so in love. I want to feel that, the real us, before all the fucking tragedy. I just want to be that girl that gets stars and magic, just one more time before we say goodbye."

Only the sound of my zipper crackling open echoes around the room as I lean down, cradling her head in my hand, lips so close to kissing that our breath mingles, hot and fevered.

"No goodbyes. Ever."

If she wants magic, that's exactly what I'll give her.

She starts to tug at my pants, but I grab her hands, pulling back and shaking my head.

"Naw, you know better. That was your first lesson. You first. You're always first."

My pants hang on my hips as I bring a finger to the strap of her sheer tank top, lowering one side before brushing my lips over her shoulder.

I drag my lips, across her clavicle, listening as her breathing picks up as I nudge the other strap down with my mouth.

"Calder."

I know, baby. I got you.

My lips travel up her neck, holding her at the nape, fingertips weaving through the red strands as her head falls back. I lick and suck my way under her chin, feeling goose bumps spread against my lips.

"Tonight, we do it all. I'm gonna touch, lick, and fuck every part of you, Sutton. You want stars, then I'll make you see 'em."

She's breathing so hard she's almost panting as she answers, "Yes."

My lips meet hers again before letting her go, bringing my hand to the front of her tank. It's draped over the tops of her tits, straps hanging down, nipples pebbled underneath.

"Where should I kiss first?" I rasp, dragging my hand over the soft material, exposing what's underneath.

The slip of cotton falls to her waist, but her eyes never leave mine. She stands stock-still, letting my eyes drift over her gorgeous body as she draws her bottom lip between her teeth, pulling her arms from the straps.

Fuck, she's beautiful, skin kissed with freckles, eyes so green they're hypnotizing, and nipples begging for my mouth.

I step in closer, our bodies almost flush. The feel of her skin grazing mine as we stand there feels like streaks of fire searing us with every brush.

My hand comes to her face, cradling it as I drag my thumb over her bottom lip.

"Should I kiss your mouth first?"

Her tongue darts out, licking the pad of my finger, making me freeze. I press it past her lips, slowly dipping into her warm mouth, letting her lips close around my knuckle.

"Suck."

A groan rumbles in my throat, watching her full lips drag over my skin as she hollows her cheeks and her head bobs forward.

My cock strains against my boxer briefs, wanting free from behind my low-hung pants. My beautiful girl might just fucking kill me tonight.

It's a death I'd welcome.

I reach between us, bringing my middle finger to the space between her tits, tracing a line down her stomach torturously slow. Soft skin pebbles under my touch as I run all the way down past her belly button, dipping just inside the band of her panties.

She grabs my wrist, twisting her head before running her tongue up the underside of my thumb.

"Someone misses my cock in their mouth. Is that what you want? To be on your knees, swallowing me back?"

She moans as I shove my hand all the way inside her underwear, cutting through her silky patch of hair, parting it as I glide over her clit. Her mouth falls open as she gasps, letting go of my thumb. I move my hand to her neck, lifting her chin as our eyes lock.

"You first. Remember." I circle my middle finger slowly, bringing another next to it as her hips move with me. "I kiss *her* first."

"Oh my God," she breathes as I stare down at her.

Our bodies are so close that my arm brushes against her stomach as I rub circles on her needy clit.

My bottom lip draws between my teeth, then glides out slowly, mesmerized by this beauty.

"Calder," she whispers. "Oh fuck."

Her body jerks, stomach contracting as I pick up my pace, rubbing the swollen bud faster. She's gripping my arms, circling her hips, as slickness coats my fingers.

"Fuck. Do you feel that?" I groan. "You're fucking soaked and throbbing. Do you know how hard it fucking makes me knowing that your pussy begs for me?"

She'll never understand the possession I feel. The straight up fucking dominance she breathes into me every fucking time she quivers under my touch.

I'm an animal stripped down to my basest fucking instincts.

I don't give a fuck how long we're apart. If any man touches her, I'll take their hands, then their life.

Her hips rock forward, eyes closed as I slow my hand and change my rhythm, dragging my fingers up and down each time a little closer to her entrance.

"Oh. My. God."

Sutton's mouth hangs open, staring into my eyes. Her tits are on display, swaying with her movement as my hand moves so slow, so leisurely, teasing under the panties that it's almost cruel.

"Fuck me," she rushes out, rocking her hips forward as my finger rims her entrance. "Please."

I press a finger inside, lips tugged up at the side as she gasps, squeezing around me.

"Yeah, baby. Tell me how good it feels."

"So good," she mewls, back arched, smashing my arm between us.

My words growl out as I move my hand off her neck, weaving into her hair, thrusting two fingers inside her.

"How fucking good?"

"Oh fuck" bursts from her lips, but my mouth seals over hers, tongue dipping inside her mouth, hungry for her pleasure.

Her arms wrap around my neck as I devour her, the sound of my fingers fucking her wet pussy echoing around the room.

"Fuck me," she says in a ragged breath against my lips.

"Come, baby. Then I'll fuck you. So it doesn't hurt."

She grabs the side of my face, holding us almost nose to nose, our lips almost touching as she opens her legs wider.

Goddamn. I wanna fuck every hole. Brand her so everyone

knows she's mine. That's how fucking deep I feel.

My fingers dip in and out of her pussy, palm rubbing over her clit, our bodies flush as she pants, looking into my eyes.

"That's it. Feel it, baby. Open those legs, and let me fuck that sweet pussy."

Her lips quiver as her body tenses.

"Ohmygod. Ohmygod."

Her pussy contracts around my fingers before her mouth opens against mine.

"I'm…I'm…"

Stuttered breaths gather as her eyes open wide. She grips the sides of my face, her entire body contracting as she drags out my name before she squeezes them shut, a whoosh of air warming my cheek.

A gush of warmth releases, filling her panties up over her clit, onto my palm.

My eyes close along with hers because it's the sexiest fucking thing I've ever felt. My forearm slows until it's not moving, veins bulging.

I drag my hand out of her panties as she sucks a hiss between her teeth, letting go of me. Her eyes are heavy, chest rising and falling as I stare down at my fingers.

I'm covered in her. My fingers glisten in the moonlight as I raise them to my lips, eyes fixed on hers as I push them inside my mouth, dragging them back out, licking her clean off me.

"More," I grunt, hands coming to her waist, forcing her back as I drop to my knee, mouth assaulting her thigh.

She gasps, contracting over me as I drag my tongue up her thigh, devouring her pleasure.

"Hold still. I'm not fucking done."

Chapter Eleven

Sutton

His mouth closes over my sensitive clit as my fingers run through his hair, gripping it as I try to step back. But he paws at me, pulling me closer, licking and sucking as I squirm.

"Oh my God. Calder, I can't take it," I rasp, bringing one hand down hard against his shoulder.

"Mine," he growls, doubling me over again.

He's an animal, dropped down to his knee in front of me, eating my pussy as I gasp for air. A slight squeal pulls from my throat as I feel him nip my inner thigh before his hands fall from my waist.

Calder stands, broad shoulders covered in tattoos, stomach muscles so hard they look flexed as he stares down. I'm panting, eyes on his, dwarfed by his size, as he wipes an arm across his mouth and reaches for me.

"C'mere."

His mouth crashes down against mine, letting me taste myself as he swirls his tongue over mine.

We're kissing frantically, as his palms hold the sides of my face. My fingertips press into his skin, gripping his hips as my feet are forced backward, each step mirroring his forward ones.

The back of my knees hit the bed, buckling as we topple down onto the mattress.

"Oh shit."

He catches us, palm pressed to the bed, softening our fall as his mouth chases me. I scoot backward, tongues dancing, lips gliding, breathless.

"Fuck, baby."

I feel it too. We're an explosion of emotion, feeling everything that's been embedded inside us like shrapnel. We're hands grabbing, nails scraping over the flesh as his hard body smothers my petite frame.

We're fucking brutal and violent, grinding against each other as my hips lift, rocking forward, dragging up his length.

"You keep doing that, and I'm gonna fuck that tight little pussy until it screams and cries thick tears all over my cock."

My eyes roll back as he licks his lips before mine part, voice husky in a way that it only gets when I want him to do dirty shit to me.

"Fuck me, Calder. Make me scream."

He exhales heavily, running his rough hand up the side of my body.

"Aw fuck, baby. My good girl's bad. Real fucking bad."

My head falls back, chin tipped to the ceiling as his lips drag roughly across my neck. His hips press forward, making my swollen clit throb.

I reach down, hand rubbing the imprint of his cock behind his boxer briefs.

"Only for you…and always for you."

Calder stills. He's hovered over me, staring so intensely into my eyes that it feels like we're sucked into an alternate universe where only we exist.

Neither of us move, overwhelmed by what we feel.

It's possession. I know because I feel it too. No matter how long we're apart, we'll only ever exist for each other.

No man will touch me. And no woman will ever touch him.

We just stay locked on each other as everything passes between us, all the love we feel, the devotion. Flashes of moments I'll never forget mix with heavy grief over what we're losing.

"I love you, Calder. Forever."

He lowers himself down, kissing me softly before whispering against my lips.

"It'll always be you, Sutton. You're mine, and I'm yours."

My fingertips dip inside the band of his underwear, dragging them over his ass as he holds himself up with one arm, helping me with the other. He kicks them off, leaving us naked, his cock nestled against my wet pussy.

I moan as my hips rock forward, legs wrapping around him. Our noses brush as Calder reaches down, positioning himself at my entrance.

But he doesn't move, bringing his eyes back to mine.

They're so full of love that it takes my breath away. *This is magic*. He's all the fucking magic, and it hurts how much I fucking love him.

I claw at his lower back, pulling him closer, lifting my hips as I do, desperate for him to make me feel something other than the sadness welling inside.

"Never goodbye," he whispers.

A shaky breath leaves my body as I nod. "Never."

Calder fills me. A tear rolls down my cheek as I suck in a harsh breath, saying, "Yes."

I'm stretched by his cock, the fullness felt in my stomach.

My body arches off the bed, hands on his shoulders as my eyes lift to the ceiling. He groans, seated deep inside of me, holding there, his eyes lidded as if he's taken a hit.

He pulls out only halfway before pushing back in, inch by fucking inch, making me lift my hips, begging for more.

"Baby, your pussy is heroin. Pure unadulterated fucking heroin. And I'll never get enough."

My hands roam gently over his chest as he leans down, bringing his mouth over my beaded nipple.

"Don't stop," I whine, pressing my tits forward.

My hips rise to meet his as he reaches behind, grabbing my knees, spreading me wide. Calder raises his body, fucking me slowly, pulling his cock to the very edge of my entrance before sinking back inside.

His eyes bore into mine as his veiny shaft drags in and out, glistening from my cum..

"Fuck. You're so tight. Touch yourself, baby."

I'm heady off the feel of his cock filling me as I stroke my clit, hips circling.

Calder's ass caves in with each thrust as we stare at each other, his rhythm gathering speed until his hips pump forward with so much force that he shakes the bed.

His fingers dig into my thighs as his jaw grinds. And my fingers move faster, gliding around my juices, before lifting my hand to his lips, watching as he runs his tongue over the pads of my fingers.

"Yeah, baby. Gimme that pussy."

Fuck. We're so intensely connected, his blue eyes so hypnotizing, it's as if the edges are blurred around us.

Our bodies are flush, already thick with sweat as we fuck.

"It'll never be enough." He groans.

Calder grabs my free hand, pinning it above my head, falling over me.

The smell of sex is thick in the air, like a fog. And the sound of our bodies slapping fills the room as he breathes heavily, mouth hung open.

I pull my hand from between us, letting that sacred space between his abs and cock create friction.

"Yes. God, yes."

His mouth closes around my nipple again, sucking the tender bud as he fucks me hard.

We're building, combusting, clawing our way toward release. His mouth leaves my nipple with a pop as he presses my wrist harder against the bed, tucking his other hand under my lower back. My hips lift as his cock pushes inside.

"Calder," I moan.

The feeling is indescribable. My mouth falls open as my eyes roll back, and my stomach tightens. Calder holds me in place, grunting, strumming something deep inside of me again and again.

"Oh…I'm…"

Everything inside of me explodes.

"Oh God," I scream, muffled by his mouth.

I'm coming. Stars in my eyes, my entire body lit up like a firework. He drops my hips, digging his foot into the bed as he grips my thigh, pulling it up over his hip, grinding into me so deep that I suck in a breath.

"Oh fuck, I'm coming," he grits out, rutting into me one more time.

My pussy strangles his cock as he jerks, coming so hard that no sound falls from my lips.

I'm silently shaking, with my hand fisted against his back.

His pants fill my ear as he drops his face to the side of mine, breathing hard. My arm is freed, so I wrap my arms around his neck, gently peppering kisses to the side of his face.

We stay like that until his arm gives, smothering me with his full weight.

Calder rolls to the side, taking me with him, draping my leg over him so he stays inside of me.

I tuck myself in close to his chest, kissing the bandage again.

His breathing slows, as does mine. But neither of us speak. Maybe he's as scared as I am.

"Say something," I whisper against his sweaty skin, tasting the salt as I kiss his chest. "Tell me what you're thinking."

He shakes his head, licking his lips. I nudge my nose against him, seeing a sad grin grace his face.

"I wish I wasn't a fucking criminal."

The memory of him sitting across from me in that confessional flits through my mind. Two people damned by our families, doomed to end tragically, unable to walk away.

He exhales, brushing his fingertips up and down my arm.

"What are you thinking?"

I scoot closer, feeling him drift out from inside of me. And something feels so sad about that. Like every connection we have is falling away.

"That I'm a liar."

His eyes close. "We're back where we started."

Calder pulls me closer, shoving his arm under me, hugging me so tight that I almost can't breathe. We're sealed, legs intertwined, arms wrapped around each other.

"Why are you a criminal?" I whisper, wanting to relive the moment, wishing I could go back and recreate it over and over until the ending is different.

"Because it's my destiny," he grits out, chest shaking.

"Why are you a liar?"

"Because I said I'd walk away. But if you tell me to follow you, right now—this very moment—I won't look back."

His lips press to my forehead, and I can feel his tears on them. A sob escapes my body as my shoulders lift, trying to crawl inside of him and never leave.

We lie in silence, just listening to each other breathe before his deep voice breaks the bubble.

"Connor will kill you. And me, if it came down to it. I won't risk you. So we have to be strong for this part of our story. Strong for each other and ourselves."

My mouth falls open as I weep, not holding back.

He kisses my head again and again before whispering, "I don't want to say goodbye either. Fuck, I already feel like I can't breathe just knowing you'll be outta my fucking reach. But Connor will do everything he promised you, baby. And you'd never be the same. I won't let that be something that happens to you. Because I can shoulder this…I will, for the both of us. I'll make it all right."

He pulls my head from his chest, holding the side of my face as I stare into his devastated face.

"So we're gonna walk away, and we're not gonna fucking look back."

My heart physically aches, a pain shooting through my chest, but I force myself to take a breath, chin quivering as I nod.

"It's not forever, Sutton. *We* are the forever."

Sunshine fills my room as I slide a hand across the empty space next to me, dragging over nothing but a cold sheet.

"Calder."

His name is whispered from my lips, but I don't open my eyes because I know what I'll see. I squeeze them tighter, plummeting back into my darkness, lost to grief again.

Because he's gone.

Chapter Twelve

Calder

"Hey. He's ready for you."

I push off the wall, and so does Roman, but Connor's guard waves him off.

"Just him."

Roman's face shoots to mine, but I give a reassuring nod before taking a step forward. It's all I can do. The hate I feel is consuming me. Trying to hold me under until I explode, but this is what I have to do to get her back, even if I want to give in and destroy everything around me.

The guard turns, opening the door to the suite and gesturing for me to walk inside. Connor's been at this hotel in New York since I was admitted to the hospital.

No part of me believes he stayed because he wanted to make sure his nephew was okay. Nah, he stayed to keep his ear to the ground and to be close enough to tighten his fucking foot on my neck if needed.

As I enter, my eyes immediately lock with Connor's. He's sitting at a desk, like a king on a throne, looking back at me with the same hardness I have on my own face.

"Nephew."

"Uncle."

I close the distance, my heart pounding, violence screaming into my ear to act in her name. But all I do is blink as the door clicks shut behind me. Connor motions for me to sit as I jerk the chair to the side and lower down, picturing myself reaching over and wrapping my hands around his throat as I choke the fucking life from his body.

"I assume you've seen her."

"Last night."

He reaches for his cigar case, pulling one out and running it under his nose as he inhales deeply.

Get her out of your head, Calder. She can't be here. You can't think about her.

"And you've said goodbye?" he levels.

My jaw sets as the muscles in my body tense.

"You act as if you gave us a choice."

His fist comes down hard on the desk, thwacking the glass on top.

"And you're barking like you gave *me* one."

I smirk, adding fuel to the fire, wanting a fight because then maybe I could get away with killing him.

"Careful, Connor, you might cut yourself. I'd hate to see you bleed."

Before I cut you open and let you spill over this fucking table.

His eyes bore into mine, the real him oozing out before he blinks and sucks in another breath, reaching for the cigar that flew from his hand. He grabs his cutter, snipping the top as he sticks it in his mouth to wet it.

"You're angry with me. And that's fair, but you're almost smart. This is your future I'm protecting. Let's be real, the more of this world you peeled back, the more she would've hated you."

All I can focus on is breathing. In, out, in, out. Because I need him to trust me, at least enough to take me home—to Boston.

"Calder, I did what needed to be done for this family, and one day you'll do the same."

One day, I'll slit your throat and burn down every fucking thing you've built.

Connor sucks in a drag, puffing as smoke billows. He points at me with the cigar in his hand as he continues.

"You put this family at risk. Almost killed the son of a supplier we're in deep with. Undermined the outfit in St. Simeon. All for what, Calder? A girl. And not just any girl—for the daughter of a man I fucking hate, who's looking to send me up the river. What exactly did you think I'd do? Because I would've done worse if you weren't my fucking nephew."

I don't offer an explanation as he stares at me. Because I want to slap his fucking mouth for even mentioning Hunter.

"Calder," he says thoughtfully, "this is your birthright. She doesn't belong here. Your loyalty has to be to the O'Bannion name."

"It is," I lie, staring into his eyes.

He shrugs, leaning back into his chair. "It's not just me…the other families, they need to know you'll be loyal too."

I let out a breath because there it is. What I came for.

My fists, squeezed together, slowly open, letting my hands feel life again.

"I said goodbye. I walked the fuck away. What more do you want from me?"

He stares me down for a long minute before stubbing out his cigar and lifting his eyes over my head.

"Tell the boys we're coming to the warehouse, and let them

know to have the package ready." His eyes meet mine again. "I have something for you, nephew. Because what I want is peace for this family."

"Yeah?" I throw back at him. "Then you show me what you showed her."

He blinks, eyes narrowing before he reaches over, grabbing his phone, never taking his eyes off of mine as he flips it over.

"Go ahead, look for yourself."

I swipe the phone across the desk, eyes flicking back to his because the fucking video was already ready. He had it fucking queued. I stare down at the triangle on the screen, before I touch it hitting play to watch my brother die.

Chapter Thirteen

Sutton

Three hard bangs on my door wake me from the dead, forcing my body to shoot up in bed, my eyes springing wide open.

What the fuck?

Another few bangs accompany a woman's voice.

"Sutton Prescott. Open the door."

"Hold on," I yell back.

I pull back my blanket and stand, eyes searching my room as I walk toward a chair, grabbing a pair of gray sweatpants labeled Madison on the sides and lifting my foot to put them on.

I'm still in just my underwear and tank top from last night.

What time is it? How long was I out after crying myself to sleep?

I step into the other leg and shift my head over my shoulder to look at the clock on my nightstand when my eyes catch, held hostage by something there.

Oh my God.

The sound of a key thrusting into my lock makes my heart stop before the handle twists and the door swings open.

"What the fuck, lady?" I bark, tugging my sweats over my ass, turning to stand directly in front of her.

The school's headmistress stands in my doorway, foreboding, with a bun twisted so tight that it makes her features look harsh and angular.

"You will not use that language here."

She walks toward me, stopping just short of uncomfortable as she stares down.

Fuck you. I'm done being intimidated.

My mouth falls open as I huff a laugh.

"I'll cut to the chase, Miss Prescott. We know your felon was here. So I hope you made your goodbye worthwhile because if he sets foot on this property again—"

I step in closer to her, blocking the view of my nightstand.

"You'll what? Have him shot? Others have already tried. What exactly do you need at noon on a Sunday? To tell me that you know I let a boy in my room? I'm a whore, didn't my parents tell you? I like to spread it nice and wide for bad boys that do terrible shit."

I bat my eyelashes as her jaw sets firmly, hands clasped in front of her.

"Get fucked," I cut before taking a deep breath and stepping backward until I feel my nightstand behind me. "I'm done with my parents' puppets. You can tell them I followed all the rules. They all got what they wanted. Now, get out because I'm going back to bed."

Her eyes narrow to slits. This bitch is mean. But I'm starting to perfect that myself.

"Your parents require you to attend mass every Sunday. Next week, you'll be ready by 8:00 a.m."

I shake my head. "No, I won't. I don't believe in God."

I cross my arms as she keeps her eyes on me for a long moment before she turns toward the door. Her voice travels over her shoulder as she glances back.

"They said you'd be a challenge." She stops at the door, hand holding it open. "I expect you to fall in line."

I say nothing, leaning back against my nightstand, hands gripping the wood on either side of me, mocking her with a sneer.

But my heart is racing, body impatient as she shuts the door behind her. I don't know how long I wait to turn around because it fucking feels like forever. But she has to be gone.

Giggling passes outside my door, making me smile as I spin around, staring down at the beat-up brown leather journal.

"Calder," I whisper.

My fingers brush over the long leather straps wrapped around it, fastened tightly like they're holding secrets inside.

I guess they kind of are.

I don't know how he got this back or when he left it here. All I know is it's mine now.

My hands wrap around the book that's as big as a Bible, picking it up in one hand and smelling the faint scent of his cigarettes, before unwinding the long leather straps with the other. My ass hits the bed as I place it in my lap, letting it fall open.

I have to close my eyes for a moment because I instantly want to cry. They drift back open as I bite my lip, fingers tracing over his messy handwriting. I flip the pages to more drawings and scribbles until I get to the last entry.

> *My life was always about you. Before I knew it.*
>
> *You saved me. Gave me purpose. Led me to be the man I was supposed to become.*
>
> *Because for an angel to walk on this earth, it'll need the protection of the Devil.*
>
> *There are a lot of empty pages I'll never be able*

to fill in, so now it's your turn. Tell me everything. Yell, scream, and cry in here, baby. Because one day I'll read it all.

Soon. –C

Chapter Fourteen

Calder

Roman and I walk in step into the dark warehouse. The sound of feet shuffling comes from the shadows as a man appears thirty feet away. He's forced forward by one of Connor's men, hands tied behind his back, a sack over his head.

"What the fuck is going on?"

My uncle smiles, stepping ahead as Roman's face turns to mine.

"C," Roman whispers because he sees what I do.

"I know," I say back as the man is forced to his knees, the sound of him hitting the cement cracking around the room.

No sound comes from his mouth, probably because it's taped shut under the hood.

"This isn't good, C. We gotta get out of here."

My head shakes because there's no walking away. I turn my face to Roman's to say just that when one by one, the lights begin to flicker overhead, clicking consecutively, sounding like thunder gathering.

Ten men stand in a semicircle around the one kneeling. They're facing us. Dead, soulless eyes behind cold faces.

This is the Council.

My eyes fall on each face, recognizing them as the heads of the different Irish families, from the East Coast to the West and all the way to fucking Ireland.

Connor runs this family, but when they meet like this, no one man is more powerful than the whole. They decide who lives and dies, who's in power, and when to take it away.

My eyes dart to the man on his knees as someone walks over and pulls the sack from his face.

"Pops," Roman breathes out heavily.

Tyler stares back at me, muzzled by thick silver duct tape.

Connor walks forward, placing his hand on my shoulder.

"This is how you show your loyalty. And it's also my gift to you. You want revenge for West. We want to know you're in. That you understand what you'll have to do from this moment on. Your father's death will be sanctioned by this council so no punishment will ever fall on you."

My nostrils flare the longer I stare at my pops. Connor turns around to address the Council, and my head turns to Roman. He's shaking with every breath, just as murderous as I am.

Our eyes meet, and a promise is made between us. No matter what happens in this room, we tear that motherfucker apart.

"Gentlemen," Connor projects to the Council, "we're here to partake in our oldest and most valued tradition. The initiation of one of our own into this world."

I step forward, but Roman grabs my arm.

"You make him suffer. Don't you fucking dare make it quick."

I nod, walking past my uncle until I'm standing in front of my father.

The stories told to me about moments like this drift through my mind. Every man that joins this family pledges their loyalty, and then when the time's right, they're initiated.

But the Irish don't fuck around. Initiation is by blood.

You beat a man to death with your bare fucking hands. Because death should always feel uncontrolled and scary. And every Irishman should know how to wield it.

"Untie him. I want him to fight back."

Connor laughs, giving the nod as my pops stares up at me.

There are no bruises on his face or cuts. Nobody's touched him.

They've left it all for me to do.

Tyler's arms are released, tape ripped from around his mouth as he lets out a growl, shaking his hands. He stands, spitting to the side of him.

"I knew it would be you they brought."

The energy in the room crackles and vibrates as we walk around each other slowly. He cracks his neck as we stare at each other.

"What's the matter, Pops? Worried that I let you win all those times?"

He narrows his eyes as we stop, just standing in front of each other, chests heaving, anger growing.

"It's gonna take a better man than you to beat me."

I lift my fist, feeling the hunger. An insatiable evil winds through my veins, whispering for Tyler's head on a goddamn platter, hissing in my ear to take his life and to make sure I'm the last fucking face he remembers before he's sent to hell.

The first swing cracks his jaw, forcing him back as men close in, surrounding us.

I should feel pain, the crunch of my bones against his jaw, but I'm not in my body anymore. I'm a demon, fed by the shouts and curses calling for his death resounding through the shadows.

His head swings around, eyes coming back to mine as he wipes a hand down his jaw, bruising already blooming under his skin.

"That was for Roman."

Pops' eyes lift over my shoulder, seeing my brother behind me before he rushes me, lifting me off the ground and grunting as he does. All the wind is knocked from my body, ribs constricted by his hold as we crash down onto the cement floor.

"Come on, Pops," I bellow, hammering my hand down into his back.

His hand slaps to my face, fingers scraping, trying to gouge my eyes. I ram my hand into the back of his elbow, hearing a pop from his outstretched arm.

"Ahh," he screams, grabbing his arm to his side.

I flip him over, straddling him as I hurl fist after fist into his face.

"Fuck you."

My teeth grind, jaw hard as my fists squeeze with so much force it feels like my skin might pop.

All the rage I feel, the hate I have for my pops, and the guilt I feel about West pours out of me like a river.

"This is for West," I cry out, hammering into his face as it swings from side to side with each hit.

I grip Tyler's hair, jerking his head up before smashing it against the concrete. Every word falling from between my lips is mangled and unintelligible.

I'm so full of hate that I'm barely making sense. I'm gasping for air, breathless, fury leaking from my body as I groan, smashing his head over and over until I hear a crack.

"Die. Fuck. Die."

Blood splatters against the ground, wetness speckling my face, making my eyes blink. But even then, I don't stop. I push off him, scrambling to my feet, throwing kicks to his gut.

His body jerks as his arm lifts, but he's not fighting back.

He's begging me to stop.

"Look at me." Every kick elicits another groan as he gurgles on the blood in his mouth. "You fucking look at me. You remember who put you in the ground."

Tyler's head falls to the side. *No. Not yet. You haven't fucking suffered enough.* I haul back and kick him under the jaw.

Men jump back as teeth and blood fly their way. My breath is heaving, spit flying from my mouth as I lift my foot, bringing it down to his nose. The crunch makes a few men turn away. More blood gushes as the yells begin to silence.

"Fuck you," I shout. "You killed him. He was my brother, you piece of shit. My brother."

Empty thuds mixed with my dark grunts are the only sounds as I kick the sides of his body.

Calls for me to stop fall on deaf ears because Connor's standing, watching, living for the monster he helped create.

Roman rushes over to me, trying to grab me, but I throw him off, lunging for Pops' body again.

"It's not enough, Romes."

He wraps his arms around me in a bear hug, forcing me backward as I try to get at Tyler.

Roman whispers in my ear, past my heaving breaths and grunts.

"It's done, Calder. West is at peace, brother. It's done. You gotta walk away now before you're lost for good. You gotta keep some good for her. For her, C."

My arms are shaking, weak from use but also high from the adrenaline. I know what I've done is wrong, but it's also righteous. Because that motherfucker should burn in hell.

"He was a kid, Roman," I say on ragged breaths as my body begins to shake. "He was our brother."

"Yeah, C. You did good. It's okay."

My legs want to give, but Roman holds me up as I gather my

strength. This shit isn't over. I hang my head, taking a breath before stepping out of his grip.

The faces of the Council stare back at me, fear along with respect reflected on them. They should be more focused on fear.

My face drops to my blood-soaked hands as I flip to my palms, eyes drifting over them and the spatters covering my clothes.

I knew what this day meant the moment I walked into this warehouse, but standing here, anointed in Tyler's blood, means I'm never going back.

This is who I am. And who I will remain.

My voice carries, filling the room as I walk back to the middle, wiping the blood from my cheek.

"You asked for loyalty. But what you got is my obligation."

I point up, high into the rafters, to a tiny red dot. "I'm not fucking stupid." I scoped that shit the minute we walked in.

Hushed voices hiss around the room, but I speak over them.

"We're all guilty, right? No man can turn on the other. But I just killed my father. A smart man might ask what I'd be willing to do to them without that obligation."

The men around the circle begin looking between each other as I turn, locking eyes with Connor.

"If you want fucking loyalty, you'll earn it. Not the other way around."

I stop in front of him, eye to eye, as I reach inside his jacket and pull out his gun. Clicks begin to echo behind me, death at my back, but Connor doesn't move.

My words are meant for my uncle, but everyone can hear them.

"You'll accept Roman as my brother. No different than blood. He's protected, initiated here, today. And you'll make sure Hunter heels."

He knows exactly what I mean. There's no fucking way I walk away from her wondering if she's in danger because I didn't kill him when I had the chance.

"This is me accepting my birthright, not cowering under your fucking coercion."

I turn around, walking past Pops' lifeless body until I'm standing in front of my brother.

My eyes dart down to the Glock, smeared in blood in my hand, before setting it in Roman's upturned palm. We're shoulder to shoulder as I turn around, staring back at the hardened faces of the men looking back.

"There's nothing left to fucking beat. Tyler Wolfe is dead. But that's not the point, is it, fellas? We good?"

The silence is fucking deafening as each man nods in my direction until it comes to Connor, who just grins.

I turn to Roman and blow out a hard breath, speaking so only he hears.

"I couldn't save West, but this is what I can do now."

I know every fucking thing he's thinking because that's what we do. He understands the gravity of what's just happened and what he's about to do.

The first man I've ever killed is my father.

There's no coming back from that.

Even if that motherfucker deserved it.

I'm all the bad shit people said I'd be, but it's the only way I protect the ones I love and get my girl back.

And now Roman's accepting the same fate.

He walks to the center of the room, staring down at Pops' body before spitting on him and lifting the gun.

The bang echoes as everyone stands silent.

Each of the men turns their back, folding back into the shadows at the edges of the room, leaving us alone in an empty warehouse.

One of Connor's guards walks forward with a sheet of plastic as Roman drops the gun on the ground. It clangs against the concrete before he looks back at me.

"You did good, Romes."

Connor looks over at his guard before he nods to us.

"Take the boys home to Southie. They're gonna need their family close now."

Year
One

Chapter Fifteen

Sutton

Tuesday—

My period started.

Of course it did. God. Why did I do this to myself? Like, hold on to this ridiculous idea that I had the tiniest piece of you—something left behind, a part of us growing inside of me.

I'm such an idiot. I just didn't want to feel like I really lost you. I knew it was a stupid idea, born from my irresponsibility. An idea soaked in desperation like a rag doused in gasoline, ready to light my life on fire.

Teen mom is exactly what I need right now. FML.

Jesus, I bet everyone could hear me in my room laughing at myself before it turned into fucking sobbing. It's like—Don't mind me, I'm just over here in the middle of another emotional breakdown. Wanna be friends?

Ugh. I can't even think about that right now.

How did I find myself here, willing to sit in this fantasy, pretending I still had you because my reality sucks that bad.

I just want YOU. FUCKING YOU.

But sitting on a toilet, crying, bleeding all over the place, has a way of sobering a person up. Because I decided that it's time to grow up. Everything feels like it's moving forward, except for me. So I have to do what you said.

Survive today until tomorrow.

***reminder to rip this page out when I let him read this.*

Basically, most of my month (October)—

"What is wrong with you? You're such a fucking psycho."

That's a direct fucking quote from the twat I checked with my lacrosse stick today. Her friends were less inventive. They threw out shit like "weirdo, slut, loser"—the holy trinity of mean girl slurs.

God, I fucking miss you today.

It's my birthday, but I don't think you know that about me—that it's in October. But, yep. I'm officially an adult and apparently starting an impromptu fight club.

Maybe Roman can join one day?...he always looked like the type.

Anyway, I hit her, she fell, there was blood.

I've never hit anyone before. Like on purpose to hurt them. There's an addictive release that happens. For a few glorious minutes, everything made sense. Nothing hurt. And the anger that's always inside was gone.

Until I was hauled to the headmistress's office, deposited in a chair, and yelled at. Now I'm pissed all over again and stuck in a week's worth of room isolation.

On top of that, it's been three months since I saw you. And I can't stop wanting to cry just thinking about that. But I don't. And that's why I hit her because all I wish is that you were here, taking me out to our field, with a pink cupcake from that bakery where you trapped me in the bathroom.

We'd sit out under the stars, and I'd blow out the candle knowing that everything I wished for would come true.

I'm so angry, Westley. Did you know you misspelled that when you put it in our phones? Lol. I watched the movie—well, I watch it...over and over.

I hate how unfair life is—I lose you, but I get to keep my shitty parents who, by the way, sent boxes of my things to me as a birthday gift.

I don't really care. It's not like I ever want to go home. But I haven't even opened the boxes. I just stare at them, wondering if what's inside will even feel like me anymore.

But I guess I'm surviving. Or maybe today, I'm slowly dying. I can't tell.

P.S. I think you'd be proud to know that I threw a mean right hook with that stick.

Thanksgiving—

So today was spent eating bland turkey with the cafeteria staff, alone, except for, like, ten other people that didn't go home. But I couldn't do it—go home.

The idea of sitting at the table and looking at my mother's face made me feel violent. And forget about the fact that any time I'm forced to speak to her, she always brings up Hunter.

It's disgusting.

She's really "keeping her fingers crossed" that our love affair's going to take off, and I'm over waiting for God to drop a piano on his fucking head.

I did do something stupid today, though. I turned on my phone.

God, I shouldn't have done it. Because I knew Aubs and Piper were probably freaking out, I also knew that my parents had PR'd that shit away. So burying my head in the sand didn't feel so cowardly.

I mean, it's not as if the world doesn't know where I am or my father's version of why.

Omg, I'm seriously fucking trying to justify being the WORST friend in a journal. Like I'll look back and be like, "Yep, wise beyond my years."

Fuck. I'm an asshole who's not ready to face them.

Because what do I say? I can't tell the truth.

How did you live like this when we were first together? Half in, half out. How did you decide what you could tell me and what you couldn't?

It would've been great if, somewhere inside of this book, you'd left some helpful hints instead of a bunch of broody existential bullshit.

If you haven't figured it out, I'm really fucking mad at you today.

I've walked around the grounds of the school hating you, blaming you for everything. Because if we'd never met, I'd still just be another clueless girl, eating turkey with fancy silver off Tiffany plates, sneaking away with her friends to some party.

Yuck. I'm sorry I wrote that.

But today is hard. And that tiny red dot next to my group message is fucking haunting me.

I miss feeling like somebody fucking cares. Ya know?

I miss you. And kinda hate you. But mostly, I love you.

(K...I turned on the read receipts, so at least they know I'm reading all the really great and amazing and funny shit they keep sending me. Baby steps.)

Calder
December

Roman throws me a towel as I suck in heavy breaths, chest heaving. I catch it, wiping my face as my muscles burn, aching from the beating I just inflicted.

"You made Connor a ton of money tonight. He'll be happy."

There's nothing Connor loves more than taking the house at his own underground fights. He does these twice a month. All of Southie comes out to watch a bunch of wannabe fighters jump in a makeshift ring and try to kill each other. And I've been his ringer ever since we got here in Boston.

I throw the towel down on the wooden bench, trying to pick at the bloodstained tape that's wrapped around my knuckles. Roman jerks my hand to him, unwrapping it.

"But damn, C. I thought you were gonna knock that guy's head right off his shoulders."

The taste of metal in my mouth has me turning my head to spit on the floor as I say, "He wasn't shit."

"Exactly. He wasn't shit. So then why almost put him in a coma?"

I don't answer. Because what the fuck am I supposed to say?

That I can't help myself? Do I tell him that every time I do another one of these underground bullshit fights, all I do is picture Connor's face or my father's or Hunter's, until I'm lost to the comfort of my rage? Because that's easier than feeling helpless and fucking lost without…

Fuck. I inhale a harsh breath and drop my head, staring at the ground, feeling my fucking hands start to shake. I can't even think her name.

"C, man—"

I jerk my fist from his grip, lifting my face to his and cutting him off.

"We've been spinning our wheels for fucking months, Romes, trying to get this motherfucker to trust us. You think I'm gonna get his attention by being a Boy Scout? I gotta do whatever it takes."

Roman stares back at me, his eyes searching mine trying to read me as usual. My jaw sets before I bring my hand to my mouth, teeth gripping the tape, ripping it off enough to grab it with my other hand.

He gives a slight shake of his head but crosses his arms.

"Everything has a cost."

I throw my hand to my side, ready to go in, to tell him to shut the fuck up, but the locker room door opens with a bang and Connor walks through.

He's clapping his hands, flanked by two men.

"Merry fucking Christmas to me."

Connor grips the back of my neck just a little too hard as he stares into my eyes, making my fingers curl back into fists.

"You're a fucking animal. And I love it. Look at all that rage inside of you. Fuck."

He smacks my cheek, stepping back.

"You're unbeatable. That's what everyone's saying. What do you think? Are you unbeatable?" He tilts his head, eyes darting to Roman. "Leave us alone."

Roman looks at me, hesitating, but I don't nod because he should fucking know better.

I keep my eyes on Connor because that's respect.

He's the boss. So who the fuck am I? Other than another asshole who listens to directions. Roman shoves his hands into the front pocket of his hoodie, walking past us out the door, not saying anything.

Connor and I stand staring at each other, his eyes narrowed before he smirks. He waves the men away, his eyes never leaving mine.

The door opens and closes again, leaving us alone in the deafening silence. I won't speak first—not my place. So I stand there trying to mask my thoughts.

I could break your neck before anyone knew what happened.

"He's protective of you." Connor chuckles.

I smirk. "He's my brother. And old habits die hard."

He's quiet again, lost to whatever thought has him drawing his brows together. I swallow, feeling a chill spread over my body as the adrenaline from the fight begins to drop.

Connor nods like he's speaking to himself before his face morphs back into a stupid as fuck grin.

"You've been working hard for me. You're trying to prove yourself, and I see that. So next week, you can start doing just that. It's easy to win, nephew. Now you're gonna lose, just because I decide."

Chapter Sixteen

Sutton

Happy New Year—

I snuck champagne. I might even be a little bit tipsy. The castaways, as I like to call them, aren't that bad here. We're like a band of misfits, left to roam these halls every holiday.

I can't believe practically half a year has gone by.

Time does not heal old wounds—people lied about that.

I'm still angry. And alone. (Maybe I'll take a leap and call Aubs and Piper tonight…liquid courage and all.)

Or maybe I'll do my new fave hobby and flip through the front of this journal until your face is all I can see. And your fingers are all I'll feel when I slip my own down between my legs until I'm so wet that I glide over my clit until I'm screaming your name under a pillow.

What a cruel world. I lost my virginity only to basically get revirginized, waiting for you to come and rescue me from this nightmare I call my life.

But what if you never come?

I thought that yesterday and started searching obituaries in New York and Boston. Because I don't know where you are. I don't know anything.

Except that I fucking love you.

Just as fucking much today as I did the night you said our not goodbye.

Life sucks. But at least I have champagne.

Calder
May

"Motherfucker," Connor thunders, tossing his glass across the room, shattering it on the wall.

Roman doesn't move because this is what Connor does. He's a fucking lunatic. Unbalanced. Moods shifting like the fucking wind.

It took five fucking months and a lot of broken ribs to appease whatever cruel ass kick Connor got off on watching me get my ass beat. But I did it because it got me in this room and one step closer to my hand around his throat.

I hang my head, sitting on the arm of the couch, and take a deep breath before looking up.

"You need me to take care of something, Uncle?"

It's not the first time I've made this offer, and it probably won't be the last. Connor runs his hand through his hair, shaking his head.

"No. No, this is street bullshit."

But as I crack my knuckles, he stares at me for a minute with a debate in his eyes. I know because I've gotten better at reading him. Not that I let on.

Connor leans back into his chair, reaching for his cigar only to smash it into the ashtray as his anger peaks again.

"I give these kids a shot, a way to better their lives. They come and work for me. Sell some product and make their lives better. They can give a little to their moms or take care of their girls." His fist hits the desk. "I do this for the neighborhood. And the fucking disrespect to not pay me on time."

I nod. "Of course. You care. You're a good man, Uncle."

The lies come so much easier now. I almost enjoy telling them.

Connor inhales harshly through his nose.

"Do you think anyone else has ever done things for these people the way I have? Their fucking bellies are fat because I created that shit they sling. I found the fucking Kellys."

He stabs his finger into the desk. "Me. I did that. And when that piece of shit Michael died, I am the one that made sure his sons had the majority vote. I turned a Forbes 500 company into my personal fucking distributor."

My entire body tenses as he says the Kelly name. He put Hunter and Tag in charge. *Motherfucker.*

I don't even notice that my fists are balled at my sides, squeezed so hard they're turning white around the edges, until Connor's eyes drop to my hands before meeting mine again. He narrows on me as he wipes spittle from the side of his mouth.

Fuck. *Get her out of your fucking head. Right fucking now, Calder.*

I let out a breath and shoot to my feet, trying to cover my tracks.

"It's the fucking disrespect," I bark. "They're stealing from you. Let me take care of this."

Roman comes to stand next to me, following my lead.

"Calder's right. Let us do this for you, Connor. You've done a lot for us over the last ten months. So let us take this off your plate."

Connor's staring between us as I put my palms on his desk.

"I'll get you your money, Uncle. Even if I have to sell someone's mother. But more importantly, I'll deliver a message that nobody fucks with this family."

Silence bleeds out as he stares back at me. I know he still doesn't trust me. I'm sure his gut tells him better…but I don't need to be his right-hand man. I just need him to put me on the streets.

His mouth slowly spreads into a smile as he slaps the desk again. *There it is.*

"You're a good boy, Calder. Loyal. You understand." His eyes pierce mine before he nods. "Okay. Pete will tell you where to go. But listen closely to my words—you bring me back something special. I want that animal I've watched on the mats. Make everyone see what'll happen when I send my angel of death."

My chest rises and falls as I say nothing, letting the last of what he said sink in—his angel of death. He wants me to bring him someone's life.

I knew it would come to this. But… *No. Focus.* I rap my knuckles on Connor's desk and give a tight nod before turning, locking eyes with Roman.

He's searching my face, digging, trying to read me. *I don't fucking have room for this, Roman.*

My jaw tenses as I walk past him because he's calling to shit inside of me that I can't let live here anymore.

Connor's so drunk on power that he just handed me the knife to place at his throat. This is what I need. What we've been working for.

Even saying that to myself, Roman's words still whisper in the back of my mind.

"Everything has a cost."

Fuck. My chest hollows as I walk out of Connor's office, with Roman on my heels, neither of us speaking until we slide into the car. He pulls out his phone to call Pete before looking at me.

His lips part to speak, but I do it first, staring out the front window.

"What I have to do today—the fucking horror that I'm about to inflict on someone I've never even met. Romes, it means that I give a little of my soul back to the devil. That's the fucking cost."

My eyes drop to my lap, looking at my hands, wishing I didn't feel her on them still as something that I heard that day at mass—the one when I waited for her up in the balcony—pulls to my mind. The priest said, *"For they eat the bread of wickedness, and drink the wine of violence."*

It's stuck with me since that day, it's why I almost left. I knew I was damned and that I would damn her too.

Because I was baptized in blood as my mother lay dying on the street, anointed in my father's blood as my hands beat the life out of him. Wickedness is my sustenance, and my thirst for violence will never end.

My face shifts to Roman.

"There isn't any fucking room inside me for *her* or the man that loves her. Not anymore. Not if I'm gonna keep her safe."

He doesn't say a word, just turns the engine over and puts it in drive as I close my eyes and welcome the numbness. Because I have to try to really let her go.

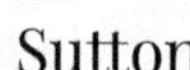

Sutton

It hasn't stopped raining—

I've been lying in bed all day, reading this journal because it's pouring outside. But I stopped to write this because I couldn't believe what I just read— YOU were not born bad. I don't care if some old lady told you that you were after you beat up her grandson.

But I want it on record that you were NOT and could NOT ever have been born bad.

I think the universe knew that you'd need to be strong enough to do what was required one day. And the only way you could be that strong was to lose a little bit of your soul. Not everyone in this world would be brave enough for that task.

And if that makes you bad, then so be it. Her grandson probably deserved it.

But you show me what it feels like to be someone's universe. And nobody all bad could do that. So, wherever you are, and whatever you're doing...tonight, someone is really fucking grateful that you know how to be "bad."

I love you, Calder. Make 'em all pay, baby. And fuck you to that old lady.

Soon.

Today sucks—

They stopped texting, Aubs and Piper.

It's for the best. But it doesn't feel like that.

I could really use some "better" right about now.

Chapter Seventeen

Calder
July

Smoke burns my lungs as I take another drag before flicking my cigarette out the window.

I motion to an alley next to the dilapidated house deep in the Southie neighborhood.

"Park over there," I grunt, staring out the window.

Roman pulls the Mustang between the houses, slowing to a stop. He glances over at me, shaking his head as I pull my gun out.

"What?" I bark.

"Nothing."

For fuck's sake. I shove my door open, then slam it behind me, uninterested in this conversation. *Again.* Roman hasn't let up since that day in the car before I shot the second person I've ever killed in my life.

I know he's worried. He reeks of it, but I've nothing to fucking say. And all the looks and the *You goods*—I don't want to fucking hear it anymore.

I tap my gun against my leg, steps ahead of Roman. Not paying attention to what's in front of me because my mind is on the shit he said without saying as I hear a gun cock.

Fuck.

My eyes lift, connecting with a beady-eyed motherfucker about ten feet away.

"Whoa," I say, nice and slow. "Jackie, don't do something stupid. Your neighbors are watching. The whole fucking street knows I'm here."

His hands are shaking, making the metal clack. Fuck, I bet he's never even held a gun. Jack Baker is just a low-level drug dealer who slings to rich kids in the city.

This isn't fucking good.

"Hey, hey, hey. Let's just put the guns away." I slowly tuck mine against the small of my back, trying to ignore how fast my heart is beating. "We're cool. I'm just here to talk."

Where the fuck is Roman?

He straightens his arms, pointing closer to my face, making me draw back.

"Fuck. Easy, man."

The gun shakes harder in his hand, and I wince.

"How do I know you're not here to kill me? I know about you. The Wolfe. You tear people apart. That's what everyone says. But not this time. I'm gonna shoot first."

Sutton.

Oh fuck. My heart stops. Her name's nothing but a whisper in my mind. But it's as if I'm suddenly awake, aware of everything around me in vivid fucking color. Because the one fucking thing I've avoided, packed down deep inside me, is the only goddamn thing I can see.

Not this way.

He's sweating as he stares at me like someone who wants to run. That look makes him dangerous and me willing to beg.

"Jackie, I really don't want to die today. I promised someone I'd make it home. So I fucking swear, I'm only here to talk."

The adrenaline pumps so fast through my body that my fingertips tingle as he stares at me. *It wasn't enough time. I've got to make it back to her. Fuck.*

He's shaking his head like he doesn't believe me as my heart beats out of my fucking chest. He's going to shoot me and let me bleed out on this dirty fucking sidewalk, and there won't be any fucking cops or paramedics to help this time.

Because in this neighborhood, nobody sees or hears anything. Especially not to help me. I did what I came to do in Southie. I'm feared. And people don't help monsters.

He pushes the barrel at me again, making my hands come up in front of me.

"Come on, Jackie. Please."

We stare at each other for the longest time as my baby plays on a goddamn loop in my mind. Over and over like a song I can't forget, humming it when I don't even realize what I'm doing.

"I promise to die by your side when we're wrinkly and fucking gray. So that we'll never be apart again."

"And I promise to love you even after death."

"Only one of us gets to keep our promise," I whisper to myself, closing my eyes, ready to die.

"Oh fuck," Jackie exhales, springing my eyes back open.

Roman crept around the back of the house, jumped the rail, and has the barrel of his gun pressed to the back of that motherfucker's head.

"Shit," I say in a whoosh, head dropping to the ground to stare at the cracked cement.

I hear Roman take his gun, saying, "Jesus, Jackie, you could've killed Calder. Get in the fucking house, ya crackhead."

But I'm rooted in my place because I can't catch my breath. That was too close. I wasn't focused. I was thinking about… *Oh fuck. No.*

My head's shaking, trying to shove what I'm feeling away, needing to settle everything that feels like it's fucking shaking inside me, but I can't. Because she's here, weighing me down.

"I can't think about you. Just get out of my head," I say quietly, still looking down.

I lift my face, not knowing what to do, eyes blinking fast because I can't stop this fucking pain in my chest. But Roman's not looking at me as he grabs the back of Jack's shirt, yanking him inside.

My fists open and close, trying to pump the blood back into them before I wipe a hand down my face. *Get your shit together, Calder. Don't let them see you like this.*

I clear my throat, giving my head a shake as I walk up the steps.

The metal screen closes behind me just as Roman tosses the guy on the couch before surveying the dump.

Roman's face screws up as he looks over at me, but I keep my eyes on Jackie. He almost killed me. This motherfucker almost took me from… My fear of her name slowly curls in over itself, turning into hate for the dick sitting in front of me.

All I want to do right now is beat Jack to death. I want to feel his bones crack under my fists until I can't lift my arms.

"Tell me why I shouldn't kill you now?" I say under my breath so only Jackie hears.

He stares at the foul mess of a coffee table, not looking up at me.

"Damn. This place is fucking nasty. It smells like old Taco Bell and stale cigarettes." Roman chuckles, oblivious to my fucking headspace. "You need to open a window more often."

My breath is calm as I exhale, reaching behind my back for my gun.

Roman peeks his head into the kitchen as I say, "Anybody else here we need to know about, Jackie?"

"No," he answers, finally looking back at me, body fucking quaking because he knows he's about to die.

Roman's smirking as he turns back toward us, something sarcastic on his tongue, but his humor fades when his eyes land on me. I know because the room is silent.

The kind of silence that worry and fear produce. The kind only narrated by the quiet sniveling coming from that dirty fucking couch.

My gun cocks as Jackie begins to plead, but Roman's voice fills the room, booming.

"That ain't happening today. Yo, you hear me, C? Put it the fuck away."

I do hear him, but I'm not trying to listen. Because she's still fucking here. Like her perfume when it lingers over my skin. Jackie's going to die because I can't forget and he almost robbed me of time.

"Hey," Roman barks.

I swallow, turning my head, our eyes locking.

Jesus. So much passes between us. But this time it's nothing I haven't seen before. My brother looks afraid again. Just like he did in that hospital room when he told me about West. But this time, it's me that he's losing.

That's what his eyes say, and I'm fucking scared he's right.

Jackie takes the opportunity to start fucking rambling, trying to plead for his life. Still, Roman doesn't look away, and neither do I.

"Everything has a cost."

Jack lets out a whoosh of a breath, running his hand through his greasy hair before pulling a used-up cigarette from an already filled ashtray. He blows on it before putting the butt in his mouth.

"Calder. Look, I'm fucking sorry about all that. Please. You said you weren't gonna kill me. So please, I got a sick mom, and my grandma just passed—"

The lighter clicks as his knee bounces a mile a minute. He looks up, blowing smoke out along with his words.

"And I got information. Shit I heard about who's selling the same stuff as Connor but cheaper. I'll tell you everything you need to know. Just don't kill me."

I drop my eyes from Roman's, tucking my gun into my pants before closing my eyes for only a second, letting myself see her face one last time before I reopen them.

"It better be good, or I'm gonna put a bullet between your eyes."

"What the fuck was that, C?"

I shake my head, still off, not wanting to answer anything as he barrels down the road away from Jack's house.

"Fuck this." Roman swerves, yanking the car into park, throwing us forward as we hit the curb.

My hand hits the dash before I'm slinging the door open, needing air, feeling fucking violent and too confined.

"Calder," Roman thunders, but I'm on the move.

I'm stalking toward a chain-link fence, jumping it to walk across a beat-up basketball court that's probably seen everything from sweat to blood to drive-by shootings.

"What the fuck, man? Calder, fucking stop."

I spin around, my shoulders so tense it makes my jaw grind.

"Just shut the fuck up, Roman. What do you want from me?"

"You can't keep doing this, C."

I could break his neck. Beat the fuck out of him. I could because I want to right now. Fuck. I turn away from him, shaking my head, voice rising.

"Fuck you. Don't talk to me about what I can't do. I'm doing what I have to. You don't know shit."

He swings an arm through the air, shouting.

"The fuck I don't. I'm standing right behind you in the same goddamn place I've always been. But now, every time you turn around, I don't recognize my brother anymore."

A guttural yell rips through my body as I kick a half-deflated basketball across the pavement before my hands link behind my head.

"That's because he fucking died. With *her* on that floor and with *West* in that fucking basement."

My mouth hangs open, watching Roman's face drop before I turn, walking the fuck away, not even knowing where I'm going, but Roman follows.

"You can't shut them out, C, and become someone else. That's not what they need."

I spin, almost face-to-face with him as I grab his hoodie between my fists.

"Don't you fucking tell me what she needs. I know what she needs. It's to be safe and not have to fucking suffer because I pulled her into this goddamn world."

He doesn't push me away, just looks into my eyes.

"Naw, man. She knew what she was doing. She knows who you are, and she loves you anyway. So the cost can't be your soul, C."

I shove away from him, but he smacks my face, bringing me angrily back as he keeps speaking.

"Because if you keep doing this, shutting her out, shutting me out, not talking about West, then when you get her back, the man you've become won't even be close to the one she loves."

My hands raise as I stumble back away from him before I'm running them through my hair. I can't fucking feel this shit. I can't. It's too much.

I tilt my face to the sky filled with clouds as I say what I never do.

"I can't just be a man, Romes. I gotta be more than that. But every time I think about her, that's all I am—a fucking guy who's split wide fucking open with grief. Because every single day that I'm away from her is harder than the one before."

His voice is lower, calmer.

"C. Loving her is what makes you strong. You're taking down an entire fucking organization. For her. She's your purpose. You told me that once. If you take that away, then all you are is a fucking animal. No better than Connor or the other families."

My eyes fall to the ground, closing them and letting myself feel. Because, fuck, he's right, and I know it. But it still doesn't make anything easier.

The sound of a ball hitting the ground lifts my eyes. Roman passes it to me hard, checking my chest.

"Let's play, like old times. Until we can't anymore. Sometimes that is all you can do, C. Just keep shit moving so you don't fall. But if you do, I got you."

I nod, bringing the ball to my chest, feeling that tightness that's always there, before I pass the ball back, letting out a whoosh of air.

"Let's go," I say without another word as he bounces it off the concrete before rushing me, because we just keep it moving until we can't.

Three hours later, we're sliding back into the car, sweaty and grinning.

"You gonna make a call about what we found out today from Jackie?" Roman says, spinning the keys around his finger.

I nod but draw my brows together.

"But I wanna do something else first."

Roman shoves the keys into the car. "Name it. As long as it's not shooting someone or beating the shit out of poor Jackie." A grin spreads over his face. "His knee was fucking bouncing fast with you staring at him."

It's sick, but it makes me laugh for the first time in forever. This feels like old times, and I'm okay with that.

"You're not the funny one. West was. Stop trying to fill his shoes. You fucking suck at it. He's probably looking down, all kinds of disappointed."

Roman shoves my shoulder, smiling as he nods, before turning on the car and throwing it into drive. We're not good with feelings, so this is how we deal with shit that fucks us up. Dark humor and jokes…and sometimes guns.

"Hey," he says, not looking at me, "You wanna go tell him about today, huh?"

"Yeah." I nod, looking out the window as we tear down the street, not saying another word.

Because my brother and I just got back on the same damn page.

Twenty minutes later, Roman and I slide out of the car at the same time, walking the distance to a gray headstone that reads:

Westley Richard Wolfe

Brother, son, friend

And the funny one in the family.

Year
Two

Chapter Eighteen

Sutton

Freedom—

I graduated today. Technically, I had to do summer school, but I did it. I can't believe it, but I actually did. Because pretty much the whole year feels like a blur.

I don't know if you know, but there was this whole terrible breakup thing I went through with this hot piece of ass. The D really went to my head. But I'm all good now.

Psych.

I did do well in one class, though. Greek mythology. I wonder why?

God. It was incredible. Like a tiny piece of you every day—a bright spot in an otherwise dreary fucking week.

It's safe to say my parents pulled a lot of strings to get me into any college.

Not going to lie—I thought about telling them to go fuck

themselves. Like try to make it on my own.

Until I realized that I had no fucking idea what I was doing.

Don't take this the wrong way when you read this, but I think the universe has a plan...you know, way past all the burning in hell retribution stuff. But an even bigger one. Like maybe to let me figure out how to stand on my own two feet.

When I lived that "padded walls life" for two weeks, all I did was wait for you to rescue me. Even this whole year, I just kept waiting for some kind of bat call that it was our time.

But I don't want to always be the one everyone needs to look after. I want to know that I can take care of myself. Regardless of who I'm standing next to (you, always you...I can almost feel future you grumbling).

Okay, now that I've shared my plan to be badass, if you could just hurry up and rescue me, that would be great. JK. But only because I have to go downstairs and do a photo op with my parents. More specifically, with my mother. Who, by the way, wore head to toe black to my graduation.

Calder...if there was a hole dug, I'd have pushed her in. Since she was already dressed for a funeral. Bitch.

Anyway, I love you. I'm pretending you're wishing me luck.

Calder
September

"I can't stop thinking about that night Roman and I took you to the docks. When we made you sit in the car and threatened to put you in the trunk. Because your ass would've definitely been in the trunk last night for the meeting we had with the Italians."

I brush my hands over West's headstone, clearing some leaves from the top. This has become part of my week. I visit my brother, tell him about shit that's going right and the stuff that goes wrong too.

I don't know if he can fucking hear me, but there's something satisfying about telling him that I'm gonna make them pay for what happened to him.

Footsteps fall behind me, drawing my head over my shoulder.

Roman's grinning behind me, cigarette in one hand, beer in the other.

"You about done talking about a girl West called first?"

I laugh, looking back at the grave.

"The fuck he did."

Roman takes a drag of the cigarette, coming shoulder to shoulder with me.

"No, he did. When we walked around to the bathrooms the first day, we saw her and her friends. West called dibs on red."

I laugh harder because of course he did. My face turns to Roman's.

"Did I ever tell you he was the one that thought of the code names I put in the phone for Sutton and me? Because I liked that movie, *The Princess Bride*. I didn't even catch on to the sneaky shit he was doing until I went to add that fucking pirate's name into her phone and…"

I don't even have to finish because Roman's laughing.

"Motherfucker." He wheezes.

"Right." I laugh harder. "She would've been walking around with *his* fucking name in her phone. But I couldn't think of anything on the fly, so I just spelled it wrong and left the *T* out."

The two of us stand there, laughing our asses off and letting ourselves heal. Roman wipes tears from his eyes, smiling wide as we catch our breath until it's silent again.

"Fuck I miss him," I whisper as Roman nods.

"Me too, brother. Me too."

Chapter Nineteen

Calder
November

The hotel suite door closes with a thud behind Roman, but something feels off. We were told to meet Connor here, but nothing else.

And guilty people worry, so right now, I'm on edge.

Connor's security walks past, not bothering to pat us down, grunting for us to follow. We do as Roman's and my eyes meet again. He mouths, "The fuck?" with confusion on his brow.

But I shrug because they left our guns on us, so we're not dying tonight. Even though there's something definitely going on. I just don't know what.

As we enter the open area of the hotel suite, my uncle's seated in a black leather chair, eyes locked to mine, surrounded by his closest advisors. I glance around at the other men spread throughout the room. All their faces are solemn, eyes fixed on us as the guard comes to a stop before turning around, leaving us in front of a low black coffee table.

Nobody speaks, all remaining in their places as Roman and I look at each other and back to Connor.

"What's going on, Uncle?"

"Do you know why you're here, Calder?"

No, you fucking dick, or I wouldn't have asked. I shake my head, glancing around again because of the grin growing on Connor's face.

"No, but I feel like you're about to tell me."

Connor's smile doubles over his face, big and wide, as laughter erupts around the room. He joins them, saying, "Can you believe this kid?"

Believe me for what?

His fat head swings back to my cautious face.

"Did you think I'd forget my only nephew's twenty-first birthday?"

Oh fuck.

The room goes nuts with cheers and revelry as my face swings to Roman, who's grinning. He holds up his hands.

"Don't look at me. I didn't say anything."

I don't celebrate my birthday. I haven't since West. It doesn't seem right to have them when he never will. So I've kept my mouth shut all week, and I thought I'd slipped under the radar. But I should've known better.

I smile, hanging my head and pretending to be happily surprised, smiling like he's a great fucking guy.

Connor walks toward us, clapping his hands as I lift my head.

"You shouldn't have, Uncle."

"Did you think you could hide from me? I know everything, Calder. And this is an occasion to celebrate."

The way that Connor said "*hide from me*" was with truthful

intent, and it requires an answer, but my mouth doesn't open. *Because yes, Connor. I do think I can hide from you. I've been doing it for a minute, you piece of shit.*

Roman slaps a hand to my shoulder, filling in all the words I don't say.

"Damn. It looks like we're in for some trouble tonight, C. And here you thought you were gonna go low-key." Roman turns toward Connor, grinning like the devil. "He never wants to bring attention to himself. You know him, always thinking about business. Never wanting to be a burden. I told him, 'Connor would want to mark this moment.' But good luck making him listen."

All bullshit, all perfect.

Connor wags his eyebrows, coming in close. "Stubborn, just like your mother." He pats both our faces. "My boys, so good." His eyes connect with mine. "And so loyal. Time to reward that."

Connor stares into my eyes for a long moment before snapping his fingers. That look felt a lot like mistrust. Fuck.

The doors behind us swing open again, drawing my and Roman's heads over our shoulders. Connor steps in between, arms slung over us as women crowd the doorway.

Shouts and catcalls boom around the room as, one by one, girls dressed in the kind of shit that puts all the merchandise on display sway their asses inside. Some cozy up to men as the music begins playing as others climb onto the tops of tables and dance.

These aren't just strippers though—they're the kind of girls that know business better than most men because slinging your body on the streets isn't something that leaves you soft.

That's why we're here, instead of a club. Connor's throwing the kind of party where secrets are kept and wives never find out.

A blonde slides up next to Roman, saying, "Hey." He drops his face to hers, reaching down to grab her ass, making her squeal.

Connor laughs, stepping away, looking back at me.

"You deserve this night, nephew. And I'm going to make sure you get your fill. Because I got ya something special."

Connor steps out into the middle of the room, spreading his arms as his voice booms over the ruckus.

"Fellas, take your pick because tonight, these lovely ladies are on me. You can have anyone you like, except this one—she's special, just for my nephew."

The doors to the suite reopen as Connor's handed a drink. He lifts the scotch as hollers from the men become deafening.

"Happy Birthday, Calder," he thunders as I follow his line of sight.

Long red hair. That's all I fucking see.

Sutton walks through the door in sky-high heels, wearing nothing but black lace panties and a bra.

"Oh fuck," Roman whispers next to me, but I give my head a slight shake as the girl with green eyes licks her lips.

This was why Connor stared at me because he knew what he'd done. This is a test.

"C. You good?"

I nod, smile still in place because that's not my girl. She's just some redhead with green eyes, meant to dig the knife in deeper.

This motherfucker. One day, I'm going to look him in the eye and watch as his life fades out. I'll be there just like I was with my father because I want Connor to see the look on my face and understand I did it all for her.

The hooker saunters forward as sick enjoyment plays behind Connor's eyes. He doesn't even hide that he's enjoying his little game, sights on me, watching my every reaction.

But all I'm giving is interest. Like a guy who's about to stick his dick in some girl that likes to fuck. Even if what I'd rather do is pull my gun out and decorate the wall with his brains.

I lock eyes with his and wink, letting my deep voice carry as the chick stops in front of me.

"You're too generous, Uncle."

Connor walks toward me, reaching out and grabbing her tit roughly.

"I'm glad you like my gift, nephew. I know how partial you are to redheads. And this one I'll let you keep."

The depth of the brutality and violence I have to swallow makes me fucking sick because I can taste the bile that's creeping up my fucking throat. *He'll let me keep?*

Roman's eyes are on me because he knows I'm about to fucking explode. He's not wrong.

Connor grabs her hair, forcing her eyes to his, and something inside of me snaps. I don't give a fuck about this hooker, but I'll be damned if Connor flexes on me like this.

My voice is rough as I reach down, grabbing the black band of her panties over her hip, jerking her forward.

"You want him? Or you want me? Because I don't fuck hand-me-downs."

Connor laughs loudly, stepping away. The chick winds her fingers around the strings on my hoodie.

"Baby, you get as many wishes as you want tonight."

The sneer across my lip is real because her perfume is Sutton's. Connor did his research. Fucking bastard.

I grab her wrists, pulling her hands off my chest before I close a hand around her petite throat.

"Then tonight my wish is for you to do as you're told. No crying or saying no. Am I understood?"

She nods, fear in her eyes.

I walk her backward, leading her by the throat as she stares up at me, all the way back into the bedroom before the door closes behind me, my fingers twisting the lock.

I let her go, stepping back.

"I'm sorry." I run a hand through my hair. "Don't let him touch you. He gets off on cruelty, which is why I said that shit. You don't have to be scared."

She smiles, relieved as she nods.

I'm already peeling off hundreds from the stack that I just pulled from my pocket as she says, "I'm Krystal."

My face lifts as her fingers pull the strap of her bra down.

"Hey, hey," I whisper, reaching out, tugging it back up. "Let's just talk."

I hand her the money as she eyes me suspiciously.

"You just want to talk?"

I nod, peeling off another couple hundred as I say, "Yeah, but if anyone asks—"

"You're the best I ever had," she interjects, biting her lip. "It's cool. We'll hang for a minute." She looks me up and down. "Or maybe like an hour, and then when we walk out, I'll tell everyone you're a real fucking animal."

I almost laugh, but I wink instead, walking deeper into the room and looking over my shoulder.

"Smoke?"

She shrugs, following behind me. I slide the patio door open to the chill in the air. So I peel my hoodie over my head, handing it to her.

I chuckle because she looks confused.

"It's cold, Krystal. Put it on."

She takes it from my hands, draping it over her head and letting it fall to her thighs because she's swimming in it. I step outside, taking a deep breath before pulling my pack out of my back pocket and offering one to her. But she shakes her head, opting to sit in one of the patio chairs, drawing her knees under the hoodie.

I light my smoke, putting my forearms on the rail, and stare up at the sky.

Fuck. Everything about that navy sky, peppered with bright lights, makes me remember how Sutton looked that night I saw her on the beach, cursing at the damn moon.

Miss you, baby.

"Wanna talk about her?"

I chuckle, looking over at Krystal. "Who says there's a *her*?"

"A him?"

I grin, taking another drag of my smoke, but she doesn't let it go.

"In my experience, men don't look at the moon unless it's the pants-down kind."

I laugh as she continues. "And they certainly don't stare at the stars. So, baby boy, you got it bad."

I drop my head down, looking at my hands hanging over the rail, cigarette burning red, smiling.

"Yeah. I really fucking do."

We dragged our asses through the door at 4:00 a.m. equal amounts of buzzed and tired. The rest of the night was easy, smooth, mostly thanks to Krystal, who didn't leave my side.

She did what she said she'd do. And it was pretty fucking convincing.

It's fucking wild, but Krystal is the easiest moment I've had in the last sixteen months. Because the only thing I had to be responsible for was loving Sutton. There was no pretense or fucking second-guessing her interest. I just got to love my girl out loud again.

I didn't even realize how much I'd missed it until I caught myself looking for reasons to stay in that fucking room.

I wipe my hands down my face, scratching my beard, body warm from the liquor as I lie in my bed, one leg bent at the knee. The joint pinched in between my fingers burns bright as I suck in a drag, holding it for a minute before releasing a thick plume of smoke.

My bottom lip draws between my teeth, dragging out slowly as my head falls back against my headboard, enjoying the tingly feeling in my body as my muscular thigh falls open.

"Damn, I'm fucked-up," I say with a laugh before I drop my head back down, eyes catching on the chair in the corner. The hoodie I wore is tossed over it. The one I let that chick wear—the one that smelled like my baby.

I blink slowly, staring at it as the thought brewing takes a minute to stick in my mind.

I drape my legs over the side of my bed before I stand and walk across my room, ass on display, over to that fucking sweatshirt.

I pick it up, turning it inside out immediately hit with the sweetest smell of grapefruit and rosemary, almost knocking me down.

"Baby," I whisper.

I bring it to my nose, inhaling as my eyes close, letting out a quick exhale before doing it again.

"Oh fuck," I groan.

I'm like an animal, devouring her fucking scent. The veins in my forearms bulge as I grip the fabric tighter, my mind drifting to the image of Sutton's body. Thinking of all the fucking places I could smell that perfume on her.

"Fuck," I grunt as my cock twitches, bobbing heavily as it grows.

My stomach contracts, abs tightening as I bring it to my neck, head falling back as I rub the fabric over me, dragging it over my throat. Licking my lips as it slides down to my chest, wanting her fucking scent all over me.

"You smell like heaven," I whisper, slowly trailing the fabric down my abs as my eyes follow, thinking about my hand in her hair as she sucked me off.

I press my cock into the fabric, rubbing my hand up and down as a growl vibrates through my throat.

"Fuck. I want to be inside you."

I chuck the hoodie, breathing hard. My hand comes to my mouth as I drag my tongue flat and wide over my fucking palm before wrapping it around my cock.

A groan leaves my parted lips as I tug down my shaft and back up, staring at that fucking hoodie. My eyes close as I lean forward, my other hand slapping down onto the wall in front of me. I roll my hips, pushing into my hand, tugging down my dick again.

"Fuck me," I groan.

I want to be inside her so damn bad, fucking her tight little pussy, treating her like the bad girl she really is.

The memory of the last time I said that to her takes over my thoughts.

"Are you my bad girl, baby?"

She looks like she's going to explode as her answer comes out husky and needy.

"Yes."

I'm stroking my cock in front of her face. Fuck she looks beautiful like this. I slide my hand up my shaft slowly, before running it down, watching her lick her lips wanting to taste my cock.

"Lemme get it wet," she whispers, making me groan.

Sutton parts her lips as I guide the tip of my cock into her mouth. Her tongue swirls over the bead of cum that crowned before her mouth covered my length, moaning her pleasure.

I could come on the spot, drip down her fucking throat as she swallows everything I give her.

"Oh, baby. I love you bad."

My hand drops from feeding her my dick, coming to her head. She moans, gripping the side of my ass, pulling me deeper into her mouth.

"Oh fuck, take it," I breathe out remembering our sixty-nine.

I'm jerking my cock, breath ragged, fingers curling into the wall as I think about all the things I wanted to do that night but couldn't.

It's so fucking real in my mind that I lose myself, hanging my head, my teeth clamped together. I wanted to fuck her, then flip her over. Run my hand up her back as she lay on her stomach, legs spread, cum on her ass as I got hard again behind her.

I tuck my arm under her, yanking her hips up as my other hand grips the back of her neck, keeping her face on the ground as she arches her back.

"Yeah, baby. Put that ass on display for me." I breathe, seeing it all in my mind.

Fuck, my cock is so hard, it almost hurts as I jerk myself, gasping for air.

My hand drags across her stomach, rounding over her perfect ass, as I use my fingers and thumb to spread her cheeks before I drop my head, spitting on her tight puckered hole. She rolls her hips as I watch the spit roll down from her tailbone before I reach between her legs, sticking my fingers in her pussy.

I dart my tongue out, licking my lips, almost hearing her moan.

"Baby, you're so fucking wet. It's dripping from you, begging for my cock to do bad fucking things to this ass."

My hand glides faster and faster as I press my hips forward wanting inside her in my fantasy. But it's not enough, so I bring my hand up again and spit into it.

"Oh, yeah," I groan, listening to the slapping sound of my cock getting off.

I gather her sweet sugar, letting her cream coat my fingers, dragging it over her tight ass, feeling it contract. I do it again and again watching as she's writhing under my hold.

"Tell me what it feels like."

"It feels like I'm your bad girl."

Her ass is red under my hand as I squeeze, growling as I push my dick inside her pussy, pumping my hips viciously. Fucking her raw. She moans my name before I pull out, bringing the glistening tip over her asshole, rubbing it back and forth.

Her pelvis rocks as my thumb slips inside, fucking that beautiful ass, before stretching her with another finger.

"Yes," she cries in my mind as I do the same aloud, eyes springing open as I pump my cock with a single focus.

I'm chasing my fucking release, lost to the filthy images playing in my mind.

My fingers in her ass are replaced by my cock. It's covered in her pleasure, mixing with the spit as I crown her asshole, spreading her inch by fucking inch, as she opens for me. I push inside, feeling her locked around my shaft until I'm seated deep inside her.

"Fuck."

She reaches between her legs, rubbing her needy little clit as my hand grips her waist, fucking her tight little ass, letting my shaft drag in and out, feeling my cock strangled until I'm thrusting into her, my body doubled over her like an animal.

Grunts and heavy breaths fill the air as I fuck my own hand.

My release builds in my stomach as I scratch at the wall.

"Yes. Take it, baby."

I'm fucking her hard and fast, one hand covering her tit as the other pulls her hair, using it to bring her mouth to mine.

My body contracts as I bite her shoulder, coming inside her, hearing her scream my name.

"Fuck," I grunt, body tensing as warm cum shoots out onto the fucking hoodie and all over my hand.

I'm panting, body jerking as I come riding out my fucking release until I drop my head back, feeling my body growing limp.

The vision of me fucking Sutton's sweet ass fades as my eyes blink open slowly. I milk myself, hissing between my teeth, as I reach down with my other hand to grab the sweatshirt. I clean myself with it as I walk to my bathroom.

I turn on the sink faucet, looking into the basin, letting out a long breath before I grin.

"Soon. Can't come soon enough, baby."

Chapter Twenty

Sutton

The day the sky fell—

Promise me that the day you read this that if Hunter isn't in the ground, you'll bury him. And my father for turning a blind eye.

Since that day, I haven't survived.

I've been swallowed whole, and I need you. Because all I want to do is disappear, even though I'm not seen.

January—

Same shit, different day since August. I go to class, I come back to my room. My roommate tells me I'm a fucking downer, and then I watch a bunch of television I can't remember.

I guess the silver lining is that I didn't disappear?

God, I don't want to write in this anymore. And I'm fucking crying all over this stupid page. And I don't want to think about when you're coming OR be reminded that I'm a fucking idiot that can't take care of myself. I just want to watch TV.

I wish you were a different person. Someone from regular parents who could just love me without all the fight to get there.

Calder
July

Fireworks fill the sky. No matter which direction I turn, color explodes, lighting my face and Roman's in streaks of gold and purple before growing dark again.

"Fuck," I whisper to myself.

"You good?" Roman asks, leaning back against the hood of the GTO.

"Yeah." I nod.

He narrows his eyes on me, but I wave him off with a grin as my phone rings.

"What's up, Unc?"

"How's the shipment?" *Wrapped up hours ago.*

"Golden."

"Any problem at the docks?"

"Nah, we're heading back soon." My eyes land on my brother as I speak. "But you know Roman. We might hit a strip club or two before we're home."

Connor laughs before coughing.

"Okay, but not too much trouble though."

"Wouldn't dream of it."

The line disconnects as Roman stares at me, chuckling. "It's not a terrible idea. It's a long drive back to Boston."

I ignore him, turning around and walking out into the field. *Our field.*

Fuck me. Being back in St. Simeon is bittersweet because everything reminds me of her. She's all over me. But I like it.

Even the smell of the ocean reminds me of her. The way it was always on her skin, like the sunshine she loves so much.

Fuck. When Connor proposed Roman and I start making some trips down here to check up on shipments, it was the first time I was happy to take a job. Although, thank God I'm only here for the night, or I'd go fucking crazy. Probably throw away all the plans and set whole cities on fire, because damn if this feeling ain't fucking potent.

If someone bottled her, I'd be a fucking junkie. I smirk to myself, because I am though—completely and totally fucking addicted.

"It's been two years since we've been back here. Two fucking years," I level, shifting my head over my shoulder to Roman.

It feels like forever and also no time at all because I swear to everything that I love that fucking girl just as much as the first day I told her.

Roman laughs. "If this situation wasn't so goddamn serious, I'd make fun of you for being pussy-whipped. Because you know your ass is thinking about her."

I laugh too, because he's not wrong. I'm always thinking about her.

Roman walks over to me, staring at my profile with a grin.

"I don't want jinx shit, but are you in a good mood? For like the first time in our lives?"

I look up at the sky as I smile.

"I've been filling pebbles in a sack, one by one. Every goddamn day. But today feels like I've got a big enough sandbag to hold them all under. So yeah, I guess that's put me in a good mood because I'm a giant step closer to my girl."

He says nothing, looking up along with me.

"You think she'll like this?"

I smile. "I think we'll die here together one day."

We stand in silence again before he pats my shoulder, saying, "It's almost time."

I nod as a breeze carries over the grass, making me remember our last moments here. She was so fucking beautiful, gifting her body to me because I'd already stolen her heart.

All the sweetest moments pull to the forefront of my mind as my lips tug into a half smile. Damn, the look on her face when she laid her green eyes on me from the hood of that car.

"I got you. Fuck. Baby, I got you. Don't cry."

She draws her head back, hands planting on the sides of my face.

"I was so scared nobody would believe us. Or that you wouldn't come."

My lips find hers before saying, "Nothing could've kept me from you."

"It's still true, baby," I whisper.

Over the last two years, it's been a methodical, unwavering fucking attack on Connor and everyone who hurt her. I've made friends out of enemies. Become a name that invokes fear and respect. And it's all happened in the shadows.

Because nothing will fucking keep me from her. I believe it so deep that I'm here, on our field, planning our future.

I drop my eyes before turning around to stare at the taped-off outline of the house to be built.

"It's all for you, baby."

I bought it all, the whole fucking plot of property. And bribed quite a few people to keep it quiet. Nobody knows it's mine, and that's the way it'll stay until this shit is over. Because one day, we'll sit out on our porch, looking up at the same stars that we fell in love under, not being able to remember ever even being apart.

"C. They're here," Roman calls.

I let out a deep breath before walking over to the car to join him. Three black SUVs come tearing down the dirt road until they slow, stopping next to each other before four men dressed in expensive black dress suits exit the cars.

"Calder Wolfe."

Dante Sovrano, the head of the Italian Chicago mob, steps forward, extending a hand toward me as I do the same.

"Nice to see ya again, kid. I was happy you called. Now, tell me how I can help. Because word is, you're the one that really runs Boston. Not Connor O'Bannion."

Sutton

July—

Happy two-year anniversary.

I was actually kind of scared to open this journal today. Still, I have things to write, and don't worry, it's not all about the television I've watched. Although there's a lot.

Shit got dark. But I crawled out all by myself.

I'm proud of that part, and I know you are too reading this.

So, on to happier news. I ran into Aubrey last month. Like actually ran into her.

She was in the city, visiting some guy she's banging at NYU, and we collided as I was coming into the dorm that she was sneaking out of.

I'm not ashamed to admit that I immediately broke down in tears. She did too.

And then she hugged me, and I cried harder because I realized nobody I love had touched me in two years. TWO.

Honestly, that was the best fucking hug I've had in forever.

(Yours excluded. I'm rolling my eyes because I know you're hugging future me.)

We're having lunch today before she flies back to London... She went to Oxford. Of course, she did.

I guess that's all. I just kind of wanted there to be one journal entry that says, "I'm okay. And a helluva lot stronger than I give myself credit for."

You've helped me learn that. Definitely a lesson less fun than the others. But I love you even more than yesterday, if that's possible. And I miss everything about you.

–Soon.

P.S. I almost scared myself at how good I was at telling just enough of the truth without revealing it fully. I was marveling at my double-life skills until Aubrey looked at me, patted my hand, and said, "One day, you can tell me the truth. Until then, we'll go with what you just said."

So I guess I'll keep working on it.

Year
Three

Chapter Twenty-One

Sutton
December

"Okay. All right. I swear, Piper. Christmas break is three days away. I have time to pack, then I promise I'll be there. Okay, bye."

I'm smiling, and it feels good, phone sandwiched between my ear and shoulder, bookbag barely staying in place over my jacket as I open my dorm room door.

My head pops up. *What the fuck?* My phone slides down my jacket as I reach for it, coming up short.

"Shit." I huff, squatting to pick it up off the floor.

"Hello to you too. Good to see your manners are still intact," my mother cuts, switching her legs, letting the other drape over.

She's seated on my bed, back as straight as a steel rod, next to my father, standing in his signature navy suit.

I place my backpack on the ground, a scowl on my face.

"What the fuck are you doing here? I thought we had a deal. I show up for the photo-ops and anything press-related, and you both stay far away from me."

"This *is* press-related," my mother snaps.

My eyes narrow. "Is it? Or should we revisit the definition?"

My father clears his throat.

"It seems as though the trouble that found Hunter during his senior year is rearing its ugly head again. The press has leaned into the narrative of 'rich kid with too much time on his hands.' Questions are being asked about his involvement with the company. There's even speculation about Michael Kelly's death. And we think—"

"Marianne thinks," I spit, anger coating my words. "Don't give yourselves more credit than you're due. But personally, I think for the first time, the reporting is spot-on. So, shouldn't you be in Tiffany Astor's room? Isn't that who he allegedly knocked up senior year? Or are you scared there's more to the story, Senator?"

The fucking nerve you have to be here.

"We think," he presses, "that it would be nice for you two to be seen out in public."

My heart stops beating as he speaks.

"The media loved when you two seemed like an item. And Hunter needs the positive press. We'd hoped to rekindle that a couple of years ago after your graduation, but—"

My hand shoots to my mouth as goosebumps pebble over my skin. I shake my head as he trails off, my stomach turning over as my body grows immediately cold. Like ice fucking cold. I stare into my father's eyes, standing silent, willing my body not to share my lunch with the floor.

They can't be serious. That day, two weeks after my graduation is the whole fucking reason we have this deal between us. The reason I almost disappeared into myself.

I know my life is not my own, but they can't actually be this indecent.

I close my eyes, remembering how they forced me to come back to St. Simeon, all to attend some "important fundraiser." And I went because as much as I hate them, they were still paying for the freedom I was desperate for. Even if it's just the scraps that life has to offer. *Something* in this hellhole of an existence felt better than *nothing*.

But I was wrong, because the fundraiser turned out to be Hunter's graduation party.

Marianne had anyone and everyone who would make Page Six in her back yard with a glass of champagne all lifted to toast the man of the hour.

But I never made it downstairs.

I wince, remembering how he smelled and how small I felt before blowing out a hard breath, opening my narrowed eyes on them.

"What's it like to be you? The kind of people who ask their only daughter to be seen with the boy who tried to rape her. Or did you conveniently forget walking into his bedroom, Senator?"

My eyes bore into his. "Did you forget seeing me struggling underneath him, crying out for you to do something? To help me." My voice rises, "Yelling, *Daddy, come back*."

"Enough," my mother snaps, making my shoulders jump as she holds up a hand, but that only makes me want to bite it off.

I stab my finger at him, my words hurled with all the anger they deserve.

"You closed the door, you fucking bastard. I begged you for help, and you fucking closed the door."

My eyes begin to water, so I snap my jaw shut, running a hand through my hair. *I will never cry in front of them.*

I turn my face back toward theirs, and the indignant looks pull a laugh from my chest. Not in hysteria, but because the goddamn nerve they possess is unbelievable.

Did I ever even know them?

I throw my hands in the air, mainly talking to myself.

"I guess it doesn't really count in your mind since he couldn't get hard. I'm sure you know that part?" I pat my cheeks as I blow out another breath. "In the future, I should really invest some of my inheritance into whiskey stocks since they were the real heroes that night."

My father stands silent, staring down at the floor. God, he used to be such a presence. He always felt a little intimidating but also safe. Now he just looks like a coward.

The thought breaks my heart, but this is the last time that'll ever happen.

Because I know what it's like to be loved and protected. I have someone who would never close the fucking door. And I will fight, scratch, and claw my way back to him.

My mother stands, drawing my attention, as I cross my arms. She looks me in the eye, saying one of the worst things she's ever uttered to me.

"Your pussy wasn't discerning enough to keep you from a criminal, so then why would it care if Hunter fucked it."

I blink, mouth falling open, dumbstruck as she continues.

"I'm not making a request, Sutton. You will have dinner together, be photographed…together, and that's that. The public wants their Romeo and Juliet, and you'll help provide it. Despite your trauma."

My hands are pressed to my chest, pushing in, feeling my heart pounding against the palm of my hand.

"Jesus Christ. What does Marianne have on you that makes you so willing to sacrifice me with such little disregard?"

"It's *who* she has, Sutton. You brought that filth into our life, and he brought with him the whole Irish mob. We all work for Connor

O'Bannion, remember? And he likes it when his dirty Senator looks good, and nobody's asking questions about the Kelly pharmaceutical company. This time, Sutton, bad press is bad."

"You could've dressed a little sluttier. You know, make the world really believe I would fuck you."

Bile rises in my throat as flashes come from a camera. I keep my eyes on my menu, smiling as I speak like I'm gunning for an Oscar.

I am, though. I will never let Hunter know that he affects me in even the smallest of ways. Because I want to take *everything* from him. That's how much I hate him. But tonight, I'm just starting with his glib satisfaction.

"Well, you've already had one Macallan and Coke, disguised as only a Coke, so I'd say the chance of you raping me is slim to none. I think we've come to learn that about you. Remember?"

Saying it out loud makes the inside of me shake. But Hunter can't see that, so it's okay.

My eyes lift to his as I shrug my shoulders like I'm flirting, batting my eyelashes.

"Hunter"—I bite my bottom lip leaning forward—"I'm a whole kind of bitch you aren't prepared for now. This version of me fights dirty. So be very careful, or I'll cut your dick off with the butter knife when nobody's looking."

"Noted." He winks, going along with the façade, but I see the worry in his eyes.

Oh, you should believe me, Hunter.

"Good, because I'd never lie to you about how much I despise you."

I giggle before looking back down at the menu.

His mother booked us a fucking table by the window at Bagatelle. A posh restaurant in the meatpacking district. I'm actually disappointed, it's just so obvious, and yet the cameras haven't stopped flashing.

Idiots.

Tomorrow, I'm sure we'll be all over the society section with this bullshit. My mind wanders to Calder, momentarily wondering if he'll see these photos. Fuck. I hate this.

The waiter comes to the table to take our order, so I choose the first thing I see because, frankly, my stomach soured the minute I saw Hunter's fucking face.

He does the same, then lifts his glass, nodding to the waiter as I turn my head from the window ticking over the other diners. *People are everywhere. You're fine.*

He takes a deep breath before leaning sideways to pull his phone from his Armani slacks.

"Seriously? Nice manners. Eat fast, and then you can go and check your phone for whatever STD's texted you lately. In the meantime, can't you just play along?"

Every word is said with a smile. I pick up my water, taking a sip as Hunter stares at me.

"Yeah, Freckles, I can play along. Like a fucking champ. Let's see if you can too."

"Eww. Don't call me that."

He chuckles, but it's dark, off in some way. My brows draw together as my lips part, but he stops the words from coming out of my mouth.

He holds his phone out toward me, covering it from the glass, so nobody gets a photo, motioning with his head for me to lean in. The smile on his face says he's flirting, being cheeky, but the image in front of me is Piper.

She's standing on a sidewalk in a tank top.

Oh my God, this was taken in L.A., but she only just got there a week ago.

My eyes dart back to his.

"What is this? Why do you have a picture of Piper on your phone?"

"Smile, Sutton."

I do immediately, and he laughs, pulling his phone away, shoving it back into his trousers.

The waiter returns with Hunter's drink, and he doesn't hesitate to take a long swig before saying, "Think of it as a reminder that we're all just puppets in a show. We all have our parts to play, Sutton, and nobody is ever out of reach."

My heart stills. *This isn't happening again.*

"I am playing my part," I whisper, quietly taking a deep breath. "I'm here, aren't I? What more does *he* want?"

He laughs, and it's genuine, throwing me off.

"Do you think I'm talking about Connor O'Bannion?"

"Shhh," I hiss before he smiles again, rolling his eyes.

"Smile, Sutton."

I do as my fingers come to my fork, flipping it over slowly again and again. Hunter's hand brushes over the white tablecloth as he speaks casually.

"I guess, in a way, you're right. I am talking about *him*. But only because he doesn't have to give any orders; everyone's fear does the heavy work."

"What are you talking about? Spell it out," I whisper.

Hunter smirks, tapping a finger on the table before he speaks.

"Our mothers understand that *he* only cares about power and money. Your fucking criminal is the power. As long as he has Calder, that organization is his. Now, my family is the money. Because we make incredibly potent little white pills. You remember those, right?"

I swallow, reaching for my water to take a sip.

"*He's* nothing without either. I fucked up, made a mess that needs to be cleaned up, and because I'm the company's future, that threatens his money. And unlike your mother, mine wants me alive, hence this fucking dinner."

My mind is racing because I still don't get what this has to do with me. *Why show me Piper?*

"But I didn't do anything. I did what I was told. I walked away."

I hate how scared my voice sounds.

"Smile."

I do.

Hunter tilts his head, extending his arm, letting his fingers skim over mine. The action sends chills over my body, my throat suddenly feeling dry, but I don't pull away, staring straight into his eyes.

Fuck you, Cunter. I'm not ever running scared of you again.

"You're so naïve. It's always amazed me that someone like Calder saw anything other than stupidity behind those green eyes."

His fingers retreat, leaving me to take a quiet, relieved inhale as he speaks.

"Freckles, they only found assurance in your weakness. Then you had to go and start acting like your life was yours. Did you think you'd just jet off to L.A. with Piper or have long lunches with Aubrey? If they can't control you, then they don't trust you. And that's a direct threat to *his* power. And I'm certain you would rather die than see your beloved hurt."

I'm sitting silent because I'm not stupid. I know Connor is always somewhere watching. It's why I don't make waves. And I know this fight doesn't truly end until Calder finishes it, which is why I toe the line with my parents.

I just have to survive until we're together.

But I just got Aubs and Piper back in the smallest way. Fuck, I just got some of myself back. And the thought of losing it all again… The lump in my throat is swallowed down as I lift my eyes back to his.

"You know," he chuckles, "if you would've just died, we wouldn't be here. So really, we only have you to blame."

He lifts his drink to me, adding, "Cheers to that, right?" before he downs it.

My eyes grow wide as I let out a half laugh, uncaring about my face.

"I could say the same for you." I hold up my water like I'm toasting him back. "It's a real fucking shame you were such a good swimmer when you got tossed off that cliff."

He sneers.

"Smile," I say, all sing-songy, reveling in my dig as I watch him force a grin.

I tap my fingers on the table, shaking my head, noticing out of the corner of my eye how close the photographers begin to close in on the window.

"So what's the point of all this? I have to ignore my friends again. Fine, done. Am I to never leave my room? Okay, whatever. Do they want me to fail out of college? What?"

The grin on his face stays, growing into a smile.

"How you didn't turn out more like your mother, I'll never know. College is over Freckles. You're officially withdrawn. They're not paying for it anymore. There are no decisions for you to make. They've decided how to get rid of both of our problematic existences."

I blink, lips parting as Hunter stands from the table, motioning between us. "Figuratively speaking, they've figured out how to kill two birds—"

He reaches into his pocket, pulling out a small blue box, eyes locked to mine.

"—with one stone."

The box flips open to a pear-shaped Tiffany diamond as he lowers down to one knee.

"We all have our parts to play. Yours is as my wife. Now say yes, because *he's* always watching."

Cameras flash like strobe lights next to me. And I see Hunter still speaking, but all I can hear is the quiet slowing of the breath inside my body. Like a countdown to my end.

I've held on for so long to the idea of *one day*. But I'm not sure anymore if there will be anything left of me when Calder comes.

The last time I write—

I can't keep doing this. Because one day, this part of my life will be a memory that I choose to forget. I refuse to honor its existence here for you to read. So just know that I have loved you, never wavering.

And I'm doing what I have to because of that fact.

I hope you find me and that I'm still whole.

Because I never anticipated that when I told you I was willing to wade through hell to be with you—that tonight, the Devil would call my bluff.

Aubrey: Why am I waking up in London and feeling like I'm in a parallel universe?

Aubrey: There are photos of Sut and Hunter dated two days ago…he's down on one knee. Piper, where are you? Did you know they were dating?

Piper: HERE! And I'm sorry, what! Was he falling, Sut? After you knee'd him in the balls for being an overall douche? Since when do we revisit HS red flags? Is this why you've been sending me to voicemail?

Piper: SUT! ANSWER US.

I can't.

Since we've reconnected, I've told the same story: Calder and I broke up, things got out of hand—there was a robbery, and my parents thought it was best to send me to Madison. I did tell them about West, but only what was reported. That lie hurt the worst.

For the most part, I stuck with the truths I could say—ones that felt plausible enough and wouldn't garner too many questions.

Jesus, I've told her and Aubrey about the depression without giving the actual reasons, sometimes blaming the season. I sat quietly on phone calls pretending to have an off day when I was really missing Calder so much I couldn't get out of bed.

And other days, I blamed school or something else just as flimsy instead of saying that I couldn't stop the memories of Hunter violating me with parental approval.

I've cried in silence all this time, but for whatever beautiful miracle of a reason, they've stuck around, accepting my half-truths, even though we all silently acknowledge the lies.

But this time I don't trust myself, because this feels too big to carry alone anymore.

Piper: *Are you still coming to LA? I'll hide you here, and you don't have to go back.*

I place my phone down on my bed and look at the boxes delivered to my dorm room today. My life is being stolen from me again.

"Fuck you, Elizabeth."

I lie back on my bed and close my eyes, just wanting to sleep this nightmare away because I'm not going to visit Piper. The only packing I'm doing is taking me back to St. Simeon.

A few hours later, more texts come through.

Aubrey: *This has Baron and Elizabeth written all over it. It stinks of social politics. WTF is going on?*

Piper: *Don't ghost, Sutton. And don't fucking marry Hunter.*

Aubrey: *Yeah. Say the hard shit this time. We're here for it, bitch.*

Piper: *I can't stand the idea that you are all alone with this.*

I pull the blanket over me, all the lights off even though it's the middle of the day. I still haven't started packing, but I haven't gotten out of bed either. I'm just staring at my phone, the urge to say something, anything, building more and more.

I have been alone through all of this, and I'm tired. So fucking tired.

Butterflies go off in my stomach as my fingers hover over the keys.

God, what do I say? Because I want to tell the truth. It's burning on the tip of my tongue to escape. I blink, shoulders jumping because I'm so deep in thought that the vibration startles me.

Piper: *Okay. I can't believe I'm asking this. But just tell us if we're team Hunter or team Cunter? That's all we need to know. No other questions until you're ready to answer.*

Say it. Do it, Sutton.

If I ignore them, I may never get them back again. Bubbles pop up right before Aubrey's message populates.

Aubrey: *I don't give AF what team you say—I'm always gonna be that fucking pirate's biggest fan. And I don't care what you say about him either because you stink of him every fucking time I see you. If love had a scent, yours would be called pining. And for the record, modern-day arranged marriages are not it, bitch. That is not a trend that's coming back. So stop leaving us on read and remember we keep secrets. All the fucking secrets. Dread Pirate Roberts for life…I like that nickname way better than Wesley…or Westley…whatever his fucking name is.*

Tears. Immediate fucking tears. I love her. She said it so I wouldn't have to. Fuck this, they can make me marry Hunter, give up school, run my life, but I'm keeping these two.

Me: *Definitely team Cunter. Arrggh.*

Chapter Twenty-Two

Calder
January

"Look at you being a grown-ass man. Sitting at the table, drinking coffee. I guess you're a whole new you in the new year."

"Shut the fuck up." I laugh.

Roman and I have been in New York since yesterday, staying in Brooklyn at a spot used for anyone who needs to lay low. Connor wanted us close to the streets, to keep our eyes and ears open, since we're here for him to meet with the Italians.

He's trying to strike a deal because they just keep taking more and more control of the drug running in Boston.

But if I had a crystal ball, I'd tell him all signs point to *"you're fucked."*

Then again, I don't really need one. *Guess who owns your streets now—me, ya' fucking prick.*

Roman pulls out the chair next to me at the kitchen table, smirking. "You should've come out last night, C. It was good to blow off steam."

"Nah, not my thing. And your hands were full, I'm sure."

"True, but what'd you do? Jerk off thinking about your girl, all alone, watching the ball drop on television? Loser."

"Fuck you," I chuckle.

I'll never admit how fucking accurate that shit is.

I lift my coffee mug, changing the subject. "That chick you brought back last night made some before she snuck out. It's in the kitchen."

He laughs, stretching his arms as he yawns his words out. "Katie might be a keeper…"

The smile on his face tells me he remembers something I don't want to fucking hear. But it makes me pause to look at him because that wasn't her name.

"Romes," I level, shaking my head, "you're not even close."

His mouth opens, a deep v forming between his eyebrows as his face lifts to the ceiling like he's thinking, and it makes my shoulders shake.

"Amanda?"

"Nope." I grin.

He crosses his arms, deeper in thought. "Jen? Jennifer?" He snaps his fingers, pointing at me. "Chrissy. It was Chrissy."

My hands cover my face as I laugh, wiping them down slowly.

"You're fucking kidding, right? Sunshine, you fucking dick. Her name was Sunshine."

He claps his hands together.

"Yes. Sunshine. I couldn't remember because I was fucking hypnotized by this thing that she could do with her leg behind her head. It was really convenient when we—"

"Stop talking," I grunt, cutting him off as I pick up my coffee and take the first swig, only to spit it back into the cup. "Damn, that's fucking dirt. Sounds like she fucked better than she barista'd."

He wags his brows, reaching for the paper that's on the table as I shovel a forkful of eggs into my mouth.

"What's on the agenda for today? What time are we escorting Connor?" he muses, spreading the paper open, making it rustle. "Do people actually read these anymore?"

"You are. So I guess, yeah," I counter, swiping the messages on my phone. "The meeting's late this afternoon. Then we drive the fellas back while Connor flies."

Roman's eyes lift to mine.

"He's gonna be fucking out of control after that meeting. A real pain in the ass all the way back to Boston. I'm suddenly glad he's a dick and making us drive the cars back. He's so fucking paranoid. We could've checked the cars that were here before he rode in them."

I smirk because I've thought about blowing him up a hundred different ways from Sunday.

My phone buzzes so I look down as a message pops up, reading it before it's followed by a photo.

"Oh fuck."

I turn my phone around, smirking as Roman lifts his brows, looking at the text.

"Stripper Chick? Is that who I think it is?"

I nod.

"Yeah, Krystal's happy to make a little side money passing on information when she entertains our local politicians. Looks like she caught a big fish."

"You sure we can trust her?"

I get why Roman's skeptical, but I nod, grinning to myself because the message above reads: I thought this might help true love conquer all. Now go get your girl.

Roman pulls my phone toward him, tilting his head to see the photo better.

"Holy shit. That's a lot of leather. He's really getting served, isn't he? Hold up, is that a ball gag?"

I chuckle.

"So much for being the leader of Christian values. I guarantee this photo isn't going on the Franklin family Christmas card."

"What are you gonna do with it?"

I look up to Roman's grin and shrug.

"I'm not sure yet. I'm weighing my options. It has to be the right move. Because I'm not just destroying a kingdom. I'm building a fucking empire. And that shit wasn't done in a day."

I flip my phone over, cracking my neck. Letting the possibilities play out in my mind.

"Why not just leak that shit. Let Prescott take the heat for being so buddy-buddy with the Lord's kinky little freak."

I shake my head.

"If I've learned anything, it's that impulse is the enemy. It's not enough to ruin everything Connor constructed. We have to be the people with the only replacements for what we take away. So that everyone comes to us ready to be led."

Roman folds the paper, shaking his head at me.

"I gotta say, C, they don't fucking know what's coming. I meant what I said earlier—this version of my brother is a grown-ass man."

I push the nasty coffee toward him with a smirk.

"Maybe you could grow up too and fuck a girl that knows how to make coffee."

He tosses the paper at me as I laugh, catching it before slapping it down on the table. I'm grinning as my eyes drop, my body immediately freezing.

My face hangs, fixed on the photo in front of me, as everything inside slows to a scalding simmer.

"What…the fuck?" I growl, spreading the pages open.

Big, beautiful eyes stare back at me—it's her picture—and she's standing right next to Hunter fucking Kelly.

Roman stares at me as my jaw fucking grinds because I can't make any sense of the words on the goddamn page.

Engaged? What the fuck does that mean?

I lift my head, shaking it. "No. Un-uh." My finger stabs down hard. "Why the fuck does that say engaged? She wouldn't fucking touch him. What the fuck—"

The sound of my chair hitting the ground is the only thing that fills the space as I shoot up, exploding in anger. My fists are balled as I look at Roman.

"Why the fuck is my girl next to that motherfucker? I said he needed to heel. I made that deal with Connor."

I throw my fist down onto the table, making everything bounce off the surface as the salt and pepper shakers fall over.

"If Connor let him off the fucking leash…to do this. No. Roman…no."

The paper rips as I ball the article in my hand, grabbing my gun off the table.

"Connor's doing this shit on purpose. Maybe it's another one of his fucking tests, I don't fucking know. But I don't give a fuck either. I'm putting a bullet in his head, and then I'm gonna finish what I fucking started with Hunter."

Roman stands, blocking my way, hand on my chest to stop me.

"C. You ain't going anywhere. Think before you do something stupid. You just fucking said impulse is the enemy."

My voice is too calm. Because I'm in that comfortable place where I stand next to death as I speak.

"This isn't impulse. This is me…protecting what's mine. Because nobody hurts her. And I know they have. I made a deal with Connor; if that little bitch Hunter is marrying my girl, it's only something sanctioned by my uncle. That means he's willing to sacrifice Sutton for whatever cruel fucking reason he's made up in his head. And he ain't holding *nobody* back from doing the same. So move your hand because I won't tell you again. I love you, but I will kill you if you come between me and my fucking girl. Make no mistake. I will put a gun in your mouth and blow you away if you try to keep me from her."

He doesn't flinch or even look surprised. I think he's known that since that night we had it out about her that she's my only priority. It's her above all. And always will be.

He turns with a nod, grabbing the keys off a table and tossing them to me before grabbing his boots.

"You better hope she fucking forgives you for what you're about to do."

The car comes to a screeching halt in front of the fucking Lotte New York Palace. The article said the engagement party was being held at an exclusive club inside this fucking place.

"Calder, man, fucking look at me," Roman presses as I throw open my door.

Cars whisk by as horns honk, but I don't give a fuck. I'm singularly focused as I stalk around the front of the SUV.

A valet rushes forward, forehead wrinkled, pointing to my car.

"Excuse me, sir. You can't just leave your car here—"

"Watch me," I growl, cutting him off, and walk past him, hearing Roman say something. But I'm not listening because I don't give a fuck what Roman has to say.

She's marrying that little piece of shit. What the fuck did they do to her? There's no fucking way that she ever agreed to this.

I can feel myself disconnecting, tearing the fuck away from any part of me that gave hope to reason because my fists want to pound into something. I just want to hit someone until I feel better. And today, that gets to be Hunter. Right before I blow him away.

My teeth grind so hard they could break as I inhale a rough breath through my flared nose.

If he fucking touched her...

My feet can't carry me fast enough as my head swings from side to side, looking for the fucking room or bar or whatever the hell it is. Some asshole rushes toward me with a shiny gold nameplate above the breast pocket of his beige suit.

"May I help you?"

I jerk to a stop, grabbing his cheap fucking suit by the lapel, bringing his face close to mine.

"What's the name of the members-only club here?"

He stutters, "Rarities," eyes darting around for security, but I shake my head.

"Just tell me where it is. Because trust me, they can't help you if you don't. I will leave you on this floor fucking bloody if you don't speak."

His arm raises, trembling finger pointed toward an inconspicuous door along the far wall.

I'm already past him, letting him scurry away to probably call someone as I close the distance to where he pointed. My hand darts out, grabbing the door's handle and twisting it before I slip inside.

It slams behind me as I stand at the top of a dark wood staircase, chest heaving as I stare down. I reach for my gun in the small of my back, pulling it out before the sound of it cocking bounces off the walls.

I don't even know if she's fucking here. But if I have to sit in this fucking room all goddamn day, I will. Tonight she comes with me, and anyone that gets in my way dies trying.

My feet are bounding down the stairs, heart racing, beating out of my fucking chest because I'm so filled with rage and sorrow that I can't tell the difference between them anymore.

A growl rumbles as I hit the bottom of the stairs, my finger brushing the trigger of my Glock.

But there's no one. The room's empty.

My head shifts around the room, walking inside. It's filled with chocolate leather club chairs and dark wood paneling, like a cigar room out of the 1940s.

This isn't Sutton.

The door I just came through slams as heavy steps fall behind me. It's Roman. I don't even turn around to know. He doesn't say anything as he comes to stand beside me, catching his breath.

We stand in silence, him trying to read me. And me going over exactly what I'm going to do to everyone—the hurt I'm going to inflict.

"She's not here, Calder. And honestly, this is fate working for you, brother. Turn around and leave because nothing good comes from this. Listen to me."

I lift my gun, pointing at nothing, sneering before letting it drop to my side.

"I'm not leaving without her."

He holds out his arms. "And then what? Huh? You're gonna kill everyone and run forever? That's not what you promised her. Walk the fuck away before everything was for nothing."

My head swings to his to say that I can't walk away. That I'm physically rooted to this goddamn spot.

"Then we fucking run, Roman," I shout. "Because I did this to her. I left her here."

A sharp gasp comes from behind Roman, spinning him around and drawing my eyes before my breath empties from my damn lungs. As if I'm being sucked into her orbit as all the oxygen is stolen from my body.

Time stands fucking still. There is no sound. No fucking existence past this moment.

Because it's her. Her—my sweet fucking girl.

Soulful emeralds stare back, locked on me. She's looking at me like she can't believe her own eyes. Fuck. Every piece of her calls to me.

I love you.

I want to say it, tell her, but I can't even open my mouth.

Her shoulders begin to shake as her lips part. She presses her palm against the frame of the door like she needs to hold herself up, before her eyes drop to my hand.

Sutton looks back, brows drawn together as her eyes begin to shine. She steps backward, shaking her head.

"Baby," I breathe.

I take a step forward before my eyes dart down too, realizing what she saw. The gun suddenly feels heavy in my hand, and I hate that it's so comfortable there that I don't feel it anymore.

Fuck. My head lifts as I tuck it back into my pants, eyes pleading with her to not be afraid. But she sucks in a breath, her hand immediately covering her mouth like she's refusing the sound. Not wanting to cry.

My heart's beating too fast because I can feel her panic. It's coming off her in waves, crashing into me, begging for me to make it better.

"Sutton."

But she shakes her head, taking another step back as she viciously shouts.

"No."

I exhale harshly like I've been punched in the fucking stomach. But before I can say anything, Sutton spins around and fucking runs.

Goddammit.

Moments crash into each other. The door she went through slams behind her as my hand shoves against Roman, who's trying to hold me in a bear hug.

Grunts and thwacks echo through the space as I reach around myself, throwing my fist into Roman's side. He loses his grip as I jerk away, shoving him off hard into a table.

"Fuck. Stop, Calder."

I tune everything out, hearing only the blood pumping inside my body as I weave around chairs and tables, throwing shit out of my way. Wood splinters and glass crashes down as my feet dig into the ground before I hurl the door against the wall, bouncing off it as I chase her.

"Sutton," I thunder.

Red hair flies recklessly down a short hall in front of me as I close the distance quickly, taking three steps to her one.

"No," she screams before I grab her arm, yanking her around, making us crash into the wall, her back slammed against it.

She sucks in a quick breath, closing her eyes as I grip her wrists, holding them up at her shoulders.

"Open your eyes," I breathe, feeling the roughness of my words.

She shakes her head, hair falling into her face as she fights against my hold. But it doesn't matter because I can feel it—all her pain, everything she's suffering. It's all over her. It's why she ran and why she won't open her eyes. She knows I'll see the pain behind her eyes because she's mine, and I'm hers.

"Open your fucking eyes."

Her chest shakes as her head hangs.

"I can't," she whispers.

I let out a shaky breath, bringing her fists to my lips, inhaling her scent as I lower my forehead to hers.

"Baby. What have they done? Tell me, and I'll take you away."

"I can't," she growls, cries beginning to fall from her lips as her hands struggle to slap my face, breaking my fucking heart.

I don't stop her, letting her wrists go as she hits me over and over, eyes on mine as she yells.

"I hate you. I hate you. I hate you." She slaps me harder. "How could you do this?"

She's weeping, her fists hitting my chest before trying to shove me backward, but I don't move. I deserve all of this and more. How could I leave her? I should've known better.

My fingertips brush her cheeks as she wails on me. I lean in, trying to kiss her, but she shoves my face away hard, shouting, "No."

I bunch my shirt in my hand over my heart, taking a step back.

God, forgive me for what I've done.

Our eyes connect, anger and love married. I reach for her, but she slaps my hand, hurling her words at me.

"Don't you dare fucking touch me. Not unless you can look me in the eyes and tell me it's all over."

Her eyes burn with rage as I wipe my hands down my face.

"Say we don't have to run or live in fear. Tell me you're here to give me what you promised. *Us* with all the magic, and forever. If you can't say that, then listen to Roman and leave."

My feet stumble backward, hands gripping the back of my neck, knocked silent. My back slams against the wall across from her as I open my mouth, but nothing comes out because I can't say any of that.

And she knows it.

She wipes the tears from her face roughly, staring back at me.

I could put my fist through every wall, scream until my voice gives, but nothing would ever strip this feeling from me. I'm hurting her.

The truth falls from my lips, in the way I can only ever share with her.

"All that keeps me going is knowing you're okay…but now you're here, and I know they're making you do this…and I keep thinking—at what cost?" My voice trails off, filled with too much anger. "Because I know the fucking cost. I've paid it."

I lift my eyes to hers, pushing off the wall.

"Don't ask me to walk away."

"Don't ask me to run," she cuts back.

I spin around throwing my fist into the wall, shouting, "Fuck," before I shove off of it, running my hands through my hair, staring at her, feeling my chest grow tight.

"Then tell me how to walk away. Go ahead, tell me how when I feel like this"—I motion between us—"it's like my soul tore from my body the minute I saw you because it was desperate to reunite with its other half. You're like a homecoming."

Her arms wrap around herself as tears stream down her face.

"How do I stop feeling that? I look at you and all I want to do is carry you the fuck out of here. Put you in the car and let you hold on to me as we fucking drive away. So tell me…how do I walk away, when everything inside of me says otherwise?"

Silence plays out between us as we stare deeply into each other's eyes, so connected that the world around us falls away and all that's left is me and this girl and the stars that measure our love.

"I love you," I breathe. "I fucking love you."

Sutton takes quick steps toward me, arms lifting as I bend down, wrapping mine around her waist and picking her up off the ground. Her lips press against my neck, arms engulfing me as we stay like that, breathing each other in, not saying a word. Because we don't have to.

We feel it all.

My fingers dig into her sides, squeezing her closer to me as I whisper against her skin,

"I won't condemn you to my hell. I'll kill them all. Your mom, your dad, Connor, Hunter. All of them. Today."

Her head rises as she brings her hands to my face, tugging it up so that we're staring at each other.

"I want you, Calder. But I also want picnics and movies and car rides in the rain. I want to hold your hand while we walk down the street. I want your last name as my own and one day to have your babies."

My eyes drop, because I can't house what I feel. It's so big that I can barely breathe. But she jerks my face, making me look at her again.

Pots clang in the background, coming from a prep kitchen, making us swing our heads to the side. As our eyes meet again, I see urgency is reflected in hers.

"None of that can happen if we leave today. You said it—we survive the best we can until we're together again. It doesn't matter what's happened or what will happen because I'm still fucking standing. And I'll be standing when you take your place. We don't run. Ever again."

Her hands brush over my beard as she glances to the side again. *Fuck.*

"Baby—"

She looks back, bringing her lips to mine gently before pulling back with the saddest fucking smile.

"I learned how to stand on my own two feet and how to be strong because of *you*. So that I can carry you too. And now is when you listen to *me*, Wesley."

I can't help the tiniest grief-stricken smile that matches hers as she uses that name.

"This part of our story isn't done yet."

Her voice cracks before she presses her salt-soaked lips to mine, letting them linger like it's our first kiss. I'm clinging to her, wrapped around her petite frame, trying to soak up every fucking last drop of her before I have to let go.

Because I'm going to. Again. She deserves forever and I'm going to give it to her. And I won't fail her again.

Her words are whispered into my ear, "Go and finish this, and then come home."

The way she says *home* almost breaks me because she means her. She's my home.

My face burrows into her neck again as she peppers kisses over my cheek. *Fuck. I want more time. I need more time.*

I inhale against her neck, wanting to take some of her with me. To breathe her in so I can carry just the smallest piece of her.

"Let me go, and walk away," she whispers again.

I know I should, but I can't let go yet.

"Whatever they break, baby, I'll spend our lifetime putting back together."

I press my lips to her neck, traveling up over her jaw and across her cheek, kissing away all her tears before I slow, letting them brush over her lips.

"I love you, Calder."

"I love you too, baby."

Our breath is shared as I lower her to the ground before I start to step back, almost unable to. But she shoots her hands out, grabbing my shirt, holding me in place. And for a minute I'm praying that she's going to tell me to take her with me. But I know better.

She's staring at my chest, not looking up as the plea in her voice almost brings me to my knees.

"Don't look back again. Promise me. It's too cruel to only give me bits and pieces of you."

I don't say anything, tipping my face to the ceiling, bottling my emotions. Shoving them down as deep as I can get them before lowering my head back down, kissing the top of her head.

"On my life."

I'll never forget this moment. This will eat at me until the day I come for her. And God help anyone that breaks even a hair on her fucking head.

My chest rises and falls in time with hers as I stare down, jaw tensed. She's clinging to me, my shirt bunched in her hands, and I know she can't let go either. So I reach out, peeling her fingers off my shirt as a sob bursts from her chest. But I give her what she needs. Exactly what I promised.

I turn around, walking back down the hall. Straight through the doorway. Closing it behind me, leaving my baby alone again.

Chapter Twenty-Three

Sutton

I'm seated on the floor, face buried in my hands, just breathing. I don't even know how long I've been here, but if I get up and try to put one foot in front of the other, I'm scared that all I'll do is run after him.

The pull is that strong.

God, so much time has passed, and even though Calder looks exactly the same to me, his presence feels even more dominant and that much more enslaving.

It wouldn't matter if today were ten years later. I am *his*.

The way his voice carried a deeper bass booming around the room melted me and woke up parts of me that felt dormant. It was all I could do not to run to him, throw myself into his arms, and let him take me away. But I knew before I listened to every word he said to Roman that he wasn't here because it was over.

Or he wouldn't have been holding a gun—no need.

I let out a breath, resting my forehead on my knees.

Calder was here to kill anyone that got in his way because he'd seen that fucking announcement in the papers. I think a part of me knew this would happen—as if I could feel his heartbreak. That's why I couldn't open my eyes. But it doesn't matter if I wanted to hide from him. I can't.

And I knew when he looked at me with that gun in his hand. The one that I have no doubt he's used before. It would just become an extension of the beautiful monster he is now.

Calder's traded his soul for me—for us. And I love him *more* for it.

It makes him all the goodness I'll ever want in the world.

And I'm greedy for more. A moment isn't enough. I want him and all the magic. And I don't care if that means that I'm damned too.

"Take it," I whisper. "Take my soul too."

My chin quivers as I try to calm my breathing.

God, when he used to say, "*If we only had tonight, would it be worth it?*" I always said yes, without hesitation. Because it was the truth. The idea of living a whole life, never knowing what it's like to be loved by him, even for the tiniest moment, seemed tragic.

Not a life worth living.

But there's a flip side to that. Now I know what it's like without him. What life feels like *because* I had him. And it's worse. If I'd never known what his lips felt like, I wouldn't beg God to let me forget. Or if I'd never felt what it was like to be safe in his arms, I wouldn't hate the feel of my own hands.

It's not that I only want him. I need him. Like the fucking air to breathe. But I need all of him, not just a piece, because that could never be enough.

The sound of footsteps lifts my head.

Shit. The staff must be showing up for today. I scramble up the wall, brushing my hair from my face, standing up straight before wiping my cheeks one last time.

But it's not a waiter I see as I smile toward where the sound is coming from.

"Hunter?"

What is he doing here?

Hunter strides up next to me, so I shift, making sure my back isn't against the wall.

"Well, well, well. Color me confused." He smirks with the kind of arrogance of someone that thinks they have the upper hand. "I thought you two were supposed to have said goodbye. None of that looked like a goodbye. I mean, I can't read lips…not that you were doing much talking."

My eyes narrow because this is a threat. Even if all Hunter saw was our goodbye.

But that's not what's beginning to settle over me like a match thrown on lighter fluid.

My eyes lock to his as my hands begin to shake.

He invaded our moment. Peeked around a corner like some kind of sick fucking voyeur enjoying our misery, again, because he's the fucking person that started it all.

Oh God, I feel violent, like everything inside of me is fucking vibrating, feeding off my hatred for him. I let out a shaky breath because I feel like I could kill him. Jesus Christ, like actually kill him.

Scratch his eyes out and wrap my hands around his throat.

How dare he stand here readied with whatever threat he thinks he's going to make.

Hunter steps in closer to me. "I bet if I were to tell Connor…"

Fuck you. Chills cover my body as I stare into his eyes.

"Or I could keep my mouth shut, and you could go about proving how much your criminal really means to you. You wouldn't want him in trouble, would you? Because I'm pretty sure they handle things way differently in that world."

I shake my head, forcing my breath to stay even as the hairs on the back of my neck stand on end. Hunter lifts his finger to my collarbone and trails over it as he licks his lips.

"What will you trade for my silence, Freckles?"

I grab his hand roughly, lifting it to my mouth, and cover my lips over his forefinger, sucking.

He groans, reaching down with his other hand, grabbing his dick.

"Oh fuck. He trained you well."

Hunter's eyes blink slowly as I smile against his finger before clamping down. Teeth slice into his skin as I bite so hard that a scream explodes from his mouth.

He shoves my face away with his other hand, sending me stumbling backward as he immediately covers his finger.

"You made me bleed, you bitch."

I spit on the floor, wiping my mouth as I laugh.

"The only thing I'll trade you is *my* silence for *yours*. Touch me again and I promise to make sure Calder knows. It would be worth all of us dying just to see him tear you the fuck apart."

I shove past him and walk in the other direction, hearing my own words in my head.

"We don't run. Ever again."

I lied—

I said I wouldn't write in here anymore but here goes because I couldn't not talk to you.

I slept on the floor of my room last night...yeah, I'm back at Elizabeth and Baron's house. No school and no money=no choices.

But it doesn't feel like home anymore except for my room. That feels like us.

I think it's why I slept on the floor last night. I literally dragged the blanket onto the floor to where you almost died. And lay there thinking about you.

Kind of morbid, right? But maybe this is my late-in-life emo phase?

Don't laugh too much at that because you really fucked us up, Calder, showing up, doing what you did today. Saying what you said.

I feel like I'd just figured out how to handle the pain. How to deal with it. But now it's compounded. So I'm mad at you...still. Before I saw you today, I'd been looking around this room a lot, wondering what was going to happen to the people we used to be. Would we ever be them again? Maybe find bits of them once we're back together.

And then you showed up and suddenly I was me again because I was seen.

So even though I kind of hate you for the torture, I also love you so much.

And I need you to know that I wanted to run after you, but that I love you too much for that. I was keeping my vow to protect you, even from yourself.

**kiss me right now while you're reading this and say, "I'm so lucky to have such a smart and beautiful girl."*

Anyway—now I'm crying because I can kind of still feel your lips. So...in conclusion, I love you more today. I want you to know that too. I love you MORE today, and I see you for everything you are.

And my favorite part of what I see is that you're mine.

-Sooner, please.

Chapter Twenty-Four

Calder

"Hey," Roman breathes from my doorway. "You good?"

My eyes lift from the chair where I'm seated, hidden by the shadows of my dimly lit room, as the beer in my hand dangles between my two fingers. It taps the side of the couch before I lift it, taking another swig.

"Am I good?" I breathe out with an empty chuckle at the end because, no, I'm not fucking good.

Roman starts to speak, but I hold up a hand, stopping him. Because there's something more important that needs to be said before I answer him.

"Romes, I should've said this shit earlier—but thank you. You tried to protect me from *me*, but more importantly, you tried to protect *her*. And I'm sorry I didn't see that sooner."

He nods, stepping inside my room as I run a hand through my hair.

"I want to kill him, Roman. Tear Connor apart for what he's done. For the way he treats people like fucking game pieces on some kind of board, just playing with them for his own fucking enjoyment. He gave her to him, Roman—"

My voice trails off as I shake my head because I have to stop talking. That's how much my blood boils. It makes me want to tear the fucking walls off this house, and I need to be clear right now because yesterday changed everything.

There's no way I'll make it another year, two, three more without her. I won't survive.

Fuck. I lean forward, elbows on my knees, holding the neck of the bottle with both my hands as I stare down at it.

"Do you know how hard it was to sit outside that meeting with the Italians and pretend I didn't want to gut him? Roman, the shit going on in my head about Connor and Sutton. Fuck. I can't stop thinking about her and what could happen, and it just makes me…"

I inhale harshly through my nose, blowing it out just as hard because I'm too volatile. I'm ready to explode, aggression readied at the surface like a bottle that's been shaken.

"What's the play, C?"

I suck some beer left behind on my bottom lip, not immediately answering because once I say it, there's no going back. And that's why I've been in here sitting in this dark room—

I've been trying to make peace between what I *should* do and what I'm *going* to do.

I should walk away, stick to the plan, not get anything messy. But that's not what I'm going to do. I lift my head, fingers picking at the label on my beer.

"When I was driving back in the other car, one of the boys said he's heard a rumor that other families were pushing for a council meeting. He didn't want to tell Connor—scared, you know."

Roman raises his brows. "You think the other families know Connor's weak?"

I nod. "Maybe. If they do, then there's blood in the water. If they don't, I need to make the first kill the messiest so they come swarming."

I hesitate as Roman stares back at me for a minute.

"I have to hit Connor where it hurts most."

He lets out a heavy breath, laying his back against the wall before shoving his hands into his pockets.

There's no hiding from him. We don't have to speak to understand each other.

"Fuck, C. That's going all in."

I set my beer on the ground, rubbing my face as I sit back, feeling the weight of my world laid heavily on my shoulders.

"You know that you don't have to do this. You could keep your head down. It can all fall on me."

His face darts to mine as his hands fly from his pockets.

"Why are you doing all this? Taking Connor down, going after the Prescotts and the Kellys. Tell me why."

My brows draw together as I grip the arms of the chair, dragging down the length of them, feeling my teeth grind together. Because what the fuck kind of question is that?

"I'm doing it for her and for West. Are you fucking kidding right now?"

He pushes off the wall, face screwed up like he's pissed.

"Yeah, me too, but I'm also protecting you, dick." His jaw tenses as he runs his hand over his head. "And I'm fighting to have a say over my own life. You're not the only one held here by this last name. So don't ever say that shit to me again. I'm not keeping my head down like some pussy. We do this together."

All I can do is nod as he lets out a breath before turning away.

Fuck.

"All right. I'm sorry."

He waves me off before looking back at me.

"So like I said before, what's the play?"

"We're gonna need eyes on her, now. Because I'm about to incite a war and topple a dynasty. And at the end—it's either gonna be me or Connor six feet under." I pick up my beer and take the last swig. "Until then, just don't let me kill him."

Roman's silent for a minute before his face matches mine. "What if we just maim him a little? Fucking dirtbag."

My chest shakes as I look at him. Because fucking Roman. He gives me a nod before turning around and walking out, leaving me alone again with my thoughts.

But there's only one—her.

Chapter Twenty-Five

Sutton

The phone on my nightstand vibrates, so I pick it up, seeing Piper's name.

"Hi."

My voice is quiet as I lie on my bed, staring out my opened balcony doors.

"How'd the fake-love engagement party go?"

"I saw him."

She's silent because of the way I just said *him*...she knows exactly who I'm talking about. No explanation or context is needed.

"Holy shit. Are you okay? Can you talk about it?"

"No. And I'm not." My chin trembles, and my voice breaks.

"What can I do, Sut?"

I wipe my fingers over my cheeks. "Just sit with me on the phone. It's nice not to be alone."

"I hate your parents for doing this to you. Forcing you to marry

Hunter, all for political gain. Try to tell me what you can. Maybe that would make you feel better?"

I close my eyes, focusing on my breathing, feeling it fill my chest and leave before my lips part.

"Imagine loving someone so much that you'd be willing to stand in the middle of hell and take on the devil just for a chance to be with them again. You'd do unimaginable things, Piper."

"Sut—"

"But it's something you'd have to do alone. Because it would be too dangerous for other people to help you. I'm in hell, Piper, so just sit with me, tell me something funny, make something up if you have to because it's just nice to hear what life can be like on the other side."

I hear her suck in a ragged breath, and I know she's crying, but she clears her throat.

"Okay, so…Aubrey had a threesome with her professor and his wife—she is now passing her International Laws of Business course. However, she's now failing her Women's Studies course. The one taught by said wife, because apparently the nutty professor only wanted to spread his butter on our honey Aubs."

I can't help it. Tears mix with laughter until all we have is laughter.

"I love you, Sut. Thank God Aubrey's a gorgeous little skank, or we'd have nothing to laugh about."

How I got so fucking lucky to have these friends, I'll never know.

"I'll have to send her pussy a thank-you card."

Piper screams, laughing, and for a minute, I'm happy.

Some of my favorite things—

I opened this journal today and just kept reading. Maybe

because it's Valentine's Day. And getting out of bed to hang out with Elizabeth and Baron was a hard no.

So I've been holed up reading and rereading the entry you wrote after that night in the car when it was raining. The night we stayed cuddled in the back seat.

We never did finish that conversation, and it's made me think about all the other things I have that are unfinished. Like College. And Us.

Jesus, we're sooo unfinished, and today that hurts a little too much. So I'm going to start compiling questions you have to answer like we did that night. All the ones you distracted me from answering. This way, we can catch up on all the things left unfinished.

I love you. Soon.

The pen drops from my hand as I grin, lying back on my bed, letting my mind drift back to that night. Trying to remember all the questions we asked as we lay wrapped in each other under that blanket, rain hitting the roof of his Mustang as the windows fogged.

"You picked tonight on purpose, didn't you? Admit it."

His fingers trail up my arm, all the way to my shoulder, and back down.

"I plead the fifth. But are you complaining?"

I shake my head as he leans in to kiss me again.

"Me neither," he growls against my skin. "I think the rain might beat the stars."

I giggle as the vibration tickles my neck, a thought springing to mind.

"Would you rather be stuck in the rain or in the snow?"

Calder pulls back, staring down at me with that smirk on his face that makes me crazy.

"What?"

I raise my brows, but he just keeps looking at me.

"Oh my God," I laugh. "Which do you like better?" He shrugs

as I stare at him. "Have you never played Would You Rather?"

He laughs, smooshing my face with his hand.

"No. Nobody plays that. You're making it up."

I shake free of his hand, laughing harder. "Lies. You totally look the type."

He darts his fingers out, tickling me, growling, "What type is that?" so I bite at his arm, saying, "A secret nerdy dreamer," but he leans in, grabbing my chin.

"I only dream about you. You're always my rather."

I smile as he brushes his lips to mine but hovers before saying, "Kiss me."

We press together, tongues dipping inside, gliding over each other's as he weaves his fingers through the hair at the nape of my neck. Kissing him always leaves me breathless.

He pulls away, looking down at me as I smile big and bright.

"Your childhood was stunted, Calder Wolfe. Everyone should have a solid list of rathers."

His face is so serious for a moment as he looks down at me.

"My choices aren't always my own. So I guess I try to never really think about what I'd want—until you. You make me want everything, Sutton."

The smile on my face feels permanent. In so many ways, we're the exact same, beholden to our names, locked in obligation. But he's been robbed of the simple pleasure of a dream.

I scoot in closer, hitching my bent leg higher over his hip. I'm going to give that back to him.

"So then, let's play." I grin. "I mean, you keep refusing to have sex in the back of this car, anyway, and it is raining. And you've already—" I bite my lip as he tilts his head, staring at me, eyes taunting me to say what he just did to me, but I'm not going to.

"Shut up with that look." He winks, and I feel more of the blush I know is already on my face creep up again. "Just answer the

question, and then you can ask me one."

He shifts us, sitting up, forcing me to straddle his lap.

"Sorry. You're making me hard."

I bite my lip, feeling shy in the best way. He smirks, reaching out and tugging my lip from between my teeth, pulling me forward so that we're nose to nose, eyes closed.

"Baby, with your legs spread like that, and that fucking look on your face, my dick was begging to grind against your pussy, to get hard enough so I'd give in and fuck you in the back of this car. But you only get the first time once, and that deserves magic, Buttercup."

I let out a long breath as he releases me, and my body falls away from him.

Jesus, he's fucking hot.

Calder drapes the blanket we brought over my shoulders, cocooning us in and keeping me warm since I'm only in jeans and a bra. He brushes the back of his hand over the fabric covering my nipple, letting his fingers gently pinch the pebbled bud.

I suck in a breath, back arched, grabbing his shirt on either side of him at his waist as he speaks.

"Let's play differently. Our way. Every kiss you give me, I'll answer your questions."

He takes his finger away, making me lick my lips.

"And what will you give me for my answers?"

"The same. A kiss. But neither of us can kiss the same spot twice or repeat what the other did. I'll go first."

I giggle as he runs his fingers down my throat to the space between my breasts. Curling his finger over the wire of my bra, he jerks me forward, pressing a kiss between my cleavage.

"Fuck," I whisper before he says, "What's your favorite color?"

"Matte black. It makes me think of this car and what you did to me on the hood of it."

He grins. "Wanna redo? In the rain?"

Heat spreads over my core as I smile, leaning forward, kissing his right cheek sweetly.

"Favorite food?"

He buries his face into my neck as he bites and licks over my skin while he answers.

"That's easy. There's this place back home called the Yankee Lobster Company. And I could eat their lobster rolls every day for the rest of my life."

He groans, pulling my jeans up, making the fabric pinch between my legs in that way that makes me gasp as my hands lock around the back of his neck.

"That's not all I could eat every fucking day."

His hand dives under my ass, forcing me forward, as his fingers come up between my legs, pressing against my clit.

My head falls back. "You're cheating."

Fuck, that feels good.

He laughs quietly against my ear as his fingers rub in small circles.

"Nobody wins this game. There is no cheating."

I circle my hips, feeling my clit throb.

"But I can't concentrate."

"Favorite song?" he whispers, taking his hand away and gripping the front of my bra again. With his other hand, he presses against my stomach, laying me back between the two front seats as he trails his fingers down my body.

I lift my face, eyes locked to his. "You forgot to kiss me."

Calder licks his lips, yanking my pants open, unzipping them slowly until my bareness is exposed. He jerks them over my ass before gripping it, bringing my pussy to his face.

"You forgot to take off your fucking pants."

I suck in a breath, eyes rolling back into my head, breaking from the memory as I reach between my legs to rub myself. I'm soaked, so fucking wet, remembering how his tongue felt on my clit. How he ate me, back arched, pussy brought up to his mouth like he was feasting.

"Oh God."

My fingers work my clit, gliding over and over, but it's not enough. I miss the way he felt inside of me, the way he filled my cunt, making me beg for more.

I reach next to my bed, sliding open the nightstand drawer, and grab my toy before pressing the button. My legs spread as I push my vibrator inside.

"Oh fuck."

My hips rock forward as it nestles inside, humming against all the right places as my other hand moves faster and faster. I draw it out of me slowly, feverishly playing with myself, opening my legs further. My mouth opens, feeling the tension between my legs as the hardness drags in and out of me.

I lick my lips just as I'm hit with the image of me, down on my knees. Calder's hands in my hair, filling my mouth with his rock-hard cock. Inching it in before pulling back, more each time until he says, *Swallow me, baby.*

It doesn't matter that I'm all alone because right now, Calder's everywhere. He's down my throat, hands on my clit, and inside my pussy. All fucking over me, possessing me, and fucking me raw.

"Oh God, yes," I pant, feeling myself tighten over the hard steel inside me. "Make me come."

My body contracts, knees drawing up as my slick, wet release gushes from me, and I moan, long and hard, doubled over before all the breath in my lungs releases, and my body becomes Jell-O. I lie on my bed, naked and still happily caught up in Calder until it fades, and I have to open my eyes again, taking a deep breath. As I do, a smile graces my face, and I lean over feeling around for the journal still on my bed, speaking the words aloud as I write them.

"God, I miss you in the most nonromantic, whorey way, Calder Wolfe. Today your dick is my rather."

Chapter Twenty-Six

Calder
March

"Hey," Roman says, looking down at his phone. "All the shit's in place. Invitations were made by Senator Franklin and accepted."

I nod, knowing what he's talking about, saying, "If this shit goes well, she won't have to do shit with that little prick," under my breath to him as I push the door open to Connor's office.

Connor's boom greets us as we walk through.

"What the fuck."

Shit spills out over his desk and onto the floor as he swipes a hand over it. He's raging again.

"Aww, I guess everything's going wrong for him," Roman whispers.

Let me just put you out of your misery and stick a gun in your mouth, Uncle.

"The Italians are undercutting me on my own streets. Those fucking greasy wops got a supplier in Chicago, making the same shit I'm making but at a cheaper fucking price. They're stealing all my business. Taking food right off my plate. And my own people are betraying me and selling for them."

Roman and I sit quietly on the couch, surrounded by other men, all watching Connor come undone.

"How'd they get by us? Huh?" he shouts.

Pete, his second in charge, stands up, glancing over at me before he does.

"We think one of the other families has cut a deal with them—to make a play for your position. That's why we're hearing rumblings about a Council meeting."

It was so fucking easy to plant that seed and watch it grow, but that doesn't mean I'm not on edge. Because all it would take is for Pete to point a finger in my direction, let Connor know I'm the little birdie that gave him that info. And bang. I'd be over before I got started.

I'd played it. Acted chill when I passed it along, pretending I didn't want to upset my uncle with neighborhood gossip. Acting like I didn't know who to go to. Letting Pete get greedy for that credit, to be held in the favor he's so desperate to have from Connor.

I knew who I was choosing; I needed a sacrificial lamb, and he couldn't be better.

Here's hoping I didn't get a little bitch too.

Connor throws an ashtray as men jump out of the way before ash lingers in the air and a thud dents the wall.

"If the Council meets, it'll be for my head. And then you'll all go fucking hungry. I need to know who the fuck's in bed with the Italians."

Fuck. The satisfaction I feel right now. I took his drugs. That was the first step.

Dante and I have been working over the last year to make him the main supplier. I obviously get a cut, and he's agreed to an equally beneficial deal for us regarding guns.

Now I'm taking all his power. Feeding his paranoia, turning his men against him without them knowing, like the one standing in front of Connor right now.

Connor paces behind his desk, breathing heavy, spit flying from his mouth like a lunatic as he mutters.

"Connor, with all due respect," Pete starts, then hesitates.

Roman turns his head, just barely lifting his hoodie, letting me see where his gun is in case I need it since mine is at my back.

Connor stops, looking straight at my patsy.

"Speak."

Pete cracks his neck—nervous habit, probably—before he begins again.

"You've put us at a disadvantage by not telling us what's been going on. If we lose control of the drugs in South Boston, we lose control of Boston. I know you know that, but you should have let me help with the renegotiation, Connor. Because now that it's fallen through, that's left us weak. So I think we need to try again. Call another meeting."

I swallow, almost seeing how it's going to play out before it does. My eyes fix on Connor, waiting, adrenaline coursing through me so fast that my heart feels like a goddamn hummingbird.

Nobody knew Connor tried to renegotiate. Only me and the Italians. And Pete, once I slipped that information in so fucking casually that he actually pretended to already know it.

Connor hangs his head, fingertips pressing into the wood like he's trying to scratch through it. His voice is low and sinister, his words said in almost a growl.

Fuck, I can feel his anger. It's like my own, just under the surface, always ready. We're alike, my uncle and I, except what he does for power, I do for love.

"You don't need to tell me what I already know. You think I'm scared of having a knife at my throat?" Connor's eyes lift, connecting with mine. "That's always the position of the king. And when it presses down, you flip it and stab your enemy in the throat."

Connor's body lifts quickly, his gun coming from the holster as a bang reverberates around the room. Shouts ring out as everyone ducks, knocking shit off tables before they hit the ground.

But I don't move. I'm sitting in my spot, staring directly at Connor as Pete collapses to the floor. This is the Connor I knew I'd get.

My uncle's lips pull into a sneer as he hurls his words out to the room, looking straight at me.

"Pete Gallagher betrayed me. Nobody knew I'd had another meeting with the Italians. Find out what family he was working with. I want to know fucking yesterday. Do you understand me?"

His voice booms through the room as everyone nods.

"Go."

Men scatter, looking over their shoulders as they hurry out of the room, but Roman and I stand, letting them all go before us.

Connor's eyes narrow on me.

"You bring me heads. Do you understand? Or I'll take yours."

I give a half smile and nod.

"Absolutely, Uncle."

He lowers down back into his chair, running his hand through his hair before he says, "And send someone to take care of the body."

Roman and I walk out side by side, silent until we hit the street.

My face shifts to his. "Gather the fellas. We're gonna remember Pete right. He died for a bigger cause."

To start a war that will burn down this family tree.

Roman nods, opening the driver's-side door before we both slip into the car. I roll down the window, putting a cigarette between my lips.

"Where's my girl?"

"The island. Back at her bitch-ass parents' house."

I nod. "We need to find the right time and send her the thing."

Roman smirks before he makes a right.

"I'm signing it from me because you ain't stealing my thunder on that shit."

I laugh before taking a drag and letting it drift from my lips.

"All right. Fair."

Chapter Twenty-Seven

Sutton

"Jesus Christ," I breathe out.

My mother and Marianne are engrossed in some wedding magazine, talking about flower arrangements as I stare down at my phone.

This has become the norm over the last month of April—they dream up a wedding that I battle, and we stand off with no winner. But I know I can only do this for so long until it comes down to actually choosing dates. And actually marrying Hunter Kelly.

Me: *Meeting number 1,785,927 in the great wedding debate is about to commence. Wish me luck. I'm proposing minimalism—example, no groom.*

The bubbles jump to the screen immediately.

Piper: *Read me clearly: If they force the whole big wedding, we all wear black. Marrying Cunter deserves funeral attire. God I hate him.*

A string of mad emojis pops up from Aubrey before her message comes through.

Aubrey: *Fuck them. Like all of them, equally and without lube. Piper—Sut's not having bridesmaids. Because I will not stand there. I'll fucking object. I'll say I've been pegging that little fucker behind her back for years.*

I bite my lip to stop the chuckle that wants to spring out, suddenly picturing Aubrey really giving it to Hunter. My eyes lift to him, seeing him staring down at his phone before another message comes through.

Piper: *But seriously, I wish I was there and not all the way on the other damn coast because I love you so much. Also—here's a good point to make. Nobody gets married before they're twenty-one anymore.*

Aubrey: *Dude—if there was ever a wedding where booze was needed.*

I blow out a quiet breath, flicking my eyes to Hunter again because I'd rather he was as sober as possible. Not that I think alcohol is to blame for his vileness. But the veil he exists behind seemed to slip so easily when he was drunk that I'm pretty sure every fucking "Coke" would just guarantee his cruelty.

Me: *K. Keep compiling the list. I'll text soon. I've got a fight to have.*

I pocket my phone, looking up as my mother's eyes lock to mine. I felt her staring at me.

"Is there a reason you look chipper, Sutton? Not that I'm complaining. It's a nice change from your usual personality. But I'd like to prepare myself for your mess if there is one."

My lips press together before I speak. *God, she's such a bitch.*

"I was texting with my friends. Nothing for anyone to worry about."

I grip the back of the couch, trying to calm my temper because it's already ready to charge at her.

"Well—" she starts, but I interrupt her, quickly changing my mind about staying calm.

"Before you say that I'm not allowed to have friends—*again*—remember what I told you. I'm keeping them. They aren't a threat, obviously, because I'm here, agreeing to marry this dick."

Marianne bristles as I motion toward Hunter.

"So there's no mess to clean up, Elizabeth…other than this shitshow of a wedding you want to throw."

My mother slaps the magazine in her hand down on the table as Marianne glares at me.

"I spoke too soon. Seems you're back to your regular self. Let's try to be less of that when you and Hunter meet with Father Michael tomorrow."

"Meet with? Not happening. I've been clear the last four hundred times that I've said this. It's either the justice of the peace or nothing."

Marianne huffs, turning her body toward me. It's rare she even addresses me, but I've never underestimated her hatred.

"I don't like empty threats, Sutton. They aren't intimidating. I prefer to be straightforward."

"Do you like the truth, Marianne? Really?" I say it dripping in sarcasm with *"Your son's a rapist"* sitting on the edge of my tongue.

I glance at Hunter, who's staring at me with malice behind his eyes as he sips his drink before smirking as he says, "Just tell it to her, Freckles, or aren't you brave enough? Where's all that bite?"

The room is silent, all eyes on him as he stares back at me. *You prick.* He's talking about Calder and his little discovery. But I know he won't tell because it's bad for both of us.

Marianne stands, drawing my eyes back.

"Yes. Why are you in such opposition to this wedding, Sutton? Tell us the truth."

I huff a laugh before I answer with one of the thousand reasons I hate this wedding.

"Because I refuse to sit through some elaborate political spectacle. One where you all pretend to cry while telling everyone a story about high school sweethearts turned into a forever kind of love." My voice lowers to a patronizing tone. "Because all this is, is a cleanup job so that Hunter doesn't end up like his father."

She swallows, crossing her arms. I'll never believe she cares about her dead husband. She's as motivated by greed and power as Connor is. That's why she wants the spectacle.

"But you're right, Marianne. I have to be there. I'm under Connor's thumb as much as any of us. I just don't give a fuck about your side agenda. So like I said, justice of the peace or nothing."

If looks could kill. She's scowling at me, matching the glare coming from my mother. I can't believe I was scared of her because she just feels pathetic now.

"Thank you for your honesty." Marianne sneers.

I nod back, going for the full bitch effect.

Because what they don't need to know is what Hunter already suspects. That the most important reason for opposing this tragedy in the making is Calder.

I won't twist the knife with photos of us kissing in front of an altar plastered on every news outlet and paper on the East Coast.

It's the only thing I can do for him, so they'll have to drug and prop me up to get me to do what they want.

"Jesus," my mother snaps, avoiding my eyes. "Someone just negotiate terms with the little bitch because the sooner they marry, the better."

I huff a laugh, looking up at the ceiling before bringing my eyes back to Marianne's.

My father stands, offering, "Sutton—"

Go to hell, Baron. My face darts to his.

"I think you should leave this one to the grown-ups. If you're confused, the kids' table's over there."

I point to where Hunter's sitting as I stare my father down. He says nothing, retaking his chair, scowling as he does.

Marianne walks toward me, clearly trying to be some kind of voice of reason, but I'm so ready for a fight.

"Sutton, sweetheart. I know this situation is impossible. It's not ideal for my precious boy either. He had different plans for his life. Dreams that have been ruined too."

I wish I had a better response, but all I manage is "Eww."

But she keeps talking.

"The whole point of this union is to draw attention away from the things we don't want the press to talk about. So far, it's been working, so yes, I admit that a big summer wedding is beneficial to all of us. And we've thought about how that can positively affect our futures."

"An announcement after the justice of the peace would do the same," I counter.

Marianne narrows her eyes, bringing her hand to her hip as she tilts her head. *Read me, Marianne. I'm not stupid or intimidated. Your dream isn't happening.*

"A small private church wedding…keeping with the narrative of two Catholic political dynasties. And you get to re-enroll in school for the fall."

My eyebrows rise, hearing my mother scoff. Wow, we really are negotiating. I hate that my happiness plays out on my face. But the idea of getting something back, even the smallest thing, makes me want to smile.

All right, let's do this, bitch.

"Done. But not a church in St. Simeon. And in the off-season—preferably December. With no bridesmaids or groomsmen."

I will not marry anyone but him in our church, where he first kissed me. No fucking way.

Marianne crosses her arms, taking a deep breath like she's thinking over her options.

"With exclusive photos from the church for specific media outlets and candids taken from your newly leased pied-à-terre."

What the fuck? My eyes grow wide, shooting my head toward my mother.

"Apartment? Tell me you haven't already leased it? Are you fucking kidding? What is wrong with you?"

"You didn't tell her?" Marianne says, eyes darting to my mother, then back to me. "You're moving in together next week."

I look around. I feel shaky, turned inside out.

"You knew," I rush out, drawing out the words as I volley between my parents, "and you're shutting the door again? I mean, I shouldn't be surprised. But I am. I actually am."

My mother screams her frustration before slapping the table and standing.

"Where did you think you'd live once you got married?"

I push off the couch, ready to meet her where she is.

"Forgive me, Mother, but I thought we were all in on the joke. That this marriage was a farce, just for looks, so we'd have separate places just like half of the other Upper East Side marriages."

She crosses her arms, turning away as my eyes shift, landing on Hunter, who's grinning as he drinks.

"Fuck you," I spit.

And without hesitation, he mouths, "With pleasure."

I can't breathe. Because all I smell is whiskey. His face feels soaked in his intention as I stare back at the harsh angles of his jaw and the way he licks his lips.

Oh my God.

It's as if he's thinking of all the things that could happen behind a locked door.

My feet start in his direction before I even know what I'm doing. But I blink, catching up as my palms begin to sweat. All those disgusting memories begin to lay themselves in front of me as I close the distance.

I drop my eyes to his hand, watching as he circles the bottom of the glass on the table, making the ice clink together. All I can think about is how much I'd like to break that glass and stick him with a piece of it.

My arms wrap around me as I stop in front of him, chills covering my body and bile coating my throat.

You filthy piece of shit. I can't wait until he makes you pay.

Hunter winks as he lifts the cup to his mouth, pausing with it against his lips for a moment.

"You're so beautiful on your back."

A hard whoosh of air tears from my body before I violently slap his fucking drink out of his hand. Whiskey splashes everywhere as the rocks glass thuds to the carpet. Someone behind me gasps, but I don't react.

I just stand there looking down at Hunter as he stares down at his shirt. His chest rises up and down heavily as he wipes the liquid from his face. Not a sound is made as I glower at him. He licks his lips, brushing the liquor that's beaded on his blue polo with his fingers.

My voice is quiet, but it's not just for him.

"If you think I would ever share a bed or a place with you after what you did, you're more of a drunk than I thought. There is no flipping this bitch. I will not back down."

His eyes lift to mine, and they're cold. So damn cold. Hunter hates me just as much as I do him. He sucks his bottom lip between his teeth, letting it drag out roughly as he stands, forcing me back a step.

But I stay rooted in my place, our eyes locked as he hovers over me until he lifts his face to his mother.

"Justice of the peace. One photo. She can have the apartment."

I blink, completely caught off guard.

He walks past me, but I've already spun around, watching him walk to the bar and blatantly make himself another drink, hearing his mother say, "Done."

What the fuck?

I don't know what to think, but the room is silent, eerily so as ice cubes fill his glass, before the sound of liquid sloshes, so I clear my throat, preparing for whatever the next fight is.

"Did we settle on a month?" I whisper, still eyeing Hunter.

He walks back, taking a large gulp of his drink, and I realize Marianne hasn't answered, so I press, voice rising, "Marianne, did you hear me?"

The first slap stings, sending a hot flash over my cheek as my head's thrown to the side. The second one knocks me to the floor.

I suck in deep breaths, not able to grab onto a thought, eyes searching the floor. My hand presses to my cheek, and it feels hot and numb. Oh my God. I'm not crying, but I can feel it welling inside. I look up as Hunter glares down at me, his bottom lip wet from the last drink he took.

"The first one was for spilling my fucking drink. And the second was to remind you of your place. I'd back down now if I were you."

Hunter steps over me, walking back to his chair as I look around the room. Nobody moves a damn muscle. My father turns his head away, wiping a hand over his jaw as Marianne looks right through me like I'm a pane of glass.

But it's my mother who takes the cake. Because she's smiling from where she's seated, as if to say, *You got what you deserve.*

I press my palm into the ground, pushing myself back to standing. My back is ramrod straight as I smooth my hair, face red from his handprint. I turn around the room, looking each person in the eye until I land back on Hunter.

"Are you done, precious boy? Because I'd like to get back to the negotiations now."

The hits keep on coming—

The title is enough said. I'm grateful that I am loved by a man who would never hurt me but possesses the strength to hurt those who do.

***take this out, don't make him live with this.*

Chapter Twenty-Eight

Sutton

"Miss Prescott, there's a delivery for you. Would you like me to bring it to your room since you're turning in for the night?"

"Call me Sutton. And yes, please bring it back."

The housekeeper nods, shutting my bedroom door behind her as I look back at myself in the vanity mirror. *Jesus Christ.* I blow out a breath, looking around the room filled with boxes, all labeled "Bedroom," reaching for the bottom of my hair as I stare at them.

How did I get here?

Sometimes that question feels heavier than other times. Because sometimes my life feels too surreal, as if I've lived ten lifetimes in a couple of years.

I moved into this apartment on May 1. And as negotiated, I'm alone. Well, almost because I've been gifted a live-in housekeeper.

One that I'm pretty sure answers to my mother—so basically a fucking babysitter.

There's a knock on my door before I say, "Come in."

The housekeeper walks back inside, handing me a small rectangular box wrapped in black paper. I look at her, brows drawn as I weigh it between my hands.

"Did it have a card?"

She shakes her head before my eyes drop down to it. I flip it over, searching the wrapping for a name. She starts to leave, but I turn my chin toward my shoulder.

"Hey, you can be off the clock for the rest of the night. I'm good here. If I need anything, I'll handle it on my own, okay?"

She nods her head as I try to smile, failing as she walks out and closes the door behind her.

I stand before walking over to turn the lock, eyes still inspecting the mystery gift. I look up, eyeing my phone on my bed, and pad over, hopping up.

Me: *Out with it, who sent me the housewarming gift?*

Aubs: *Not it.*

Piper: *No, ma'am.*

Nobody else knows I'm here. This is weird.

"Who sent you?" I whisper to myself.

My fingernail picks at the corner of the wrapping as another text dings.

Aubrey: *Take a pic and send it to us. I'm curious now. What does it look like? How big?*

I laugh, ignoring her text as I push my finger in past the paper and tear it open. Pieces of wrapping fall around my legs as I lift the box, freeing it from the rest of the paper before brushing it all to the floor.

It's a small dark wooden box with a hinged lid, so I flip the top open, and a folded white note comes into view. I'm grinning because it feels all mysterious as I pick up the paper, revealing what's underneath.

Oh. My. God.

A gold switchblade with an antique wooden handle is nestled on a bed of black silk fabric.

What the hell?

I can't help but chuckle as I pull it out, feeling something on the other side of the handle, so I flip it over, and my mouth falls open.

True Love is embossed onto the wooden handle in Shakespearean letters.

A full laugh bursts from my chest as I pluck at the fabric, ensuring nothing else is inside before my eyes dart to the note.

Here's to true love, mama.

And slicing anyone's throat that comes between it.

Mama.

I gasp as I drop the note, covering my mouth.

Roman. You amazing, incredible man.

I love him almost as much as Calder because he did this for my beautiful monster. My eyes begin to tear as I squeeze my hand around the knife's handle, using my fingertips to pull the blade open, feeling its weight and its intention.

It shines like a deadly treasure, making me smile even bigger until a bigger realization hits.

He knows where I am. Oh my God. My Romeo knows where his Juliet is.

Suddenly and all at once, this place feels like home. Because Calder's with me.

I lean over, grab my phone, and snap a picture of the blade before sending it to Aubrey and Piper.

Me: *Someone sent me True Love.*

Aubrey responds immediately.

Aubrey: *Arrrgggh motherfucking arrrgggh.*

I let out a laugh, scooting back into bed, and put my phone on the nightstand before I crawl under my blanket. I'm snuggling, lying on my side as I tuck the covers up under my chin and stare at my present.

"I love you forever. Until we're dust and bones and even after that."

My eyes close, and for the first time in a long time, I'm not scared. Because Calder is out there, and he's coming for me.

Chapter Twenty-Nine

Calder

"Senator."

Sutton's father stares at me from the back seat of the police car, hands cuffed, fear behind his eyes.

"God help me."

My head tilts as I look at him, fingers coming to my beard scratching my skin.

"Why do men like you always try to pray at the end? You hope for mercy."

He swallows hard, not speaking, leaning back as much as he can in the car. So I squat down in front of the door, eyes locked to his. "God isn't here, Baron, and I have no mercy to give you."

I stand, jaw tensed as I look between the two crooked cops I paid to bring me Baron, and motion my head to the side. One of them reaches inside the car, grabbing Baron by the collar, but he struggles, shuffling his feet and fighting being pulled out. His protest almost makes me laugh.

"No. Please. What are you doing?"

I smile, taking a step back as they pull him out, tossing him back against the car, letting his body bounce off.

He's breathing heavy, sweat already beading on his brow as he stands hunched over, leaning to the side. The cops turn back, giving me a nod before they walk away.

"Do you know why I'm here, Baron?"

He doesn't speak but judging by the way he's already fucking shaking, he knows exactly why I'm here.

"You know, I made a special trip to New York for this very moment."

His face shifts to the cops, then back to mine. I chuckle, running a thumb over my bottom lip before I turn my head and watch them walk, knowing they're going to turn a blind eye to whatever I do.

We stand silent while Baron drowns in fear, breathing quickly, the further they get down to the end of the alley. My mouth tugs into a grin as I speak calmly, eyes still on them.

"They can't help, you dumb motherfucker. Tonight, they're going to deliver you to a holding cell, and then some friends of mine are going to string you up and let you hang."

My face turns back to him, inhaling, almost immediately fucking drunk off his fear. *This is for you, baby. For the fear you felt when they locked you up in that fucking hospital.*

I take a step toward him as he cringes.

"The interesting thing about hanging, Baron, is that it's a slow death. The life is wrung out of you, but your body never stops fighting to try to free itself."

I take another step closer, feeling the always simmering rage begin to boil over like lava cresting the mouth of a volcano. Violent intent oozes through my veins, pumping inside of me like blood as my chest rises and falls.

"I imagine it's a lot like what my baby felt like in that fucking hospital." My voice grows louder, hand darting out, gripping his throat, squeezing hard.

He sputters, body jerking, but his hands are cuffed as I squeeze harder, feeling the muscles in his neck constrict as I speak.

"She had to fight to survive the hell you stuck her in, against the lies you fucking told her."

My teeth grind, veins bulging on my forearm with force as I crush his trachea. I dig my fingers in hard, closing my eyes, listening to the squeaks of air desperate to fill his lungs as I lean in closer to his face. My cheek almost to his.

"There's a peace born from the brutality of righteousness. I've waited years for this moment—to kill you in *her* name. And on the day I meet my maker, I won't pray. I won't ask for forgiveness. Because this is what you fucking deserve."

I release him, stepping back, sucking in a deep breath as he does the same. He bends forward, coughing, spit falling from his lips as he gasps for more air.

"Fuck," I bellow as I stare back with the cruel hint of a smile.

"I have money," he snivels as he begins to weep.

My feet rush back to him again as I grab him by the hair, jerking him forward so I can whisper in his ear. My words are ground out with the evilness I feel.

"You made her pray, you motherfucker. You forced her down on her fucking knees in front of that worthless piece of shit and had photos taken. Fuck the money, your life is the price you'll pay for that."

I yank his head back roughly as he squeals like the fucking pig he is. Tremors, guided by hate, ripple through my body. The rage can't be contained anymore because I don't want it to be.

He put her on her knees. So I'll do the same to him.

The fingers I have weaved in his hair squeeze as I growl, pulling the strands as hard as I can, watching tears stream down his face before I thrust him down.

Baron cries out in pain as I look down at him. He starts to mutter a prayer, and it makes me laugh.

"You have to be sorry to receive forgiveness. Beg me. Confess your sins, say what you've done to her."

His body shudders, sobs rolling over him.

"Please, Calder. Please don't kill me. Elizabeth made me do everything."

I can feel my heart racing as I stare at him. His head hangs as I let it go. He hunches over, ass falling onto his feet as I stand there looking down on him in that dirty alley.

"Confess," I whisper, eyes hooded, feeling my nature begin to lead.

His face tips up. "Please let me live. I'll tell you anything you want to know."

I step back from him, eyes narrowed, feeling possessed with the need to draw his fucking blood.

His shoulders shake uncontrollably as he begins to speak, "I'm sorry. I'm so sorry."

I draw in a breath and spit on him, listening as his cries grow.

"What are you sorry for?"

I want to hear it. Hear the fucking words from his mouth because I want them to make me cruel.

He's pleading incoherently, rocking in place, so I step forward, smacking the side of his head, watching as he falls over onto the asphalt. My boot presses down on his face, grinding his cheek into the rough concrete as the gravel in my voice echoes.

"Make your peace with me, you motherfucker."

His words come out from under my boot.

"Okay. Okay. Please."

I step back, fists balled as he cries his words out.

"I turned my back on my daughter. She needed me, cried out for me to help her, but I shut the door because I was scared of what Marianne Kelly would do. Scared of Connor O'Bannion. I was a coward, so I shut the door and let Hunter..."

Shut the door... Let Hunter...

I'm shaking, vibrating. Numb to time and the world around me. Because in my mind, I'm back in hell, gathering that black smoke, letting it wind around me. The same way my hand wraps around a piece of rusted scrap metal next to a trash bin.

His sobs grow louder as my face tips to the night sky. A guttural sound, almost demonic, rips from my lungs because everything inside of me breaks, shatters into a thousand pieces fracturing my soul.

He let him hurt her. I felt it on her that day at the hotel—the sorrow. This is what she wouldn't tell me. My brave, beautiful girl.

"Baby," I whisper, sucking in a breath as I stumble back.

He let that filthy cocksucker put his hands on her.

My feet carry me forward as my mind replays his words over and over until I hear *heaven or hell, heaven or hell* hissed deep inside the recesses of my mind again.

"Hell," I grit as I throw myself down, shoving the metal into Baron's side. It slides into his flesh as I blink from the splatters hitting my face. Drawing the scrap metal back out and shoving it in again and again, faster each time until I'm stabbing and grunting as blood blooms over his white dress shirt. He's gurgling on his own blood, drowning in it as I watch.

My face leans down close to his ear so that I make sure he hears me past his choking.

"You failed her. Now go and get a place ready for your wife. Because I'm gonna gut that fucking bitch for what she's done."

He coughs, blood spattering over his lips, but I draw back

slowly, kneeling next to him, staring as his pupils begin to grow and the gurgling grows silent. I wait there until his lifeless eyes stare up at the sky, then I reach out and close them.

"You don't deserve to see her stars."

Sutton

The sound of glass shattering yanks me from sleep, making me kick my legs, scurrying up to sitting as a shriek leaves my lungs. I'm shaking, blinking a mile a minute, pointing True Love at my bedroom door.

My chest rises and falls quickly as I search the space, but nobody's here. *What the fuck?* I lower my hand, running my other one through my hair, glancing at the clock to see it's eleven p.m., just as a crash echoes again.

Holy shit. It's from the living room.

Before I think twice, I hurry out of my bed toward my bedroom door, unlocking it as I swing it open.

"Greta?" I call out for the housekeeper. "What's going on? Is everything okay?"

I'm halfway down the hall as my eyes land on her. She's standing in a bathrobe, arms wrapped around herself, looking back at me with red-rimmed eyes.

"What's going on—" I whisper, confused, but I'm met by a different voice.

One that has my feet slowing their pace as my head swings to the side.

Hunter's voice thunders as he charges toward me.

"This is your fault, you fucking bitch."

"What are you doing here?" I yell.

My feet stumble backward as I thrust the knife up, eyes wide, panic welling. He slaps it from my hand, hard, as I scream before he grabs the back of my neck.

He forces me down, bent over, my eyes to the ground. Glass shards cover the floor, scattered everywhere as he guides me down the hall like I'm on a leash, and his hand is the collar.

"What are you doing?" I cry, gripping his wrist for support as I stumble over my feet.

My shoulders lift as he tightens his grip, his fingers digging into my skin. He forces my bare feet over broken glass toward the television, pulling me to a stop, breathing hot, heavy breaths into my ear as he grits out his words.

"Listen."

I'm standing in front of the television, body trembling, blinking through the tears pouring from my face.

"Hunter—"

He grabs my arm, jerking me still.

"Stop fucking crying and listen, Sutton."

I wince, feet stinging, but I hold my breath to try to stay quiet as I shake. Hunter walks to the television, turning it up as the news anchor's voice fills the room.

Breaking News: Senator Baron Prescott of New York has been found dead along with two NYPD officers in what police are calling an assassination. Possibly associated with the O'Bannion crime family in which he'd had a long history of legislating against. This was following his surprising arrest during a sting operation conducted by the NYPD. Senator Prescott was arrested with Senator Thomas Franklin of Maine and other prominent figures. Charges were issued, including soliciting an act of prostitution and distributing drugs for sex. No official statement has been released by the Senator's office or family as of yet.

My hands press to my chest as everything feels like it's going in slow motion. "My father's dead," I whisper, unbelieving of my own words. I wait for them to taste bitter on my tongue, for the humanity I should feel to kick in. But I feel nothing.

That's not true. I feel relief because this was Calder. I know it like I know my own name. This was his first move, the single domino that starts the topple of the others.

"Miss," I hear behind me.

My head swings to see Greta, hand lowering from her mouth as shock plays over her face.

But I don't say anything. Because there's nothing to say. Calder took his life for me, but I still hate him. So all I can do is take his legacy. I'll never speak his name again. I won't grieve him or say kind words, especially out of obligation.

He may be dead, but now I'll make it so he never lived.

"Get the fuck out. And keep your mouth shut or I'll find you," Hunter yells at Greta as he comes from my room, tossing a bag at my feet. I didn't even see him leave.

I stare at him as he stalks toward me again, glass crunching under his shoes, but I don't move. Hunter stares down at me, taking heaving breaths of air as my lips tug into a smile.

"He's coming, Hunter. And you should be afraid."

"No. Sutton, *you* should be. Because I promise there won't be anything left for him when I'm finished with you."

Chapter Thirty

Calder

My fingers tap on the gun in my lap as I stare at my uncle asleep in his hotel bed. I've been here, sitting in this chair watching him for the last twenty minutes. And it's taken a lot of fucking self-control not to just pull the damn trigger.

I could blow his brains out of the back of his fucking head before he even woke up. But that's not the plan, and it's also too generous.

Plus, I already went off course with the way I killed one man tonight. *Fuck you, Baron.* So I need to keep my head because Connor needs to stay alive. But I can't trust that he'll just show up to the Council meeting, or that he won't do something stupid, not after he hears about Baron.

I'm going to have to take him.

But son of a bitch, if the tap of my finger on the side of this goddamn Glock doesn't sound like the ticking of a clock. Like the countdown to the end of his worthless life.

The shit you will suffer, you filthy prick. Angels will weep watching my cruelty.

"Connor," I whisper, before barking louder, "Connor."

His hand's already reaching under his pillow before his eyes open.

"Uh-oh." I grin, holding up *his* gun that's in my lap. "You looking for this?"

The darkness always on his face seems to multiply as he slides his hand back, sitting up slowly. I'm watching the look in his eyes volley between confusion and suspicion.

"Calder," he breathes calmly, furrowing his brow. "What the fuck do you think you're doing? Why are you in New York?"

Goddamn, it feels like I've waited forever for this moment, so I take a minute before answering to really look into his eyes, searching them, because I don't ever want to forget the look in them as I answer.

"Betraying you, Uncle."

The silence fucking bleeds out, down the fucking walls and over the floor. It banks the room in unease and fury. I can almost taste it. Our chests rise and fall together, eyes locked like two fucking lions challenging for dominance.

"You came here to meet with the Italians again, except that's not what's happening. I just needed you in the fucking city. So my friends helped."

"You," he grits out. "It was you. All this time…running my drugs," he snarls, eyes narrowing on me. "It was never another family."

I was always right under your nose.

I grin, eyes locked to his, breathing faster but not answering. The evil inside me is being fed by the contempt in his eyes because now I can finally hate him back, right in the open.

He shakes his head, so many expressions crossing his face as he begins piecing it all together. In all fairness, it wasn't hard to see. He just had to look. But that's where our genius lied—we fed him lies for what he craved.

His invincibility.

"You told Pete about the meeting so I'd believe a war was happening. You knew I'd lose it—"

I tilt my head, smirking.

"Anger is predictable. So is greed. You have both afflictions in spades. So sacrifices were made. You always said that one day I'd do what was needed for this family. Guess you were right."

His eyes shoot to his bedroom door as my grin grows.

"Nobody's coming, you piece of shit. They don't work for you anymore. Haven't for a minute now."

His face swings back to mine, mouth hanging open as he stands slowly from his bed. He's staring at me the way I'm looking at him—with predatory fucking intent.

I draw my bottom lip between my teeth, dragging it out roughly as I push slowly from the chair, digging my fingers into the fabric of the arms.

Fuck, I feel so animalistic that I could bite down on his fucking throat and rip it from his body. That's how much I want to kill him right now.

"This was always going to happen, Connor." I take a step forward. "You took her from me." My teeth grit as I repeat his words back to him. "Kept her close. Isn't that what you fucking said?"

He's walking toward me as well, our stares never breaking.

"You don't know what you're doing, boy. The mess you're making."

We stand only a few feet apart, tension rippling off us, jaws tense, chests rising and falling in sync. His eyes search my face, drifting down to my hands, which are still stained red with Baron's blood as I narrow my eyes.

"I killed Baron Prescott. Stabbed him to death in an alley and linked it to you. Because she's mine. Just like your fucking throne."

Red begins to crawl up his neck as his fists ball at his sides. But I'm not done.

"Don't worry. I won't let you go to jail because I plan on sending you to hell."

He's fucking snarling, looking at me like he could rip me apart with his bare hands.

I breathe out a whoosh of air, feeding off his energy as I tip my face to the ceiling.

"Fuck I wish you'd try," I say aloud to my own thought before lowering my face to his again.

He takes a step back, then another as if I can't see he's walking toward the door. *Oh, run, Connor. The boys will have so much fun chasing you down.* He stabs a finger at me, reaching for the handle behind him.

"The Council will never approve my death, Calder. And when they don't, I'll have your fucking head. Mark my words."

I smirk. "Guess we'll just have to find out"—I raise my phone to show the time—"in less than forty-eight hours. The Council was more than happy to meet sooner. In fact, I think the Irish are already here from Dublin." My words rush out. "You or me. Me or you."

I can't help myself. I close the distance between us, standing almost chest to chest, backing him up against the door.

"It was for her. Always. Remember that when Roman's cutting you open. He's gonna take his time, keep you alive. I want you to feel every cut you made to her heart."

He says nothing as I put the gun under his chin.

"You don't get to walk this earth while she's on it."

I use the gun, digging it into his chin as I step back and guide him away from the door. My other hand reaches for the knob, opening it and letting Roman walk inside.

He grins as he lays eyes on Connor.

"Hey, Connor. You can go easy, or I can have some fun taking you outta here. I'd really like for you to pick the second option because I wanna make you bleed before I get to slice you up."

Chapter Thirty-One

Sutton

"What the fuck did you do to her?"

Tag's voice carries past the bathroom door, the one I'm hiding behind at the Kelly house in St. Simeon because Hunter forced me from the apartment barefoot and in my nightgown after he attacked me.

God, his hands were everywhere, pulling on my skin, ripping at my nightgown. He was trying to tear it off my body and do God knows what, and the only thing that stopped him was his mother, who walked into the apartment.

I begged them to leave me, even saying my mother would need me. But Hunter just kept insisting, saying this was my fault and I had to pay the consequence.

My shoulders shake as I try to push the memory out of my head, cleaning the scratch marks marring my cheeks, reddened over my freckles.

I stare into the mirror, looking back at red-rimmed eyes and his handprint along my jaw where he slapped me. My hands drop to my chest, and I pull the fabric back in place from the rip in my nightgown.

The stinging on my cheek smarts, so I turn my head to the side. Jesus, he drew blood. The red gashes are scrawled over my cheek from just below my eyes to my nose. He looked at me as if all he could think was to hurt me in the cruelest ways possible.

Not just hurt me—make me stop *being*. He tore at me like he was trying to rid himself of my existence as if I were a piece of paper with a story he couldn't read anymore. Something that needed to be destroyed, burned… Hunter wanted to make me disappear.

A bang on the door makes me jump.

"Sutton. Get out here. Now," Hunter shouts.

I take a deep breath, staring at myself in the mirror. They're afraid, scared to death that Connor's coming for them too. Like they think he came for my father. But I know better.

This was Calder.

"Just survive tonight," I whisper to myself.

I just have to make it through tonight. Calder has someone watching because he sent me the knife. *He'll find you, Sutton.*

Tears stream down my face as I stare in the mirror because the reality of my situation lies heavily on me. No matter how much I tell myself that Calder will come, I don't really know if he will. But the thing I *do* really know is that given enough time, Hunter will kill me.

The salt from my tears stings my cheeks, but I wipe my face, shaking my head, and take another deep breath.

No. I survive. That's the only outcome I choose.

There's another bang before the door crashes open into the wall as Hunter charges in. I scream, ducking as my hands cover my head, but he grabs my hair, yanking me out.

"I said to get the fuck out here."

"Hunter," Marianne yells, but this time he ignores her.

My shoulder bounces off the doorjamb as Tag steps in front, yanking Hunter's hand from me, pulling strands of hair with him. I'm staring down at the ground, trying to stop my body from shaking, but I can't because I'm so fucking scared.

"What the fuck are you doing, Hunter? If you make her any fucking uglier, how are we supposed to travel? She's a walking red flag. Jesus, little Kelly. For once, think before you act. I don't even know why you still want her anyway."

I glance up as Hunter's jaw tenses, so I take a step back because my breath is coming out too fast. He's beyond angry.

The others are worried about Connor, game-planning how they evade his wrath if this is what's happening, but every piece of me sees that Hunter couldn't care less. This is about him and Calder, and using me to level the playing field.

"Why wouldn't I want her. She's the queen. The players protect the queen, and I have a feeling, Tag, that Connor may be willing to trade me something for her—like my life." Hunter's face twists to me. "But that doesn't mean I can't have my fun first."

Tag looks at me and frowns.

"Sutton, just go upstairs and stay out of the way until we figure out what to do or what's going on. Got it? You're making my brother crazy."

I nod, taking quick steps backward, jumping on this opportunity to get as far away as possible, but as I turn, chills creep over me because Hunter says, "Go to my room. Nobody else's. I mean it, *Freckles*."

My stomach tries to turn over as I look back over my shoulder, swallowing every bit of hatred I have, and nod, but Hunter's tongue darts out over his bottom lip.

"Come here."

Oh God. I turn back around slowly, trying not to wince as I walk back, stopping in front of him.

He's looking down at me, saying nothing as my heart beats out of my chest.

"Are you afraid of me?"

I don't lie as I stare at his chest.

"Yes." His fingers trail up my arm to my shoulder, then over the tops of my breasts until he lifts them to my face. He brushes my hair behind my ear as he leans in so close that his breath warms the lobe.

"You should be afraid. I'm not done making you hurt, but if you promise not to scream, I'll be nicer tomorrow."

A soundless sob wracks my body as my lips part for me to suck in air because he's pressed a kiss to the cheek marked by his fingernails before turning his back to me.

I'm standing there, frozen by fear, body so rigid that I'm not even shaking anymore as he casually looks over his shoulder and says, "Go to bed, Freckles."

I turn, body so cold, heart beating so hard it may explode as I take step after painful step up the stairs and into Hunter's room. He's going to come up here. And this time, he will finish what he started.

The panic inside me is screaming to be heard. *What do I do? What do I do?* The rest of me is trying to go numb and prepare myself to not feel so that none of it will hurt. But as I close the door behind me, there's a louder voice. The one I've grown and nurtured.

The survivor.

My head shifts around, eyes pausing on his closet…shoes?

"No, too big," I answer myself because there are too many thoughts, too many fears in my head that I need to say everything out loud, or I won't even hear it.

I look to the other side of the room, sucking in a breath as I see a window. But really, all I see is a tree outside that window.

"Go."

The carpet's softer on my feet, so I hurry toward it, face shooting to the door as I think I hear someone coming up the stairs.

"Fuck."

Adrenaline pumps through me as I run smack into his window, unlocking it before I lift it open. My hands shove the screen, jutting it out enough so that I can grab it and pull it inside.

I glance over my shoulder again, feeling my entire body break out in chills from the ocean breeze that drifts through the gaping space. My head peeks out, and I look down to the ground then back to the tree, swallowing hard.

Dammit, it's close, but I'll have to drop to the branch. I'm on the second story, and if I fall, there's no way I'll be able to run.

Not on a broken leg or ankle. But if I stay here…

So before I second-guess myself, I hitch my leg over the frame before doing the same with the other so that I'm sitting.

I'm almost panting as I look out into the night.

"It's okay. I've got this. It's okay."

My hands grip the wood as I roll over to balance on my stomach, as I strain to let my foot feel for the branch closest to me.

My toes just barely touch bark before I let my stomach scrape the windowsill until I can almost feel the balls of my feet resting against the oak. So I drop. I let go, hitting the branch so hard the wind is knocked out of me.

But I hold on, gritting my teeth so that I don't make a sound.

The breath inside of my lungs burns as it releases, but it doesn't matter because I can't stop. Hunter, Tag, Marianne…any of them could find me at any time.

My legs burn, muscles aching as I begin to climb down and out of view, balancing and weaving under branches until I get to the lowest one, which is still high off the ground.

But I don't hesitate to drop down, feeling the sharp pain reverberate through my legs, making me clamp my hand over my mouth so that nobody hears me as I fall to the ground.

I press my palm into the grass, taking deep breaths as my fingers dig into the dirt below, but I push myself to stand. Everything hurts, so I take careful steps, limping as the pain fades. Until I grow stronger and stronger, carrying me into the shadows away from that fucking house and everyone in it.

"Where do I go?" I whisper. "God, where do I go?"

My words keep coming as I run down streets I know like the back of my hand, but somehow, nothing looks familiar. I look around the darkness, feet stinging, eyes thick with tears, feeling so lost. I stumble, knocking my battered body into a fence just as I hear bells.

Stuttered cries fall from my lips because I know that sound. My face lifts in the direction they're coming from as I run faster and faster toward the only place I know I'll be safe.

I'm running over the concrete, across the paved street, until my feet rush up steps.

There is no pain anymore. All I can feel is hope.

I slow, grabbing the sides of my nightgown as I stare up at the stained-glass angels in front of the church. *Our church.*

"Calder," I breathe as I reach for the door, eyes darting to a gold plaque affixed to the wall next to the door that's never been there before.

I can endure all these things through the power of the one who gives me strength.
—Philippians 4:13

It's as if reading this was an answer to his name.

The door creaks as I open it and slip inside, feeling warmth envelop me. Until now, I didn't even realize how cold I was, but my skin is like ice, goose bumps pebbling my arms.

I walk inside, staring up at the rafters. God, it's exactly how I remember it. My head shifts around, looking from place to place, almost seeing us again.

"Lamb, are you okay?"

I jump, startled, eyes wide as I turn around scared, but a woman, petite with the kindest blue eyes, stares back at me. Still, my first instinct is to run, so I stumble back toward the doors, but her words rush out.

"You're safe now, sweet girl." Her eyes lower to my outfit, taking me in as she looks back to my face. "You've endured so much."

She holds her arms open, and I don't know why, but I rush into them, letting her wrap me in her warmth. My shoulders shake as she soothes me, running her hand down my hair.

"Shh, now. Shh."

The sound of a door opening from inside the church makes my head lift, but the woman cradles my cheeks, whispering, "Go now. Upstairs, to the confessional. Hide there. Everything will be okay. You can endure all things through the power of the one who gives you strength."

I nod, staring at her, repeating the words from the plaque in my head as I turn. My feet carry me quickly as I make my way to the familiar stairs, hurrying up as my white nightgown sways against my legs.

The moment I'm at the top and slipping into the confessional, it feels as if I can finally breathe because I'm back in the room I remember in my dreams.

Calder

"You gonna stay awake all night? It's 2:00 in the morning. Go home. I'll keep him here."

Roman means back to the field house because we're standing outside my old room in Tyler's place on the island. We needed to keep Connor someplace nobody would come looking, just in case.

"Hey, did you check in on my girl?"

Even though I ask, I know he would've told me if something was wrong.

"Yeah, earlier. Before Baron. The housekeeper said she was already turning in for the night. No Hunter around. We're good until the Council meeting."

I blow out a breath, tired and worn down from the day, as I look back at my brother. Everything I've done in the last two, almost three years feels like it's finally catching up with me.

Because tomorrow, I'll be judged. I'll stand before the Council and make my case—my life, my allegiance, in exchange for Connor's life. I can't help but wonder if between Connor and me… if either of us would really be more deserving of life than the other.

Except I know I want her, so whether I'm worthy or not, I'd do it all again. My eyes close for a moment before I look past Roman, feeling stripped down to the barest bones of the truth.

"Tomorrow decides if I live or die. But if I *die*, then promise me—"

He shakes his head, holding up a hand for me to stop. "No. Quit that shit. You'll take care of your own girl."

"Roman."

His jaw tenses as he looks back at me. We stand there staring at each other because he doesn't want to lose another brother, and I don't want to leave my girl. But we both know that's what could happen. It's why I'm waiting to get her. I need it all in place so she doesn't have to spend even one fucking day in hell.

He gives a tight nod before looking away.

"If I protect you, then I protect her. I remember our deal, and that shit counts even in death, brother."

I bring my hand down to his shoulder, patting it.

"Call and check up on her later, when normal people are awake, will you?"

"I got you."

I let out a long breath before I turn my back and head out. Because there's nothing more to say. Roman knows what to do. We hold Connor until the Council meeting. If I walk out, then we go get Sutton. If Connor walks out, he gets Sutton.

It's that simple. But tonight, at least, she'll have peace.

I cross the lawn, heading to my Mustang, then pull open the door and slide in. The engine growls as I turn the key before I pull out and slow at the end of the driveway.

My head swings to the left, the way that takes me to the field house, but I don't move. I sit, letting the car idle as I look to the right.

I can see the tracks off in the distance, the ones I cross into downtown St. Simeon, and something about it keeps calling me.

I need to make my peace.

The tires turn right, taking me down the street. I grip the steering wheel almost on autopilot because the call is so fucking loud. I need to fucking make my peace with God. Not for myself, but for her.

I need to know that if I'm going to die that he'll have her back.

My mind begins to drift between all the sweetest fucking moments with my girl. I let them wash over me as I pass by familiar places, smiling as I drive past the basketball courts, remembering how nervous she looked when I walked around the corner or the way she stared at me when we played basketball.

I'll never forget that. I'd had plenty of girls look at me, but the way Sutton stared like she could feel my thoughts…it was different because I could feel hers too.

I slow to a stop before turning the engine off, staring up at the Gothic-looking church. My hand wraps around the handle, pushing open the car door before I slide my head out and stand.

"Fuck," I whisper, feeling her everywhere.

The keys bounce in my hand before I shove them into my pocket and walk across the grass, thinking about when I snuck back just to fucking kiss her that day. I follow that same path, walking around the side of the church, reaching for that same handle I twisted to sneak in the first time.

It opens, making me hesitate for a moment before I slip inside. The familiar smell of frankincense and myrrh waft in the rafters as I look to my sides, seeing an empty church.

I walk through the hall that connects to the church's main room, letting my hand drag over the pews as I pass between them to the center aisle.

Fuck. I stand staring at the crucifix above the altar.

"I'm not sure I even believe in you anymore, but she does. So tell me how to make peace with you because I need you and every good thing in the world on her fucking side if I go."

A throat clears behind me, making me spin around and reach to the small of my back. But the priest staring back at me just smiles.

"Father," I offer, relaxing.

"Calder Wolfe. It's been a while."

My eyes narrow. "How the fuck do you know who I am, priest?"

He frowns before answering, probably because of my language.

"I met your father once or twice. And you, but I saw you up there." He turns and points to the balcony. "I remember because I lost an outstanding communion volunteer that day."

My lips tug into a grin as I chuckle before I change the subject.

"Why is your church open in the middle of the night, Father? Or do you lead mass in your pajamas now?"

"Our doors are always open for any lost soul. But currently, I'm here because the bells rang. Probably just some kids messing around."

He puts his hands behind his back before smiling. "Take the time you need with God, Calder Wolfe. But come and visit me tomorrow for confession. For now, I'm going back to bed."

I smirk as he walks past me, the doors clanging behind him as he leaves.

"The Devil and God in the same room," I whisper, eyes landing back on the balcony.

I walk back out to the hall, wanting to see it all again, even if it's only a memory. I take those familiar steps, eyes catching on that basin of holy water as I ramp it up, taking two stairs at a time until I land on our balcony.

It's completely the same, untouched, from the bookcases to the goblets and stored containers of oils.

And there's still that damn confessional. I close my eyes, wanting to see her face as I say, "Baby."

Chapter Thirty-Two

Sutton

"Baby."

My knees are drawn up as I hug them, pressing my face down as I hold my breath because I'm hearing things. Goose bumps grow wild over my skin, but I'm warm. I'm so still like I'm trying to be invisible, waiting for the footsteps to retreat. But then I hear the voice again.

"I miss you."

I gasp, my body rocketing toward the confessional door. My fingers scramble, throwing it open before I burst from my hiding place.

My hand clamps down over my mouth because I don't want to scream or cry. Because if this is a dream, I don't want to wake up.

"Sutton?"

Calder steps toward me, brows drawn together deeply as he

shakes his head, his hand already reaching for me. But I run. I launch myself into his arms, wrapping mine around his neck.

"Baby. Oh my God. How are you here?"

He's engulfing me, holding me off the ground as we hug, wrapped tightly around each other so there is no start or end point between us.

"You're here. I can't believe you're here."

"Let me see you. Are you okay?" He tries to pull back, but I won't let him go. "Okay. It's okay. I've got you, baby. Let me make it better."

I wrap my legs around him, needing him close, never wanting to let go.

"I prayed for you," I whisper, kissing his neck, feeling the smooth warmth of his skin on my lips. "In the confessional. I prayed you'd come for me."

He holds me there, one hand under me, the other around my back, swaying back and forth.

I don't even know how long we stay like that, but his hand runs down my hair as he kisses the side of my head, saying nothing, just loving me.

"Sutton. You need to look at me now."

I shake my head against the crook of his neck because a part of me still doesn't believe this is real. Maybe I've died, and he has too, and this is someplace we get to meet.

"Baby, look at me. I promise I won't disappear."

I blink before I pull my head back. Our eyes lock, but the instant sorrow on his face makes me hate myself. I should've been stronger because this is breaking him.

His fingers brush over the marks on my cheeks so gently that I barely feel them. Soft kisses rain down over each mark as he catalogs the bruises and rips on my nightgown. He brushes my hair from my face, trailing his fingers over darker bruises down toward the back of my neck. His hand lowers over my arm, reaching behind him to my calf before feeling my bare foot locked at the ankle behind his back.

"Baby," he rushes out as if weeping on the inside as his face tilts to the ceiling.

But as he looks back to me, the muscles in his jaw ripple, his eyes shining.

Calder looks deeply into my soul, voice so low that my breath stops.

"Who did this to you?"

My tongue darts out, tasting the salt left behind from my dried tears.

"They all did this to me. You're the only one that protects me."

Calder's eyes grow cold. There's so much anger behind them, but I can't help but think how beautiful it is because it's fueled by his love.

"Tell me it's over," I rush out, already knowing what he'll say.

"I can't."

I crush my lips against him, needing to feel his kiss. To taste him.

His tongue slips inside my mouth as I pull him closer, curling an arm around his neck as he turns us and begins to walk.

"What are you doing?" I breathe, pulling away.

Calder looks at me with so much love that it knocks the breath out of me.

"I'm stealing you back."

I can't help how my chest shakes as my hands come to his cheeks.

"This isn't the plan."

His feet stop as he holds me up and takes one of my hands, bringing the palm to his lips.

"I will never leave you alone and unprotected ever again. *You* are coming home."

All the emotion I've held on to, everything that I've pretended not to feel. All the sadness, the rage, all the goddamn grief—it explodes from me, exorcised from my body as I cling to him.

I weep as he holds me tightly to him, letting me feel for the first time in almost three years. It's as if I've been turned off, the lights dimmed so as to never be seen. And now he's here, and I can't hide, but really, I don't want to because he's the only one that can make it all better.

With just his arms wrapped around me and his lips against my hair.

Because he's my home.

I bury my face into his neck as I'm carried down the steps. He whispers about stars and magic, love and forever to me as I cry, never breaking his stride as he walks through the entrance of the church.

His lips press to my head as he speaks.

"I love you. You are so strong and brave, and I'm so proud of you, baby. But let me take care of you now. Let me make it better, my sweet girl."

As he says the last part, my head lifts, tears still in my eyes as I look around, searching for the woman.

"Wait, there was a woman here. She helped me, and I need to thank her."

Calder slows, looking around before he rubs his hand over my back.

"No, baby. There's nobody here except for the priest and me."

His arms hold me close as he walks us out to his car, but I suddenly cling tighter. I don't want him to let me go. I can't be away from him.

"Baby, what's wrong, what's wrong, what's wrong?"

My head shakes against his neck.

"Please don't let me go."

I feel him release a whoosh of breath as he hugs me tighter.

Calder walks over to the driver's side and turns sideways after opening his door before saying, "Just unhook your legs."

He lowers us, my feet only touching the ground for a second before I'm pulled inside the car, straddling him, arms still firmly around his neck.

It's the way we were so many years ago the first time I was in this car.

I feel him lean to the side, but I don't move, hungry for more of the peace he brings me. The sound of ringing fills the car seconds before a deep voice answers.

"What up, C?"

Calder's voice vibrates through his body as he speaks.

"Send a couple of the guys over to the Kellys'. Tell him to hold everyone there until I arrive." His hand strokes my hair as he whispers into it, "Is your mother there?"

I shake my head, closing my eyes as he says, "Sutton's mother is missing from that crew. Send someone to grab that bitch. I want them all there together."

"Done. But you want to tell me what the fuck is going on?"

A kiss is pressed to my head as the engine turns over.

"I found Sutton at the church, Roman. Something went south with our contact. I'm taking her home."

There's silence before he says, "I got you. Give our little mama a hello."

The line disconnects as Calder puts the car in drive and pulls out, keeping one hand on me and the other on the steering wheel.

"Better now, baby?"

I nod into his neck, feeling his hand stroking me from my head to my back.

"Only until we get to the highway," he breathes out as the feeling of déjà vu washes over me.

But my eyes stay closed, our hearts beating in sync as we drive. Until I finally connect the dots. I lift my head as the car slows to a stop. Goose bumps spread over me as I look into his eyes.

"Time to buckle up now, Buttercup."

I feel like I can't catch my breath as I ask, "Where's home?"

He leans in, brushing a tender kiss to my lips before saying, "The only place it should be."

Chapter Thirty-Three

Sutton

The minute we pulled up, I barely waited for the car to slow before I threw off my seat belt and scrambled out into the middle of our field.

Deep, gasping breaths fill my lungs as I stare up at the stars. Even though the dark blue sky is getting lighter, they're still looking down, twinkling like they didn't want to miss out on seeing me either.

God, this is more than a sky or stars. This is our magic. The place where I dreamed of a love that would last forever and he promised all those damn stars in the sky.

This is our forever.

"The house is the other way," he whispers, coming up behind me.

I spin around, staring up at him.

"I'm…" There are so many endings to that sentence—broken,

battered, scared, exhausted—but the only one that matters is the one I say, "…yours. Forever."

Calder cradles my face, staring down at me as the universe finds its place again.

"I'm yours too, baby."

He lowers his face, lips pressing to mine as we linger until I lift to my toes, dipping my tongue inside his mouth. His fingers weave into my hair, holding my head as our tongues dance over each other's, tasting and teasing, getting reacquainted, effortlessly falling back into rhythm. I was made for kissing this man.

My head changes positions as our kiss deepens, my hands gripping the front of his shirt as I arch toward him.

His hand comes to the small of my back, his fingers bunching the fabric of my nightgown before he pulls back breathless, the wind knocked out of him just like me as our foreheads touch.

I have so many questions to ask him, but right now, I just want to be loved, to feel him everywhere until nothing else exists but him.

"Take me inside," I whisper.

Calder sweeps me off the ground, tucking his hand under my knees and cradling me. He walks toward the house as I stare, lips parted.

It's so beautiful and warm. It feels like a place where love would grow. I can see us sitting on the porch, having picnics on the field, making a family. He built me everything I've ever wanted—a place meant just for us.

"You built us a home," I whisper.

"I did."

My chin trembles. "How do I even begin to say thank you?" I don't mean to say it aloud, but it comes out without permission. He stops at the door staring down at me as a grin begins to grace his face.

"You don't." He hugs me closer, leaning down to kiss my lips.

"You don't ever say thank you for getting everything you fucking deserve. You are owed beauty and magic. And, baby, you better demand it from me every goddamn day for the rest of our lives."

He opens the door carrying me across the threshold as I all but climb him, sealing my mouth over his. Calder shifts me so that I can wrap my legs around him as the door closes behind us.

We're moving—he's carrying me, but I'm lost in this kiss. Our lips glide, dipping in between each other, and dragging away as his hand splays against my back. His right hand is on my ass, fingers kneading as he growls into my mouth.

I jostle against him as he climbs the staircase, pulling myself closer, wrapping my arm around him. My other hand stays on his cheek, wanting the feel of his skin under my fingertips.

Our heads tilt and turn, tongues rolling over sloppily as we devour each other.

Calder's hand runs up my back and into my hair pulling it, so that our kiss breaks, forcing my chin up just as his mouth assaults my neck. I moan as his lips drag over my throat.

"Yes."

We walk through a doorway as he guides my face back to his using my hair.

"This is our bedroom."

"I love the décor," I breathe out, voice husky, only looking at him.

He laughs, deep and rumbling as I'm placed to the ground. But our eyes don't part because right now, he's all I want to see.

I draw my bottom lip between my teeth, and the longer we stare, the faster my heart beats and butterflies unleash from their cages inside of me. I'm nervous.

I'm not the same girl I was the last time we found ourselves in this place. So much has happened, and I'm scared of everything and nothing all at once. I think that I'm afraid to let myself feel because what if it's ripped away again and I'm left with a huge gaping hole that only he fills.

A piece of me knows that I can't survive that anymore.

I know that all of my thoughts play out on my face because his brows furrow as he steps in so close that our bodies are almost flush. I'm dwarfed by him, leaning forward to place my forehead on his chest.

His voice is quiet as he strokes my hair.

"It ends tomorrow, baby." I smile even though he can't see me because I never say anything. He always just knows, even after years. He knows what I'm feeling because he's feeling it too.

Calder takes a deep breath before I feel his lips press to the top of my head.

"I tried to give you peace—"

"I can only find that with you," I say, cutting him off. "That's why fate intervened."

An empty chuckle shakes his chest like he believes what I'm saying. As if he feels the truth like I do. Tonight brought us together because we needed something only the other could give.

I step back to look up at him, but his fingers lift, tracing over the scratches on my face. He's searching my eyes, with an equal amount of rage and love as his brows draw together deeply.

"Show me the way you need me to love you, baby," he whispers.

My heart stops. He knows what Hunter's done. I can see it in his face, feel it in the tenderness of his touch. I stare back in awe of everything he is before I grab his hand, pressing it to my face, then to my chest.

"You know how to love me. Fuck me, kiss me, make love to me. I want everything you give, Calder Wolfe. Because there is and will only ever be *you* and *me*."

His eyes meet mine, and so much passes between us. One day I will tell him everything, but that shit doesn't get to exist here. Not in this room. Or in this moment.

Calder lifts my hand to his lips, kissing it before he steps past me, making me turn as he leads me to a door at the far side of the room.

He opens it to a large bathroom, turning on the lights but leaving them dim. I'm standing, staring around the room, taken by all the details. The beauty in just a bathroom, from the white-gray marble to the matte black fixtures that accentuate the floor-to-ceiling double shower.

But the sound of water draws my eyes to the corner. Calder's sitting on the edge of a clawfoot tub, his hand testing the water as it runs.

I take a hesitant step onto the tile, feeling warmth, but he's already walking back to me, hands coming to my waist.

"Let me look at you now."

I blink up as he bunches the fabric of my nightgown, raising it over my body before slipping it over my head. If I were broken or battered, I'd never know because the way Calder's staring at my body only reflects beauty.

His hand comes to his mouth, wiping over his beard as his eyes drift over me.

"You have never been more beautiful." His blue eyes lift to mine. "My strong, brave girl."

He leans in, kissing my chest, bending lower to my stomach, pressing more kisses as his arm hugs me in. My head tilts before dropping down, bringing my face to the top of his head.

Calder's lips move from bruise to bruise, ones I don't even feel but are speckled over my body until he falls to his knees in front of me.

His hands hold my hips as his cheek lays against my stomach, letting me feel the ragged breaths he draws in.

"Never again, baby."

His ass lowers to my feet as his face sweeps over the small tuft of hair on my pussy.

"Oh." I gasp, hands on his shoulders as he presses a kiss right to my center.

The feeling almost knocks me over. Makes me feel greedy for more.

"Again," I breathe out, fingers weaving into his hair.

It's been so long since I've felt his mouth on me that I'm instantly overwhelmed as Calder's tongue cuts through my hair, licking up my wet center, gliding over my clit.

"Oh my God."

My stomach contracts, but my body begins pulling back because it's all so sensitive. The counter hits my ass as I lean back, but he chases me, tugging me back by my hips to his face with a growl.

"More."

The sound of water filling the tub bounces off the walls as I'm pinned between Calder and the counter. My legs are nudged open by his broad shoulders, already shaking as he licks and eats the most sensitive part of me like an animal.

His mouth feels everywhere as his tongue rolls over my clit, flicking and sucking, pressing his face in harder as my hips circle. My leg is yanked over his shoulder as his palms splay over my stomach.

Calder's holding me right where he wants me.

"Calder. Oh God."

He moans, vibrating against my clit as he sucks the swollen bud, letting it go with a pop as he looks up at me, his face glistening with my desire.

"Look at me, Sutton. Watch."

My eyes lock to his as he presses two fingers inside of me, hitching my breath.

"Fuck," he groans. "My fingers fucking missed you."

He juts them in and out, switching between quick thrusts before slowing again. We stare at each other so fucking lost to this feeling that everything could be on fire and we'd never know.

"Fuck me," I whisper, combing my fingers through his hair.

My stomach contracts as he pulls out, suddenly standing. He's breathing hard, staring down at me as he trails the wet fingers over my lips before his mouth crashes down to mine again. He grabs my jaw, tilting my head as his tongue swipes over my bottom lip, making him groan.

"Fuck."

He draws back, eyes narrowed on me.

"Put your fingers on that wet pussy and show me what you learned to do without me."

Calder takes a step back, then another as I stare into his eyes. My hand lifts, but I can't help it—I feel shy. The way he looks at me like he sees all the places I hide. I'm wholly exposed past my naked body.

His head tilts as the gravel in his voice stirs everything inside of me.

"Are you my good girl or my bad one tonight?"

He reaches down, eyes still on mine, turning off the tub as he gives me a wink.

Oh fuck. My eyes close as I step open wider, bringing my fingers to my lips, pushing them all the way inside my mouth, and suck.

"Mmm," he rumbles as my eyes reopen.

He reaches behind him, dragging his shirt over his head.

"Baby, you keep sucking those fingers like that, and I'm gonna feed you my cock to let you remember what it feels like to swallow me back."

My hand drops past my stomach, through my folds, emboldened. Wanting him to see. My fingers flank my clit as I begin rubbing in small circles, pressing my hips forward. My tongue darts out over my lips watching his hands run over his abs.

God, he's so fucking primal. The way his head lowers, eyes narrowing as he watches me, lips parting with his focus.

"Spread yourself open for me."

I part my fingers, letting him see my swollen clit as he licks his lips before I tip my head back and play with myself.

The sound of Calder kicking off his boots and socks fills the room before my body starts to feel warm. I close my eyes, wanting more of the feeling, coaxing it to grow bigger as I hear his belt buckle.

My fingers rub faster and faster, back arching as whimpers fall from my lips. I'm gripping the edge of the counter, digging my nails into the marble as my core begins to tighten.

"Eyes," he growls.

Without hesitation, they spring open just as Calder grabs my wrist, stopping my movement.

"*I* make you come."

My chest rises and falls as I pant. He leans in, kissing my cheek, then my nose before pressing his lips to mine.

"This is *my* reunion with her. Hands off now, Buttercup."

He dips down, picking me up and spinning us around, walking to the tub.

The water's hot against my skin as he lowers us down, stinging before it soothes my feet and body. I'm straddling him, feeling his hard cock between us as he reaches to the ledge next to the tub, grabbing a washcloth. He dips it in the water, soaping it up.

I can't stop looking into his eyes because the love reflected is so powerful that I have to keep catching my breath.

Neither of us speaks as he begins slowly washing my body.

"I love you," I whisper, staring into his eyes after a moment.

Water cascades down my chest as he runs the cloth over my skin and down my shoulder. He dips it into the water again, running it down my leg and over my calf, before gently cleaning my feet. It doesn't hurt. Nothing ever hurts with him.

He repeats the same thing on my other leg before dropping the damn rag outside the tub and pulling me close. My arms wrap around him, bodies flush as he buries his face into my neck. We stay there just breathing as his fingers urge me closer as if we can't be close enough.

Calder's palm is against my spine as his other hand holds the back of my head. I feel the warmth of his breath against my flesh as he peppers kisses to my neck, traveling over my jaw until we're face-to-face. His ocean blue eyes bore into mine as I cling to him.

"I love you, Sutton."

His voice is barely above a whisper, but he doesn't even have to say it because I feel it. It's washed over me like the fucking water bathing my body.

He loves me. It's all the life I ever want to live.

I reach down between us, lifting myself up, seating the head of his cock at the rim of my pussy. We're locked on each other. Never breaking eye contact as I lower down slowly, feeling the inside of my pussy drag over the thickness of his cock.

"Fuck, baby," he groans, hands running up my waist.

Calder's hands grip me tightly, stopping me in place before he locks eyes with me, controlling the movement. Taking it achingly slow.

I could come right here, right fucking now, all because of the look on his face. His jaw is so tense the muscles in his neck are strained as heavy breaths come from his nose. He's fucking wrecked by the feel of being inside of me, forcing himself to hold back because he's savoring it.

It makes me want to shove his hands away and ride him fast and hard until he's coming undone.

"You feel so fucking good. Let me feel that pussy on me nice and slow."

His mouth falls open, breath wisping against my nipple, as he leans forward, taking it between his lips before tugging me down farther.

I gasp, completely filled by his thick cock, swallowing hard. Water sloshes as my hands press against his shoulders, rising up before rocking down again.

"Oh, fuck." He grunts, pressing into me each time I lower.

We're moving faster, craving the closeness as his cock slides in and out. Our mouths taste every fucking spot we can reach, as his hands slide up my waist to caress my tits.

I moan, pushing them into his hands as he runs his thumb over my nipple.

"Yes."

Slickness builds inside of me making Calder groan. His hands drop to my waist holding me still, as he fucks me harder from the bottom, rocketing water from the tub.

I lean down, gripping his hair, pulling his head to the side, sucking his neck. I bite it and lick, wanting to leave marks all over him.

The sound of his foot squeaking against the basin accompanies a low, "Out."

Jesus, he all but growls it, lifting us in one big motion from the tub, spilling water all over.

His cock falls from me, but it doesn't matter because I wrap my legs around him, writhing against him. Calder steps out, stalking from the bathroom taking us straight to the bed.

As my back touches the mattress, he's over me, having never let go before his body lifts.

"Oh my God." I gasp.

I'm struck by the picture in front of me.

Calder's kneeling between my legs, his dick rock hard above

my pussy. He's holding one of my legs open from behind my knee as my other is draped over his hip. We're beautiful.

"This is your last lesson." He grins.

His tongue glides over his bottom lip as he looks down between us and back to my face.

"This pussy is mine to do with as I please. I will fuck it until it cries for me, and then I'll kiss it better. Because, baby, *I* was made to fucking worship you."

He crowns my entrance before thrusting inside deeply.

I suck in a breath, gasping his name. "Calder."

His hips rock, pounding inside of me, ass indenting at the sides with each movement. He's powerful and dominant, bathed in tattoos and graced with the bluest eyes that are so connected to mine as he fucks me raw.

"I'm so fucking wet for you, Calder."

My hips meet his movement as I drag my hands over my tits, feeling the slick warmth grow in my center.

"Aw fuck, baby. Drip for me."

The smell of sex is thick in the air as our wet bodies slap against each other. Calder throws my leg over, so I'm flipped to my side before he comes behind me, pushing back inside of me. Our bodies are flush, my back to his front as he draws my knee toward my body fucking me deeper. His dick strums all the right places, hitting deep in my belly with every thrust.

His beard scratches my neck as he whispers in my ear, "I fucked myself picturing your pussy. How it would taste, feel on my fingers again. I fucked every part of you in my mind."

I'm moaning as he pushes inside over and over, rocking our bodies together. His hand covers my breast, pinching the nipple between his fingers, rolling it as my body aches for more. My hand holds his wrist, pulling his fingers to my mouth, rolling my tongue around them before I suck, hollowing my cheeks.

"There's my girl. You want me everywhere. In your mouth, your pretty little cunt, and that ass. Don't you?"

My mouth drops open so fucking turned on as my body undulates.

"Fuck. Calder. I want to come."

My hand lowers between my legs, but he grabs my wrist, quickly sliding my arm out, forcing me onto my stomach. My legs are shoved open, feeling his tongue hit my clit.

"Oh my God," I scream, feeling my body shudder.

His arms are hooked under my legs, keeping them open as he eats my pussy from behind. I'm breathing so hard, I feel like I might pass out, but his face tears away as his dick hammers back inside.

He reaches around my throat gently, pulling me upright as I'm fucked hard, bouncing forward.

"*I* make you come," he growls.

I can barely catch my breath. I'm panting, needy, wanting all of him.

Calder reaches around me, his fingers pushing through my tuft, rubbing my clit. It's not slow or easy. It's demanding. I'm treated exactly the way I want, like his.

He isn't just fucking me or making love to me. He's laying his claim.

My hand closes over his, around my throat, chin tilted up, as he brings my mouth to his. I'm filled, building while he strokes my swollen clit.

Everything begins to curl up inside of me, compounding, rising as my stomach tightens.

Oh God, I'm covered by Calder, his tongue in my mouth, his cock gliding through my slickness. It's thrusting, pounding in and out of me, over and over as his fingers rub.

"Oh… I… Calder… Please…"

I'm begging as my eyes roll back, and my body is gifted what it's praying for.

"Oh my God," I scream against his mouth before my breath is held.

My body explodes as my eyes squeeze shut, shaking and tense.

Calder engulfs me ramming his cock inside me as I come harder and harder. My body is rocketed into the heavens, his name launched from my lips.

The crest is so high that my entire body slumps as it leaves me, a long breath whooshing past my lips.

"You're mine," he growls, pulling out of me, rolling me over on my back as he jerks his cock.

Calder shoves my legs open, spreading me wide as he stares at my pussy coated in my own release. He tugs viciously on his cock before releasing thick white ropes onto my clit.

"Oh fuck," he grits out, tensing, marking me as his.

His jaw is tight as his chest rises and falls quickly. I lick my lips, breath slowing as I lift my head, looking down to see his release on me.

Calder groans as he milks himself before lowering his hand. He drags his thumb between my folds as I let out a breath, gathering the cum before hooking his thumb inside me to push it in. His other fingers spread cum over my clit, and through my folds, breathing heavily as he does it.

His eyes meet mine again, and I'm hollowed by his possession. My palms press to the bed as I push myself to sit, bringing my face to his, capturing his bottom lip between mine before letting it drag out slowly.

"Now I'm baptized in you."

Chapter Thirty-Four

Calder

We've fucked too many times and too many ways to count. The sun's already up but I can't get enough of her.

I reach for her, never wanting her too far away again, so I drag her naked body closer. Our legs intertwine as we lie there, staring at each other, bodies slick with sweat, married together in our release.

I grab her hand, bringing her fingers to my lips, taking one between my teeth.

"Animal." She grins, but I growl, making her giggle.

It's the most heavenly fucking sound. I let her finger fall from my mouth as she begins playing with my beard.

"What happens today?" she whispers, leaning in to kiss my chest. "You said it all ends tomorrow."

I inhale deeply, humming the exhale before I answer.

"I have to go before something called the Council. Think of them as a jury. They decide the life and death sentences of this family. So they'll decide between Connor and me."

My head is lowered, watching the thoughts cross over her face before she looks up.

"And if they choose Connor?"

I open my mouth to answer her, but I hesitate because I don't want to tell her the truth. I can't. Fuck.

Her hand brushes over my chest as she leans in, kissing it again.

"Your heart's beating so fast."

"I'm scared."

It's so honest it hurts to say.

She blinks a few times, not looking at me before she lifts her chin.

"Of the Council?"

I shake my head.

"Of leaving you."

She says nothing, just stretches her arm across my chest, holding me closer. My fingers trail up and down her arm as we sit in silence, just listening to each other breathe, drowning in the bittersweet moments. Fuck, I just got her back.

Minutes tick by, weighing us down deeper until she takes a breath.

"We won't leave each other. You promised me that we'd die together, remember? So no matter what happens tomorrow, I'm following you everywhere you go, Calder Wolfe. So let's have right now, for us, until we know what today will bring. "

My chin drops as I look down at her. "I'm gonna marry you."

"Yeah, ya are."

I tuck my hands under her armpits dragging her up my body, growling as I kiss her again.

"I love you. But if I'm celebrating my possible last night on this planet, then I should get a last meal."

She laughs, leaning in to kiss my lips. "And what would you like to eat?"

"Your pussy."

I roll her onto her back as she squeals, but a clang from a box I had on the nightstand makes her jump.

"Oh shit." I chuckle. "It's okay."

She smiles, relaxing as I lean over, surveying the mess.

"What was that?"

I'm half off the bed as she laughs, anchoring me with her legs wrapped around my waist. But I press a palm to the floor before I pick up the box, muscling myself back into bed.

I shift around so that she can sit as I lie on my side, placing the container between us.

"This is something special. These are all the things I have left to remember my mother. Some are random trinkets. Others are things she specifically left me. The only thing missing is the coin."

I watch her as she smiles, but it's sad.

"You're lucky," she whispers. "I know that sounds weird, but..."

My brow furrows. "Do you want me to let her live?"

Sutton's eyes cut to mine as she stares back into my eyes because she knows I'm speaking about her mother, but she just shakes her head as she looks back down, sorting through the belongings.

I won't push her to tell me what they did when we were apart, and I'll never let on to some things I already know. Because they're hers to tell when she's ready.

But goddamn if I wouldn't move heaven and earth for this girl.

She's pulling things out to look at them closer, the sadness in her eyes fading as they flick to mine. She holds up a postcard that says Memphis.

"She always wanted to go to Graceland. Obsessed with Elvis."

Sutton grins, putting it back inside, reaching for something else before she looks up at me.

"What makes you think the Council will choose you over Connor?"

I run my finger down the slope of her nose and over her freckles as she blinks back at me.

"Because I did everything he did without taking from people. We're alike in so many ways. But this life is about family. We do wicked things, but in the end, we're supposed to protect our own. I remembered that because of you. Connor looked after himself alone. So I took everything away from him—the drugs, the money, the power—and I made it better. People respect me as much as they fear me."

She grins. "Like an Irish Robin Hood, huh?"

I chuckle, looking inside the box too. "Not exactly, but I like it." My eyes drop, seeing a folded picture. I pull it out and open it, staring down at the old faded photo, smiling before I hand it to Sutton.

"It's so faded, but people always said that we had the same eyes."

She's grinning as she looks down at the photo before her fingers come to her lips.

"Baby?"

She pales, blinking quickly, eyes darting to mine before she shakes her head and whispers, "Holy shit." She laughs as tears spring to her eyes.

"Whoa. Hey. What's wrong?"

I'm already sitting up, pulling her into my arms, but the smile on her face feels like it arrested my heart. Her hands come to my face as she straddles me, fingers brushing over my beard.

"You wouldn't believe me if I told you."

My head tilts as I lock eyes with her. "Try me."

Her eyes search mine before she leans forward, brushing her

nose against mine.

"I just think destiny works in amazing ways. And if you ask me, your eyes are identical."

My brows draw together, but she kisses me deeply, and she doesn't stop until I've forgotten what the fuck I was going to say.

My eyes dart to the clock, hating this fucking moment because of how she looks—hair wild and laid out over the pillow, body covered in one of my T-shirts because she got cold last night. Fuck, she's perfect. This is perfect.

I take a deep breath, letting my chin lift before I step back from the bed.

"It's almost over."

The butt of my palms wipes my eyes as I turn, walking away, but the minute I touch the handle, I look back, staring at my girl. My beautiful girl, with emerald eyes and hair like fire who landed in my life like a goddamn earthquake, shaking it up and leaving me destroyed. I wouldn't have it any other way.

Because what she tore down, she rebuilt.

"I love you, baby. And I'll kill every motherfucker there if they try to keep me away."

I pull the door open, eyes locking to Roman's, who's already standing guard outside the door.

He gives me a nod as I pass him, but I stop and look at him.

"Did you have her things brought home?"

"I did. And I thought you could use this later. For Hunter."

He hands me the knife we had made for her. This is his way of saying I better make it out.

All I can do is nod before leaving my brother in that fucking hallway, looking after my heart.

Chapter Thirty-Five

Calder

The room is dark and ripe with the scent of death. Because the call for it is oozing off the men standing around us. This is it. What it's all come to. The Council will decide who leads this family. And who dies.

"On your knees."

Connor and I drop directly across from each other, eyes locked as a gun presses to each of our temples. My teeth grind as I look at him because I want to grab the fucking gun at my temple and shoot him with it.

But I won't. Because even if I die, Roman's going to make sure Connor does too.

The head of the Irish Chicago family—the MacGregors—walks to the center of the room, standing between us.

"Only one of you will leave here alive." Connor's eyes lock to mine as the man continues. "Now's the time when you convince us of which."

This is tradition. These ten men stand in the shadows, all silent until they vote, and then bang, one of us goes down.

"Answer this, Calder Wolfe…why should this family"—MacGregor looks around—"these men, why should we follow you?"

Fuck. Time feels like it stands still. All I ever heard growing up was shit about my birthright into violent delights, to a family that did wicked things with sometimes dire consequences. I hated it. I ran from it.

I ran to her.

And somehow, deep in the vastness of finding love, I also made peace with the devil inside of me.

Birthright meant nothing to me. Even as I walked in this door, it's always just been a means to an end. But as I look around this room, at the faces of the men who stare back, I'm suddenly struck with the enormity of what my life means.

This family will protect her and the babies I fill her belly with. It will leave a mark, take lives, and better others. And it should only be led by me.

I reach up, bringing my hand to the gun at my head, lowering it as I stand. Unease sweeps the room as I look at each man inside this warehouse.

"I don't expect anyone to be led. I expect that we'll walk together. Side by side like brothers in arms." I step toward Connor, jaw tensed before I speak, "Because what I took from him, I'll give to you."

The men around the room exchange glances, because he keeps them hungry so they obey. But I'll keep them fed so they're loyal. I take another step feeling anger begin to course through my veins, pulling my fists closed tight as my voice is gritted between my teeth.

"I own his streets—the ones he abandoned and turned into

ghettos." My head shifts to MacGregor. "I run his fucking drugs, but I'll make sure that everyone gets a piece. Because that's what this family was built on. Our violent loyalty and understanding that no man is ever above being Irish."

Connor's inhaling through his nose like a bull, face red as he glares back at me. I crack my neck as I look back.

"Get off your fucking knees and face me like a man."

Tension bounds through the walls as the gun held to his head is lowered. Connor stands, his chest heaving, snarling as he stalks toward me.

But I'm fucking ready. It feels like I've waited my entire life, building, culminating to this moment. It's right in front of me, mine for the taking.

We stand toe to toe, ready to kill as his hand darts out, gripping my throat.

"You think these men will turn on me? After all I've done for them? I know what's right. I am King, you little prick."

My fist swings down across his face, knocking him to the ground as I hover over him. The sound of guns cocking echoes through the silence.

But I won't be stopped. My words are growled, bellowed from within me.

"You've only done for you." I heave out breaths as I lower my voice, body stilling as the comfort of killing wraps itself around me.

Connor's staring up at me, fear in his eyes as he wipes the blood from his mouth.

"There is no longer a king. Because my family will be a fucking army. And Uncle, I will take my place by any means necessary."

My eyes are narrowed on Connor. I could kill him right here. I take a step just as my head is pushed sideways by the cold hard steel of a barrel to my temple. MacGregor steps into view sneering.

"The only means are the ones we give." He presses the gun

harder as my heart pounds. "We decide who lives and who dies. Who's in power and who's starved."

Connor is yanked, forcing his back straighter as his lips tug into a grin, before a heavy hand pushes on my shoulder.

"Get on your knees, Calder."

I drop, glimpses of Sutton flashing through my mind because I'm either going to be anointed or annihilated.

Chapter Thirty-Six

Sutton

My eyes drift open slowly as my hand slides over the bed, reaching for Calder. But I already know it's empty. There's only the sunlight shining through the window, hitting the sheet and leaving a streak of brightness to spotlight his absence.

I just lie there, staring at the crumpled white sheet, scooting closer to smell it.

My eyes close again, picturing him lying next to me, a smirk on his face as I trace my finger over the tattoos on his chest.

"Please come back," I whisper.

A knock on the door shoots me to sitting, eyes wide open. My heart's beating too quickly as I drop my eyes, seeing that I'm still wearing Calder's T-shirt.

Another knock brings Roman's voice. "It's just me, Sutton. Roman."

I let out a breath, running my hand through my hair.

"Come in," I say quietly, hating that I'm so unnerved.

Roman peeks his head around the door, meeting my eyes.

"Hey, mama."

He must see the look on my face because he shakes his head. "Hey. Hey. Hey," he says as he walks inside, beelining to me.

Roman is scary and intimidating, but at this moment, the way he holds my face in his hand—it's everything I need. I'm gripping onto his wrist, staring up at him, just needing the anchor he's giving because…

"I'm so afraid I'll lose him," I whisper, finishing my thought.

He shakes his head.

"C fought death for you. You really think a few gangsters are gonna get in his way? This is what he knows, baby girl, and if shit doesn't go his way, then I got you. Because you ain't alone anymore. You are a part of him, and that makes you my family."

I smile up at him, letting him pull me into a bear hug.

"I would trade my life for his," I say on a ragged breath.

"Me too."

I hug him tighter for what feels like forever until he lets me go, giving me one of those Roman nods I remember. They say so much without saying anything at all.

He clears his throat. "I'll check on you later."

I nod, sinking back into the bed, and pull the sheet up before I close my eyes again and pray.

I don't know how long I've been asleep, but the sun's lower in the sky, shadows cast across the walls in our room. I roll to his space, still empty, so I close my eyes again, but a knock on the door reopens my eyes as I sit up.

"Haven't we already done this?" I tease quietly as Roman walks inside, holding a bottle of water in one hand and something in a bowl—maybe soup.

"You need to eat and stop grieving. He'll be pissed when he comes back and you're all hungry and sad."

I run my hands through my hair before smacking down on the blanket a little too hard.

"Don't do that."

His face swings to mine as he puts the bowl on the nightstand.

"Do what?"

"Act like he went to the store. Like he'll be right back. Don't do that, Roman."

He looks down at the food, placing my water next to it before he gives a quiet growl. God, it reminds me of Calder, so I scoot back into the bed and roll over so my back is to Roman.

But I'm nudged, and I only move because I feel him sit down on the bed.

"Can I tell you something?"

My brows furrow, but he can't see that, so I shrug as I stare at the wall.

"Every year while you've been apart, I went to see that old witch."

My chin meets my shoulder, eyes fixing to his.

"Why?"

He crosses his arms, leaning back against me as he stretches his legs in front of him.

"I don't know. At first, I thought maybe she'd cursed us." He pauses, giving a sad chuckle. "Because of West dying and all."

My teeth find my bottom lip before I whisper, "I'm so sorry about West, Roman."

He doesn't look at me, just gives my shoulder a gentle tap of his fist before he continues.

"The thing is, she always said the same thing. It was stupid. But everything felt pretty out of control, so I figured fuck it, what's the harm? I thought maybe I'd go one day, and she'd say you were over him."

I poke his back, scowling, but he grins, still speaking. "Then I could tell him you'd moved on, and maybe he wouldn't be so fucking lost without you."

His face shifts to mine. "Because he was lost. My brother hasn't looked like himself since this morning when he left. You breathed life back into him."

I shift, roll over, and push to sit up again.

"Or, fuck, I kept thinking best-case she'd use her hoodoo voodoo to tell me something we could use against Connor. But it was always the fucking same. Until it wasn't."

I grab my water, twisting the top before taking a sip.

"What did she say the last time?"

He motions to the soup, so I pick up the warm bowl and take a bite.

"She told me that men were like fish—the great ones devour the small. But that Calder was the ocean, and he'd swallow everyone whole. She said death wasn't waiting for him. It was listening for his instruction."

The spoon slides out from between my lips as I frown.

"What does that mean?"

He chuckles, and he looks out the window. "I have no fucking clue, but I do know what's important about it."

"What?" I answer weakly.

"She never said he'd lose, Sutton."

The sun's gone down. The house is dark.

And I'm standing in front of the window, drawing the curtains, because I can't bear to see the stars.

There are none anymore, not without him.

The bedroom door creaks open as I turn to look over my shoulder.

"Is he dead?"

"We haven't heard anything yet."

My chin trembles as my arms wrap around me as I almost double over. Roman rushes to me, but I hold out my hand, stopping him as I stand back up.

"No. Just leave me alone. Please. Let me do this part alone."

Roman reaches for me, but I step away, so he drops his hand.

"There's no way to prepare for this." My voice is so shaky as I look back at him.

Roman nods, taking a step backward as I turn around and stare at the fucking curtains. My eyes search over the fabric, thinking about the spot I can see on the other side of them. The place on the field where he made love to me, took my innocence, gave me his heart.

The door closes as my shoulders fall, letting my head hang.

Silence crashes around me as I stand there, my fears fighting hope, our love threatening death. I don't even know how long I've been there, but it's long enough that I'm cold. Even though I don't feel it because goose bumps spread over my arms, and my chest feels hollow.

Calder.

The sound of the door opening again makes my chest shake. Because Roman's not speaking behind me. And there's only one reason for everything to feel and be so quiet.

"He's gone," I whisper.

Tears drop to the floor, but the sound of heavy footsteps lifts my head just as Calder rushes past me, tearing back the curtains.

"They're gone. I'm right fucking here, baby."

I gasp so loud that my hands shoot to my chest. He grabs my

wrist, yanking me into him as his mouth crashes down on mine. I'm sobbing, kissing him back with the same fierceness, arms crawling over his shoulders and wrapping around his neck as he picks me up.

He pulls back, breathless, drops of blood splattered on his face, body infused with the smell of gasoline as he stares at me.

"It's over, Sutton."

It's over. The words don't come out. They linger inside, flicking switches, igniting sparks as I begin to shake, gripping his shirt in my hands. Calder looks out of the window as I follow his line of sight, immediately knocked still.

From our window, a fire burns like the fucking sun, set against a backdrop of stars on top of that black glass of the bay. Oranges and reds color the sky, reflecting off the water.

"Oh my God," I rush out.

I'm breathing quickly, watching the fire rise and grow, flickering in my pupils. I can't look away. It's as if everything taken from me is being reborn from the ashes of that fire. I can feel it inside of me like I'm coming back to life.

"It's over," I breathe out, breath doubling in speed until I'm almost panting. My skin tingles as Calder bends, placing me back to the ground, whispering against my skin, lips touching my neck.

"Yes, baby."

His face touches my cheek as I watch the fire, and my ragged breaths turn to cries.

"Thank you." I shift to bring my lips to his. "I love you so much."

His hands cradle the sides of my head as he kisses my face. The blood on his hands is on me now, but I don't care, because I want to share this with him.

No part of Calder isn't also a part of me.

Our lips touch as I say, "Connor?"

He tips my chin up to look into his eyes.

"I promised his life to Roman. And he's gone to take it."

We stare at each other so deeply because, at this moment, I feel free. My lips part, wanting to say something, ask questions, but I can't find the words. But I don't have to because Calder always knows what I need.

He licks his lips before his thumb brushes my cheek.

"I faced death today but then I wielded it. Because everything I do, I do in your name."

My eyes close feeling the peace before he gifts it to me.

"I tied them to chairs."

I suck in a breath because I want to know. I want to know it all. I need to know that they suffered because I did for as long as I can remember.

Kisses are pressed to my skin, hands weaving into my hair.

"I put them around the dining table and made them watch…"

My T-shirt is lifted over my head as I stare up at him. His lips meet mine before he draws back, lowering his head to my neck, kissing the bruises left by Hunter.

"I castrated him. I cut him over and over and then fed him the filthiest fucking piece of him."

My shoulders shake as Calder brings his mouth to mine again, almost feeding me the air I need. I'm gripping his shirt, back arching toward him, wanting more of him as our eyes lock.

"I made him eat his cock until he choked, shaking from the fucking shock. Then I took his hands for laying them on you."

Air fills my lungs as I inhale harshly, reaching for his face. He takes my wrists, kissing my palms, smearing the blood from his cheeks to my hands. His forehead lowers to mine as I close my eyes, listening to the love in his voice.

"I threw him on the table and taped all their fucking mouths shut because they never listened to your cries." His words grind out between his teeth. "So nobody got to hear theirs."

Calder's lips press to mine before pulling away but staying so close that they brush mine as they speak.

"I burned them alive, baby. Nobody will ever hurt you again."

I lift to my toes, kissing him so profoundly, pouring my love, gratitude, and life into this one solitary moment before my eyes open. I look into his—ones bluer than the ocean and the sky—as I say the only thing that matters anymore for the rest of my life.

"I am yours. And you are mine. Forever."

Chapter Thirty-Seven

Calder
One year later

She's been walking around the field for an hour, picking flowers, staring up at the clouds, pretending not to watch me as I sit on this porch reading. But I can't keep my eyes off my girl.

But that's nothing new.

I look up again, staring at her red hair that's hanging wild and free down her back, just the way I like it. She tucks some behind her ear, glancing over at me, then looks away as her hand comes to the slit in her long baby blue dress. It's the kind with skinny straps that hugs her body in all the right places, falling all the way down to her ankles.

Fuck, it makes me want to do bad damn things.

I look down again, having lost my place for the three hundredth time before I chuckle, not lifting my head as I shout.

"Stop tempting me and let me read."

I hear her laugh, and it stirs everything inside of me.

Because that's what she always does—reminds me I'm alive.

I close the journal, *our journal,* and put my eyes on her again. She gave this to me today as an anniversary gift. But I know it's making her nervous for me to read it because my girl hasn't stopped playing with the ends of her hair or biting her perfect bottom lip.

"How much more do you have to read?" she shouts back, still standing too far away.

My head shifts to the side, to the guards that are always watching. They make her feel better, and that's all that matters because I'm still the scariest fucking thing here.

"Hey, get inside, go make yourself a sandwich. We're fine."

"Okay, boss." One of them stops and grins over at me. "Should we shut the curtains?"

I smirk as I stand, giving him a nod, my eyes staying locked on my baby. The journal drops to my chair with a thud just as the door closes.

She's already smiling, with her hands clasped behind her back, just waiting for me as I take the steps down to the grass, making my way toward her.

"You sent the guys inside."

"I did."

I stop in front of her, bringing my hand to cradle her face as my thumb brushes her bottom lip.

"So I read that you popped some chick in the face with a lacrosse stick, huh? Who knew my girl was such a fucking bruiser. I should put ya in the ring."

She laughs, holding my wrist, leaning her cheek into it.

"I mean…full disclosure: I'd think twice before messing with me." She tries her hand at a Boston accent, "Imma ringah."

My laugh cracks my chest because I taught her that word when I told her about the fights I did for Connor. I tuck my hands under her armpits lifting her to my eye level.

"You wanna tell me what's got you so nervous. Because you were all excited an hour ago for me to read."

Her hands are on my shoulders as her brows draw together. Damn, she's fucking cute when she's thinking.

"Wrap," I growl.

She reaches down, hiking up her dress, and hooks her legs around my waist. My arms close in around her as I walk us farther out into the field, just letting her hug me.

It only takes seconds before she takes a deep breath and whispers, "Better."

I shift my face, kissing the side of her head, nudging her with my shoulder, so she looks up at me.

"If you carry it, then so do I. You get me?"

She nods. I know she understands. Sutton and I don't know how to not be full fucking disclosure.

"And baby, there is nothing in there I don't already know."

She's staring at me, so thoughtful as her fingertip traces the constellation on my neck.

After the Kelly housefire, the world turned upside down. But it all stood back a comfortable distance because my girl was with me. And nobody was crossing the line to try to get to her. Not reporters, not lawyers, nobody. Not even the cops.

It gave her the room she needed to find peace. And with that peace came all her truth. I listened, never interrupting. I kissed her when she needed it and let her scream when she couldn't hold it in.

That beautiful girl bared her soul to me, and it was a fucking gift.

She takes a deep breath before giving me a little frown.

"I know. But—"

I say nothing, letting her find the words she wants to say.

Because I can see them sitting back there behind emerald eyes that speak to me before she does.

"A part of me wants to forget it all. To burn the book like none of it ever happened. I just want to fill all the pages with this"—she motions around with a hand—"with our magic. And our dreams. I needed that journal because I didn't have you. But now I do."

I lean in, rubbing my nose over hers.

"And you don't want it to follow you here."

Her eyes lock to mine as she blinks, so fucking stripped down and honest.

"Exactly. I don't want it anymore. I just want to let it go, and I didn't realize that until you were reading it. Because you reading it makes it all that much more real."

I pat her ass, lowering her to the ground, and take her hand.

"Then, baby, let's rewrite history."

I've turned, making my way across the grass as I tug her behind, listening to her laughter like it's my favorite fucking song.

"Hey," I bellow toward the front door, seeing one of my guys come out quickly. "We're going downtown."

"Choose."

Sutton's got a journal in each hand, eyes volleying between them as we stand in the tiny bookstore in downtown St. Simeon. She told me once that this was the store she was standing near the first time she saw me driving down the street.

Fuck me. The way her eyes lit up made me realize I couldn't take her from here. She loves it, so Roman stays in Boston, and I'm here for all the New York shit.

"I can't pick."

She scowls before grinning, weighing them between her hands. So I grab them from her, wagging my brows.

“Then we’ll get both. One for me, and one for you.”

She hurries up behind me as I walk toward the counter, setting them down to pay. Her arm wraps around my waist as mine rests over her shoulders.

“Will you let me read yours?” she whispers absentmindedly, playing with some trinkets.

I chuckle. “Of course, I will. But only if you write about me in yours at least once a day.”

She pokes my side shaking her head, humor crossing her face.

“Deal. But you’re going to have to try harder to be interesting. Because you’re really just a completely uneventful person with no life. It’s all broody—who am I? What’s my destiny? Blah, blah, blah.”

I laugh, as I turn in toward her, tickling her stomach, but she squeals, sealing her body to mine in a bear hug.

“I’m gonna put you in a headlock with that smart mouth.”

I’ve got her tucked against me, hugging her as she laughs, but I’ve stopped because my eyes are staring out of the large shop window. Because looking back at me is that old woman—the one that told Sutton her fortune, and me about my destiny.

Eyes I remember as cold now stare back with kindness. Her eyes drop to Sutton as my arms tighten, and I press a kiss to the top of her head.

A small smile comes to the woman’s face before she cranes her neck as if she’s looking at the display on the table. It’s one we didn’t check. The books are neatly stacked, arranged for people passing by.

Her finger points to a book in the front, but I can’t make out what the design is. But as a v forms between my eyes, she gives me a nod and walks away.

“Your heart is beating fast,” Sutton whispers, kissing my chest before resting her chin on it to look up at me.

I’m still staring out of the window at nothing as Sutton chuckles.

"Hey, are you okay?"

I nod.

"Yeah, but do me a favor? Go check out that table, just in case you see another journal you like. I have a feeling there's something there for you."

I point to where the old lady did before Sutton furrows her brow, a smile playing on her face.

"You have a feeling, huh?"

She saunters off as I throw some money on the counter because the cashier's already bagging up our purchase.

My eyes are on my girl, watching her peruse the books until pure fucking joy lights her up. Her eyes are wide open, teeth showing from her smile as she holds up a thick black leather journal.

She hurries, flipping it over and back.

"Oh my God. Look at this one."

I take it from her hands, shaking my head. Son of a bitch, that fucking witch.

On one side, there's a sun engraved in gold and on the back a moon. I open it thumbing through the pages.

"Oh my God, there are tiny stars on the bottom of the pages." She whispers like it's the best thing she's ever seen. "And we can both use it because it's double-sided."

I put it on the counter as the salesperson picks it up, looking at Sutton.

"These are the best."

The girl opens it, then flips it over and opens the other side—like two books in one.

I grin, taking the bag, lacing my fingers through my girl's hand, watching her marvel over the journal. I couldn't have been led to anything more perfect.

My mind starts thinking of all the notes I'll leave her. The moments I'll replay for her to read. Fuck I need to buy a hundred of these.

She opens the front cover as we begin walking out back toward the car, squeezing my hand.

"Oh wow, it's inscribed."

She holds it up to me as my face turns down to hers.

"Write about a love that defies the stars. Write about yours."

"It's as if it was meant to be. Like fate," she whispers, leaning into me.

The car door is opened for her, but as she gets in, I tug her back. "It's not fate, baby. Or destiny. We're bigger than all that shit."

Her eyes close like she's letting my words soak into her skin before I lean in closer.

"But when we get home, I wanna show you something that is your destiny."

She laughs before leaning forward, pressing her lips to mine.

"And what exactly would that be?"

"The back seat of the Mustang."

Sutton bites her lip, so I reach up and tug it free before grabbing it between my fingers and pulling her into another kiss.

She's breathless the minute I draw back as her husky voice breathes, "I thought back seats were for bad girls."

Goddamn. The way she's looking up at me—she looks just like heaven and I can't fucking wait to show her how fun sinning like hell is. I suck my bottom lip between my teeth, letting it slide out slowly before I answer.

"They are."

Chapter Thirty-Eight

Sutton

"Marry me."

I roll my head to the side, staring at him because we've been lying in this bed all day, wrapped up in each other, celebrating our five-year anniversary.

"When?"

His hand reaches between my legs, cupping my pussy as I draw my bottom lip between my teeth. God, he's good with his hands. Two fingers slip inside me as his other hand grips the inside of my thigh, easing it open as he tilts his head to watch.

"Fuck, your pussy is pretty."

I exhale heavily, lifting my hips, gasping as he leans down, pulls his fingers out, and licks them before closing his mouth over me.

"Fuck, Calder."

His tongue makes a slow figure eight around my clit, teasing before he gently flicks his tongue up and down, making me shudder.

"Marry me."

It's hummed onto my pussy, lifting my head, my hooded eyes on him. "When?"

He growls, making me chuckle before he crawls up my body, his cock sandwiched between us. I smirk, but he just stares at me.

I'm not giving in. We do this all the time. He asks, and I say, "*When?*" and then he never gives me a date. When our nightmare ended, he'd asked me to marry him, and I'd said yes immediately—but once life calmed down, and I found my footing.

I wanted to be his wife, but I also wanted to stand on my own two feet. So I went back to school and graduated early this year and started a nonprofit for women in abusive situations. I did it with my inheritance—seemed like a fitting end to their money.

I became a woman that could take care of herself and still had a fucking lion at her back.

Two, actually. Roman's my family too.

Because it was never going to be enough for me to just rely on Calder's empire. Not if I was going to stand next to him. Because it *is* an empire. There is no doubt that Calder was born for this, because he is the Irish mob and all that it implies.

But he deserved a queen. And I deserved to become one.

"Just tell me when," I whisper, lifting my lips to kiss his beard.

He shakes his head, so I reach down and grab his ass, making him smirk as he presses his cock against me.

"Baby, I'm not choosing for you. That's not something that happens ever again. *You* tell *me*. Until then, I'm gonna fuck you until you're sticky and sweet, and then I'm gonna lick you fucking clean."

Not something that ever happens again. That part hits me so hard that my eyes bore into his. He's still always giving me what I need. My whole life before him was decided for me, but he sees me.

Everything is on my terms now.

I blink up at him, remembering our moment last night. He was chasing me outside, promising dirty rewards when he caught me, but once he did, he tugged my face to his and told me he was proud of the woman I've become. It will forever be one of the greatest moments of my life.

Because Calder never says anything he doesn't mean.

"Ask me again," I rush out.

His hands trail up my naked body, stopping between my breasts as he locks eyes with me.

"Marry me, Buttercup."

I'm already nodding.

"Yes." I lift, kissing his lips. "Now."

He smiles, drawing back, searching my eyes.

"Now?"

I nod faster as he brings his hand to my throat, leaning in to kiss me again, growling his words into my lips.

"I've been waiting for you to say that for too fucking long."

I chuckle, wanting a deeper kiss from him, but he leans over me, grabbing his phone and letting me go. I'm staring at him, confused but laughing as he peppers kisses over my face, his weight almost crushing me.

"What are you doing?"

He ignores me, speaking into his phone.

"She finally said yes. But it's tonight. We'll see you in an hour."

I'm blinking, staring back at him, shaking my head.

"What are you doing?"

Calder wags his eyebrows and rolls out of bed, walking his gorgeous bare ass to the closet before he comes out with a slinky white gown. It's spaghetti-strapped and almost backless. And honestly, everything I've ever wanted.

"Where the hell did you hide that?"

"Baby." He winks. "I'm a fucking criminal."

My hand covers my mouth as I laugh, trying to process what's happening.

"Get dressed. Don't ask questions. And don't peek." His eyes dart to the window. "You've got an hour. Then I'm hauling you out over my shoulder. Because you said yes."

"Wait." I'm laughing, naked in the bed, but he's already got basketball shorts on and is walking out of our bedroom.

"Calder," I yell after him.

But he just bellows, "Get your pretty ass dressed, baby."

Oh my God. I scramble out of bed, wanting to look outside, but the moment my toes touch the floor, he's shouting again.

"Don't fucking peek, baby."

I bite my lip, grab my dress, and behave like the good girl he wants as I walk into the bathroom and get ready.

Almost to the minute, there's a knock on my door. So I check myself out in the mirror, beaming because I've never felt so beautiful. I kept my hair down, and I'm barefoot because that's what I've always wanted.

I don't have to peek to know he's planned this in our field. The only place it should be.

I walk to the door and open it, still smiling as Roman extends his arm.

"Well, look at you, in a suit."

"No tie," he counters with all the broody grumpiness that never leaves him.

"Still, you look very handsome."

He leans in and kisses my cheek. "Thank you. And if you wouldn't mind, I'd like to give you away."

My heart almost explodes because he can't even look at me. After all, Roman and feelings don't mix, but I could hug him to death.

He clears his throat. "I always wanted a sister, and you've been…you know. I'd like to be the one that walks you down the aisle if that's okay?"

My eyes are already glistening.

"I love you too, Roman. And I'd really love for you to do that."

I take his arm, following his lead as we walk down the stairs, but I almost scream when we hit the bottom because Aubrey and Piper are staring back at me.

"Oh my God."

Piper grabs my hand, pulling me away from Roman.

"I can't believe this is happening. It's kismet. What are the chances we'd all be in the same place, at the same time?"

Aubrey hands me some wildflowers as I smile, hugging her.

"The chances are good, Pipes. Considering their anniversary is in July and we always spend it here on the island."

"Whatever," Piper counters, rolling her eyes. "I'm just saying it's all fate and destiny."

She hugs me too, my smile planted on my face. Piper starts talking to Roman, and Aubrey takes my hand, staring at me.

After everything happened, she's who I told everything to. I always felt like a third wheel with her and Piper when we were young, but I realized that none of us worked without the others. But Aubrey is the friend that can shoulder the kind of story I lived.

She pulls me in for another hug, tears in her eyes before she reaches up and tugs my hair.

"You look amazing. And bitch, this was all most definitely your damn destiny."

Piper snaps her fingers. "Wait, we have to do the thing, Aubs."

"Oh yeah," she breathes.

Piper reaches inside her purse. "So, your something new is the dress. This is your something old." She hands me Calder's mother's rosary, wrapping it around my wrist like a bracelet, letting the cross hang down over my middle finger.

Aubrey wipes her eye as Piper looks at her. "Did you just shed a tear, Miss Cold Dead Heart?"

"Allergies." She winks before taking off her diamond drop earrings. "Now, if Piper would shut up, I'd be able to tell you this is your something borrowed."

I take them, laughing as I put them in my ears, hearing music start playing from outside.

Piper looks at us, eyes growing wide. "Shit, we forgot something blue."

Aubrey snaps her fingers like she's trying to think, but I reach out, grabbing their hands.

"I got it. Hold on."

They're staring at me like I'm crazy as I hurry back up the stairs and grab the one thing I can think of before I rush back down.

"Okay," I whisper, laughing and breathless.

Roman walks back to where I'm standing, eyes dropping to Aubrey's for a moment before he offers me his arm again.

The girls walk ahead as we follow out to the porch and straight to Calder. There are no frills, with the exception of a framed photo of West on the railing of our porch. And candles, so many candles lit everywhere, illuminating the dark field, making everything glow amber.

Calder is standing next to Father Paul.

His blue eyes shine against his all-black dress shirt and slacks. God, he's so fucking gorgeous that I almost can't breathe. I lick my lips as he wipes his eyes.

So strong until he sees me.

We walk step after step until Roman slows us because I'm not even paying attention. The moment my beautiful man put his eyes on me, I was lost—tethered to my other half, where the outside world becomes only a myth.

Roman takes my hand from his arm, giving it to Calder.

Our hands join, eyes locked on each other as a breeze blows up from the water. It's a gust, rippling my dress, sending pieces of my flowers up into the air as the candles blow out.

We exhale simultaneously, tipping our faces to the sky, because without the candles, Calder and I are surrounded by a blanket of stars.

"I understand you have your own vows," Father Paul whispers.

The smile grows on my face as our eyes meet again and petals drift downward.

Calder's hands are shaking, chest vibrating, overtaken with emotion.

"I vow to always love you above all others. No matter what."

My eyes close, remembering where we started as I repeat what he's said.

"I vow to always love *you* above all others. No matter what."

He brings my hands to his lips, kissing them over and over before saying, "I will always protect you, even with my life."

God, we came so close to that, and we've made it through all the bad parts, scratching and clawing our way past destiny and fate, to this—to us. We're stronger than any of that. We're indestructible.

"And I will always protect you, even against yourself."

I'm crying, tears falling down my cheeks as he lets go of my hand, stepping in closer as he wipes them from my face.

"Baby, I promise to die by your side when we're wrinkly and fucking gray. So that we'll never be apart again."

My hands cradle his face.

"And I promise to love you even after death."

He's silent, staring down at me, so deeply connected that I'm not sure if he's speaking or it's his soul making promises to mine.

"Not even death does us part."

"Forever," I answer as he leans in and grabs my face before

kissing me like it's the first and last thing he'll ever do.

A throat clears, pulling my lips into a grin against Calder's. We don't separate, staring into each other's eyes as Father Paul whispers to us.

"You have to wait for me to declare it."

Calder growls, making me laugh.

"I'm not good with impulse control when it comes to my girl, so declare it already."

He's already lifting me off my feet as the priest pronounces us man and wife. Calder's mouth crashes down on mine as yelps and howls echo in the background.

He pulls away, arms wrapped around me.

"Can I get you pregnant now?"

I laugh loudly, nodding, reaching inside my bra and pulling out my small, round birth control case.

"I needed something blue, and it was the first thing I thought of."

He attacks my neck, taking a bite as I squeal before popping me up, right over his shoulder, as he turns, stalking back toward the house and grunting, "Right now. We're doing it now."

I never thought in my wildest dreams that I'd marry a man that would not only make my dreams come true but that he'd redefine the idea of them altogether. He carries me up the stairs, placing me to my feet as he closes the door behind him.

My hands fall on his face, and I swear the entire glimpse of our lives passes before me.

Our happiness, children, joy, pain…a lifetime. But no matter what I see, through it all, he's by my side. And I'm by his. It took us five years after we parted to get to this moment, and I wouldn't do it any differently.

He kisses me softly, brushing my hair from my face as I look up at him…my husband.

"You are mine, Calder Wolfe. And I am yours. Promise it again."

"Forever and ever and ever, baby."

Chapter Thirty-Nine

Calder
Thirty years old

"Look at you," I whisper, not really sure if the words have come out. My face lifts to Sutton's. "She's beautiful. Look at all her hair."

My wife is smiling from ear to ear, exhausted after laboring with our daughter for too many hours. It's moments like this that make me feel small, holding this tiny little life after witnessing my beautiful girl birth a miracle from her body.

I have nothing to offer that could even compare to what they've brought to my life.

So I just keep protecting them with mine and my whole fucking army.

A nurse asks Sutton if she should get the boisterous crew in the hallway, making me chuckle.

"Yes." She smiles.

I stand, carrying another piece of my heart to my wife as I sit down next to her. The tiny little life in my hands suckles as she lies peacefully sleeping.

"Are you crying?" Sutton breathes.

"I do every time."

She inhales deeply, "Well, I don't care how Catholic you like to pretend we are. This uterus is officially off-limits."

I grumble, rubbing my nose over the tiny one in front of me. "Did you hear that, Saoirse?"

Sutton laughs, hitting my arm. "We are not naming her Saoirse."

I hold her up, facing Sutton.

"Come on. She looks like one."

"She looks like someone who nobody can pronounce? It's not happening. Unless you're moving us all to Ireland."

I lift my brows.

"Don't even think about it."

We're laughing as the door swings open, and my boys come running in, along with Aubs and Piper behind them, Roman trailing behind with a grin.

"West," Sutton warns as our oldest jumps up on the bed, smiling like the devil.

The room fills with giggles and excitement because all three of Saoirse's brothers have prayed nightly for a sister. Roman helps the other two up as I give them a look to be careful of their mother.

"Fellas, this is your sister. And your job is to protect her for your whole entire lives."

West reaches a finger out, and she grips it with her tiny little hands, making his little eyes shoot to mine.

"I promise, Dad. Forever."

My jaw tenses, holding back my emotion as I look to Sutton, whose emerald eyes stare back into mine as she mouths, *Forever.*

I don't deserve this kind of happiness, or maybe I do, because I was willing to fight for it, no matter the consequence. All I know is that I love this goddamn girl, and nobody will ever take her from me.

And I will keep building this empire for my children so that one day she and I will look down from the stars and watch our legacy thrive as they stare up at us and tell our story.

Sutton
Fifty years old

God, he's so handsome. I laugh to myself because I'm not sure I'll ever stop thinking that. He's aged in all the most perfect ways, like a damn fine wine. The man is just as much of a presence as he was when we were young.

Calder runs his hand through his hair, tattoos a little more worn, his smile just as bright as he sits outside with two of our grandkids, letting them look through the telescope.

"Grandma, Grandpa said he brought you here when you were younger and made you see stars."

My mouth pops open as Calder's booming laugh fills our sky.

"This one's a filthy liar, baby. You can't trust him. I said I brought you here to see *the* stars."

"No, you didn't…" rings in unison behind him.

They both giggle as he grabs them, tickling their sides. I lean a hip against the doorframe, smiling, just marveling at our life well lived.

My husband is a dangerous man, a fallen angel, but still, he came from heaven. And that's exactly what my life has felt like.

I've never felt alone. Always been loved, worshipped even.

And from that, we have a legacy, not of hate or violence, but one from love.

A few years back, I stopped into that tea shop, the one where I had the tarot reading when I was a kid, because I saw a flyer just like before.

At first glance, it looked like the woman hadn't aged, but I came to find out it was her daughter. She told me her mother used to tell her the story of our love. How it was so powerful that it punched a hole into the world of the living, letting Calder walk in both because not even the devil could keep him from me.

We laughed, treating it as a story told by an old woman with magic in her veins and too much age to tell the difference between what's real and what's not.

But as I walked away, I looked over my shoulder just like when I was seventeen, feeling that indescribable pull to him. Because my life tells me her story is real.

Our love has always been too big to contain.

"Hey," he whispers, making me blink up into his blue eyes. "You thinking about me again?"

"Absolutely."

"Then kiss me."

I smile before I push to my tiptoes, pressing my lips to his as he picks me up and places me on his boots, and we dance to music only we can hear.

Calder
Eighty years old

Her gentle face lies next to mine, pillow caressing her head. She's so fucking tired. My baby held on for so long, waiting until every one of *her* babies made it home to say goodbye.

Always my brave girl.

She's always been the strong one our entire lives together. And last year, when the doctor told her she had six months, she smiled at me, smoothing tears over my wrinkles, saying, "Don't you be sad. It's better this way. Now I can make sure they let you into heaven."

But I'd sell my soul for one more second with her. Just one more. One lifetime isn't enough.

"Baby," I whisper as I stare at her peaceful face.

Sutton left me only a moment ago, body stilling as she released her last sweet breath like she was giving me her soul to keep.

"Dad."

My name comes from behind me, but I'm not leaving my girl. I'm going to lie here until God takes me too.

"Just leave him. Let him grieve, West," Saoirse says.

The door quietly shuts as I run my shaky hand down her long hair that used to be red, now silver. My eyes close as I lean in, kissing her lips one last time.

"I promised you all those years ago that we'd go together so we'd never be apart."

My chest shakes as I take her still-warm hand in mine, doing the thing I swore I'd never do again. I pray.

"Our Father, who art in heaven. Hallowed be thy name."

I see her in my mind, smiling, running through the field as I chase her. So beautiful, so alive, and so filled with love.

"Thy kingdom come. Thy will be done. On Earth as it is in heaven—"

A pain shoots through my chest as my mouth opens. I gasp feebly for air, tears falling from the creases of my eyes.

My eyes close, body sinking into the mattress as I exhale.

Sutton.

Her name is all I can feel. But I can't open my eyes. Everything inside of me pulls to a surface I can't see, but I dig my heels in, fighting it like I'm holding myself down.

"He's not breathing," I hear somewhere in the distance, but I turn my back.

Baby.

Suddenly, warmth fills my body as my eyes finally blink open.

Sutton looks up at me, eyes so green, red hair blowing in the wind. She looks exactly how she did the day I first kissed her. I look around as she laces her hands through mine, bringing them to her lips, pressing kisses to the palms before she looks up at me.

We're in our field.

My eyes drop to hers as the edges around us blur, and she smiles.

"You're here."

I cradle her face, bringing my lips to hers, feeling warmth on her lips, almost tasting the sun.

"Not even in death, baby."

The *never* End to a kind of love story we all deserve.

Gretchen Eddy.
Jennifer Mirabelli.
Katie Friend.
Amanda Kay Anderson.

Those are my acknowledgements. When I tell you that the process of writing is hard, it's grueling. It humble in ways most could not handle—me included. But these women held me up, reminded me I was badass, sometimes told me "You're better than that." Because, Yeah I am. They pushed me to write the best fucking possible story in me.

I love you guys forever. You'll never know the impact you've had on my life.

Also thanks to Erica Edits, Sandra from One love and Ellie McLove , Sarah Plocher, and Rumi Khan for the countless hours and dropping everything they were doing to edit because I decided to change the whole end of the book. You legit held me down.

Thank you to everyone that read this story, bloggers, crew, readers…and whether you loved it or not, it means something to me that you took the time to pick up something I created.

About the Author

Trilina is a USA Today Bestselling Author who loves cupcakes and bourbon.

When she isn't writing steamy love stories, she can be found devouring Netflix with her husband, Anthony, and their three kiddos. Pucci's journey into writing started impulsively. She wanted to check off a box on her bucket list, but what began as wish-fulfillment has become incredibly fulfilling. Now she cant's see her life without her characters, her readers, and this community.

She's known for being a trope defier, writing outside of the box and creating fictional worlds that her readers never want to leave.

Connect with Trilina and stay up to date.

www.trilinapucci.com

facebook.com/trilinapuccibooks

twitter.com/trilina_pucci

instagram.com/authortrilinapucci

amazon.com/Trilina-Pucci/e/B07BQFYLKB

www.ingramcontent.com/pod-product-compliance
Ingram Content Group UK Ltd.
Pitfield, Milton Keynes, MK11 3LW, UK
UKHW020419250726
13967UKWH00007B/2719